From the heart of Krynn . . .

Amid the turmoil of the War of Souls . . .

Bertrem, member of the Aesthetic Order and heir
to the great Astinus, master chronicler of Krynn,
has once again sent forth his agents to gather
information about the lives of the ordinary
people of Ansalon.

In this time of war and upheaval, they bring
forth letters, memoranda, diaries, and
conversations that record moments of fear, of joy,
of laughter, and of heartbreaking sorrow.

The story of the War of Souls, as told by the
common people of Krynn.

For more about the world of Krynn . . .

Bertrem's Guide to the War of Souls

Volume One

Bertrem the Aesthetic

with the able assistance of
Jeff Crook, John Grubber,
Mary H. Herbert, and
Nancy Varian Berberick

BERTREM'S GUIDE TO
THE WAR OF SOULS
VOLUME ONE
©2001 Wizards of the Coast, Inc.

Distributed in the United States by Holtzbrinck Publishing. Distributed in Canada by Fenn Ltd.

Distributed to the hobby, toy, and comic trade in the United States and Canada by regional distributors.

Distributed worldwide by Wizards of the Coast, Inc. and regional distributors.

Cover art by Jeff Easley
Maps by Dennis Kauth
First Printing: September 2001
Library of Congress Catalog Card Number:

9 8 7 6 5 4 3 2 1

ISBN: 0-7869-1882-9
UK ISBN: 0-7869-2669-4
620-21882

U.S., CANADA,
ASIA, PACIFIC, & LATIN AMERICA
Wizards of the Coast, Inc.
P.O. Box 707
Renton, WA 98057-0707
+ 1-800-324-6496

EUROPEAN HEADQUARTERS
Wizards of the Coast, Belgium
P.B. 2031
2600 Berchem
Belgium
+ 32-70-23-32-77

Visit our web site at **www.wizards.com/dragonlance**

To my fellow researchers in
the Great Library
of Palanthas,
without whose assistance
this volume would not have been possible.

Silvanost

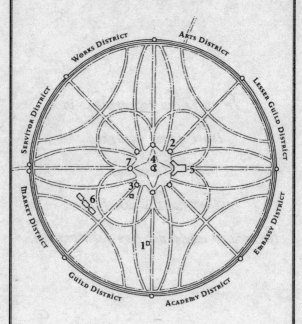

Works District
Arts District
Lesser Guild District
Servitor District
Market District
Embassy District
Guild District
Academy District

1: House Woodshaper
2: Temple of E'li
3: Temple of Solinari
4: Temple of Astarin
5: Palace of Quinari
6: Wildrunner Barracks
7: Tower of the Stars

N

0   4 Miles

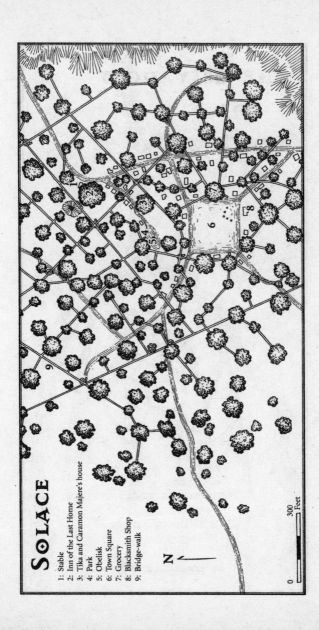

SOLACE

1: Stable
2: Inn of the Last Home
3: Tika and Caramon Majere's house
4: Park
5: Obelisk
6: Town Square
7: Grocery
8: Blacksmith Shop
9: Bridge-walk

N

0   300   Feet

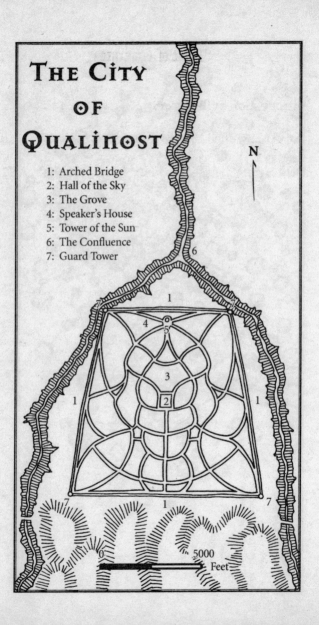

THE CITY

OF

QUALINOST

1: Arched Bridge
2: Hall of the Sky
3: The Grove
4: Speaker's House
5: Tower of the Sun
6: The Confluence
7: Guard Tower

N

0   5000
        Feet

Table of Contents

Introduction by Bertrem

War, sad to say, is the midwife of history.

I am an old man now, and as I sit in my chair by the window, pen and ink on the desk before me, facing a clean, well-scraped parchment, there comes into my mind the endless procession of campaigns and battles, raids and counter-raids, victories and defeats, that has been the story of my world.

In the street below I see people passing to and fro, some of them stopping to look up at the great Library of Palanthas, and I think to myself, how many of you will be alive a year from today? How many will see a good old age and will dandle grandchildren on your knee? How many will fall and lie unmarked and unremembered in a far-off grave?

Bertrem the Aesthetic

War, alas, is upon us once more—this time more terrible than almost any in my memory. Even as I sit here, rumors assail my ears: of a great army of Dark Knights, led by a strange, red-haired young girl, sweeping across Ansalon; of threats and rumblings among the Dragon Overlords; and—only this morning—of a cataclysmic disaster in the elven land of Qualinesti.

Amid this swirl of death and destruction, the great Library of Palanthas stands as a bulwark, strong and indestructible. Mayhap there will come upon Krynn a devastation such as that unleashed by the gods in the Cataclysm. Perhaps it will even come at the hands of this "One God" trumpeted by Mina, new leader of the Dark Knights. But until such an event should come to pass, the brothers of the Order of Aesthetics pass to and fro along the book-lined corridors of the library, preserving for future generations the wisdom of the past.

After the strange and inexplicable turn of events that followed the end of the Chaos War, when the contents of the library, together with its master, Astinus, vanished in the night, I and my fellow Aesthetics have labored long and patiently. Slowly, slowly we have rebuilt our collection, drawing upon sources throughout Ansalon. Once again, the library's shelves are filled with leather-bound volumes.

Yet we are but a pale shadow of the magnificent library that existed under the stern but just rule of Astinus. The extent of our loss becomes clearer every day.

It may seem strange to some readers that while Ansalon trembles around me, I stay here and patiently chronicle the passing years of a new age. This, though, I learned from Astinus, who was unmoved by the great events that surrounded him, valuing clarity, detachment, and accuracy above all other qualities. I have striven to emulate him in this, but it is hard when the world totters on the brink of some dreadful abyss.

A week ago I arrived, as usual, at my desk in the early morning. The sun had not fully risen, and the room was suffused with that cool, lemon light that is so conducive to reading and writing. The room was warm, and the air was pleasant, so instead of working, as I should have been doing, I sat quietly, half dozing, gazing out the window at the street below. It was largely empty; a few merchants wheeled barrows with their daily supply of goods along the cobbles.

As I watched the dust motes dancing in the shafts of sunlight, it seemed to me that a faint breeze swept through the still air of the library. The dust whirled and swept around me. Light darkened, as if a veil had been cast over the sun.

From the street below, I heard faint voices crying. At the same time, I heard the hurrying footsteps of my brothers, their voices raised in alarm. I joined them and ran forth through the library's great doors into the street.

People poured from the houses, looking aloft. Many, dread filling their voices, cried that a dragon had come upon Palanthas. Others wailed that the

Dark armies of Mina were at the city's gates. Still others claimed they saw a flaming mountain coursing across the sky.

Yet none of these calamities were fulfilled. Instead, the air blew across us, and it seemed to many, myself included, that in that soft wind we heard a wailing of distant voices, crying out in grief and anguish as they perished from this world, their tongues forever silenced. And from beyond the distant miles came a deep roar and rumble of destruction.

Silence followed. It was a terrible silence, one heavy with menace. Yet none knew from where the fear came. Then, all at once, a bird sailed overhead, gliding from the southlands, and from its beak came a cry so clear and full that it seemed to blow away all our terror and fill many in the crowd with joy, as if some great weight had been lifted from their shoulders.

Many of the citizens of Palanthas came to the library that day and the next, seeking enlightenment concerning these portents, but the brothers of the Aesthetic Order turned them away, telling them we knew no more than they. So matters remained for many days. At last, this morning, a messenger arrived from the south. It was a dwarf, weary with travel, his clothes stained and torn, his face lined with the weariness of many long miles.

The brother in attendance at the door of the library, Brother Mark, the most stunningly handsome and intelligent of all my brothers, brought him to me. He stood on the rug, shoulders bent but head held high and a light in his eyes.

"What news do you bring?" I asked him.

He lifted a hand. "News, Brother Bertrem, that will shake this library to its foundations. News worthy of songs and celebrations. Beryllinthranox, the great green overlord, is dead!"

I started from my seat with a cry of joy, but he continued.

"This news is accompanied, however, with considerable sorrow. The green dragon fell in battle with elves escaping from Qualinesti. She was challenged by Lauralanthalasa herself, Hero of the Lance, queen mother of the Qualinesti people. Laurana, standing alone on the Tower of the Stars, wielded the dragonlance against Beryl.

"She did so at the cost of her own life. Beryl fell upon the Tower, crushing it and Laurana. In her agony, the dragon fell upon the city of Qualinost. What she did not know was that the elves, with the help of my people, had burrowed tunnels beneath the city to aid in their escape. When the dragon turned, thrashing in pain, the tunnels collapsed and the river poured in. Many elves and dwarves were destroyed as they fled through the tunnels."

I could scarcely find my voice to ask, "And what did the Qualinesti find when they returned to the city?"

The dwarf's eyes glinted with tears as he replied, "They found nothing, because there was nothing to find. Qualinost is no more."

Silence filled the room, heavy with sadness. For centuries the elven city had endured, and now so much that was beautiful has passed away, never to come again. I felt my cheeks grow wet, but I remembered the lesson taught me by my master, Astinus: the true historian is always calm, detached. I turned my head for a moment and blinked, then turned back and asked, "Where did the elves go?"

The dwarf shrugged. "Under the leadership of their king, Gilthas, they have begun the journey across the Plains of Dust toward Silvanesti, where they trust in their cousins to aid them."

"Silvanesti!" I cried in alarm. "Do they not know that—" I broke off, biting my lip.

The dwarf looked at me. "What? What should they fear?"

I was torn between my duty as an historian and my duty as a man. Silently I struggled for a few minutes, then replied, "Silvanesti, we have heard here, is under the control of the Dark Knights led by the girl Mina. I doubt the Qualinesti will find comfort there."

The dwarf looked at me, swaying on his feet with weariness. "I cannot warn them," he said sadly. "They are traveling secretly, and I doubt I could reach them in time. They must discover the truth for themselves."

He left, and I made arrangements for him to be lodged near the library and his needs tended to. I thought much on his news. That the green dragon had been destroyed was a miracle beyond all our hopes. Yet the other great overlords remain: Malystryx the Red, Onysablet the Black, Khellendros the Blue, and many lesser dragons as well.

There is still much work for heroes to do.

To play the part of a hero is not my task. Rather, I must chronicle the events of the age. In this spirit, I have compiled the following notes on the land of Ansalon in this time of war and destruction. My reporters are members of the Aesthetic Order. They have fulfilled their tasks admirably. From their travels they have gathered diaries, letters, poetry, and much more. Their aim has been to show how, in this time of upheaval, the common folk live. In this, as I have remarked in a previous volume, I differ from Astinus, who was entirely uninterested in the lives of ordinary people. I cannot help but think that in a time when so many of those same ordinary people have been overtaken by great events—the siege of Sanction, the deaths of Cyan Bloodbane and Beryllinthranox, the destruction of Qualinost—such an account is needed more than ever. Here, then, is my offering. I make it with profound thanks to those whose diligence created it: Jeff Crook, Nancy Varian Berberick, Mary H. Herbert, and John Grubber.

May the light of Paladine shine upon you always.

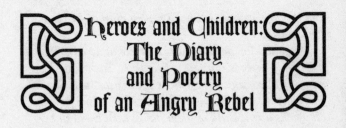

Heroes and Children: The Diary and Poetry of an Angry Rebel

Bertrem's Note

Brother Crook has been deeply interested for some time in the poetry of Ansalon and, indeed, has worked diligently to rebuild the library's collection of poems. His weakness for modern poetry, as opposed to the great classic collections, has on occasion borne correction, but for the most part his industry and expertise are to be admired.

His notes on the poetry of Genin Crystáltust are enlightening because they show the service to which even verse has been put in these dark days. I have allowed him to include here not only a selection of Genin's poetry but extensive excerpts from her diary, because of its relevance to the history of our times. The notes that accompany the diary and poems are by Brother Crook.

As Krynn's longest lived race, the elves are one of the greatest repositories both for knowledge (facts, events, dates) and commentary available to the historian and social philosopher. Whenever one chances upon personal accounts of a time, even of a modern time, written in the hand of an elf for whom the recent past may stretch back over seventy years, it is like finding a diamond in the coal scuttle.

Occasionally, one discovers a personal account that is more than mere history. It is literature. Such is the case with the diary and poetry of Genin Crystáltust. Genin was born into these momentous times, and like few others, she is a true child of them. With each entry in her diary we witness the suffering of an entire people through the words of a single young woman. With each poem, we progress with her through the relative innocence of the pre-Chaos world, the confusion of the world after Chaos, and the horror and loss suffered by those involved in the bitter struggle to free Qualinesti from the grip of the Knights of Neraka and the green dragon Beryllinthranox.

A large number of pages at the beginning of the diary are missing. As hinted at in the first surviving entry these pages were destroyed by fire during the invasion of Qualinost by the minions of Chaos. The first entry of the diary dates to just after the Chaos War, but much of what is written in this segment deals with the hopes and dreams of a naïve young elf who had set her heart upon winning the love of the Speaker of Suns, Gilthas of House Solostaran. She was little aware of the events passing in the outside world, not unlike much of her older, wiser kin, but this can perhaps be excused in one so young, so soon after the shock of seeing her home destroyed. Yet even these show a young woman still struggling to come to terms with her shattered world, as she tries desperately to cling to that which has been irretrievably lost—her love for the handsome young king, their old way of life among the courtly niceties of a former day.

The fires of the Chaos War first shaped Genin Crystáltust into a poet and rebel. The destruction and loss of her home robbed her of her innocence, as evidenced by the sudden maturity in the style and subject matter of her later poetry. Sadly, we have only fragments of her poetry and few written in her youth. In these, one glimpses a world that is no more, through the eyes of a lovesick, misunderstood child.

Mother gave me these two books for my Eleventh Day of Life Gift twenty-three years ago. They were bound here in Qualinost by Uncle Dorthinion, who makes books of this sort for the recording of diaries and journals and such. Mother suggested that I keep a diary with one of them, as she had kept one when she was a girl my age, and a poetry journal with the other, since I showed a fancy for poetry quite early and was fond of scribbling verse into the margins of her volumes of Kierloth and Merturan.* This I did, but not faithfully, I must admit, but I am glad now that I was lax in my promise, for it is fewer pages that were destroyed when the—I cannot say it, I cannot bear to remember that horrible day. Has it only been two years?

Father says that I lack patience. I should never become a Woodshaper until I learn some patience, he says. It is because I was born in a time of sorrow, when we elves were in exile in Qualimori, during the humans' War of the

---

* Two famous poets of Qualinesti. Kierloth lived during the Age of Dragons, while Merturan was almost contemporary, having died a few years after the War of the Lance. The works of these two great poets is readily apparent in Genin's verse, especially in the poems written before the Chaos War. Both poets are famous not only for their romantic poetry, but also for the shortness of their lives—both died violent deaths at relatively young ages. Kierloth died in the destruction of Istar at the age of 109; Merturan was slain by a green dragon in 354 AC at the age of 112.

Lance.* I wish I had been born sooner, so that I could be happier. I was not born in my homeland.

Now that I am older, though, I have changed my mind about the diary. Diaries are for silly little girls. When I told him so, Father said that perhaps I should keep a journal instead. Father says that this is an important time in the history of our people. I should say so! Everything has changed, and the feelings I recorded in the diary and poetry of my youth are an embarrassment to me now. To think that I should have fallen in love with *him*, honored *him* with my heartfelt prayers and verse, with my tears that he should be so long away from his people, and to have so worshiped the woman he called his wife—the witch! I see now the foolishness of youth, "the wayward heart so easily stirred by simple beauty."** He is revealed at last, the treacherous traitor of his people! It makes my blood fairly boil. I am glad that he is dead. It was he who led the minions of Chaos into our beautiful city. I do not care what the others say. If I saw him starving in the street, I think I should not even allow him to lick the dust from my shoe. Thank Paladine that Speaker Gilthas was there to thwart his plans to betray our nation and destroy us all. I shan't write his

---

* During the War of the Lance, as the dragonarmies neared their borders, the elves of Qualinesti evacuated their homeland for the safety of Southern Ergoth, joining their Silvanesti kin already hiding there (351 AC). They called the region of Southern Ergoth that they occupied Qualimori.

** The reference is obscure.

name, nor hers either, for they are cast out of the light. If I wrote their names here today, I should have to tear out this page tomorrow.[*]

But tomorrow, Gilthas of House Solostaran is to have a Spring Dawning ball. Father says that we are to attend! I shall wear my white dress with the pink roses on the cuffs, and a silver net in my hair, the one Theonathas said made me seem woven of starlight and dreams. The cheek! Still. . . I shan't talk about it, it only makes me angry that I gave him one of my poems. I would that I had it back or had burned it at his feet! I'll wear the silver net, and I hope he sees me in it tomorrow. May the sight of me blast his eyes.

I hope I do not have to sit with Mother in the carriage.

SPRING DAWNING DANCE—13ᴛʜ DAY OF THE MONTH OF SPRING DAWNING—2 SC

I am so weary that I believe I shall faint! It has been a day that I shall never forget, for all the centuries to come. I have seen him, and he is glorious, more beautiful than I could have imagined. Speaker Gilthas of House Solostaran. His name

---

[*] Genin is speaking of Porthios of House Solostaran, and Alhana Starbreeze, queen of the Silvanesti elves, who were married in 362 AC, when Genin was approximately eleven summers old. Like with many elven girls, it appears that Genin fell in love with Porthios at the time of his marriage, both for his own sake, and for the sake of Alhana, who is accounted among the most beautiful of all elves. At the time of this entry into her journal, Senator Rashas had exposed Porthios' and Alhana's intention to sign the Unified Nations of the Three Races treaty. Most elves viewed this treaty as a direct threat to their nation's sovereignty. Led by Senator Rashas, the Senate of the Qualinesti cast Porthios and Alhana from the light, making them dark elves. As such, they became non-entities, shunned by their own people. It was forbidden to even speak their names.

shall always be upon my lips. His hair is like sunlight falling through aspen leaves upon bur-
nished gold, his eyes deep sad pools of dreams.
When I saw him in his yellow robes of state take
the sun medallion in his fine hands and look
upon it with reverent eyes, I felt my knees go
weak! He so looked a king in every fiber of his
being. He is a poem come to life.

What is more, never again can anyone call me a
child, for Speaker Gilthas is younger even than me!
He is only nineteen, they say! The next time Mother
tells me I am too young to do something, I shall
remind her that Speaker Gilthas is younger than me
and yet he is king! They say his marriage has not yet
been arranged. Thank Paladine that Father has never
let Mother disgrace our family with one of her fits.

But I am beginning in the middle.

Linnet roused us to an early breaking of our fast.
She is very pretty in the mornings, with her silver
hair, but her facial tattoos truly are beastly.* I
once thought them charming, but the older I get the
more barbaric they seem. To think I once tried to tat-
too an oak leaf upon my cheek. If it hadn't hurt so
much, I might have ruined my natural pale beauty,
Mother says. She is fond of saying those sorts of
things, reminding me of my obligations and my fail-
ures at the same time. But she always apologizes
when she is feeling better.

---

* The Qualinesti often kept Kagonesti servants. Linnet appears to be a female
servant especially charged with the care of Genin and her sister. Her brothers most
likely had their own servant. The Kagonesti, being a rather barbaric offshoot of the
race, are fond of facial tattoos, though the practice had already begun to fall out of
favor among the younger Wilder Elves.

外

Father says we mustn't protest, for it is Paladine's will. But I hardly think so, for where is Paladine now? I have heard that he no longer answers the prayers of his priests, but when I mentioned it to Father, I thought he might actually strike me! After he had regained control of himself, he told me I mustn't blaspheme, that I must have faith and courage. Yet I hardly think it is worth it anymore, after all that we have lost. Why did Paladine not aid us? Why did he not answer my prayers? Was I not faithful to him?

I've digressed again. I am terrible about straying from my point. I fear I'll never be able to debate in the Thalas-Enthia.* Thank goodness, Ardian** will fill that role for our family.

After breakfast, Linnet helped me with my dress. Valursa became quite jealous of the attention Linnet paid me. Oh, and the compliments! The honey that flows from her Kagonesti tongue is collected from strange flowers, but it is sweet nonetheless. Valursa wore pure white—the imp! And light sandals, because she is so vain about her feet. As if *he* might notice her feet in all that crowd! Linnet tried to press some color upon Valursa for modesty's sake, but as she is the eldest sister of course she knows better. At least she had the decency not to wear flowers in her hair, for it is ratty enough without looking like she just crawled from the glades. Linnet could do nothing with it. "You hair ahs a mind ov its own, Valoshin," she said, in her

---

* The Senate of the Qualinesti.

** Ardian is one of Genin's older brothers. She had two, including Chrysostomus, also called Sosti later in the text, who was her senior by some forty years. Ardian was four years Sosti's junior.

peculiar way. She calls Valursa *Valoshin**; it is simply hilarious! I am thankful that I have Grandmother's hair—lively, glossy, and obedient!

When Father came to retrieve us in our room (how I hate this new house, having to share a room with Valursa!), he asked Valursa to please ride with Mother in the carriage. Valursa was only too glad, for it is a tremendous walk from our house to the Tower of the Sun, and she was only wearing her sandals. I had my supplest boots, of course, for I am not such a fool as she. And though it is fitting that I appear charming, for Father's sake if not for my own, it is also fitting that I wear the boots of the Woodshapers, for I shall be one myself in twenty or so years. It seems such a long time, but Linnet says it will pass more quickly than a summer. What a foolish notion! I shall never be fifty, I think.**

Father and I left first, much to Valursa's chagrin. Linnet did not come with us, though she complained most stridently. If she had come, I should have died of shame. Many girls are perfectly happy to parade around Qualinost with their Kagonesti *slaves* in tow, but I think it is a barbaric practice, just as keeping

---

* Valoshin (Kagonesti)—peahen. Valosha is the peacock. It is obvious, from Genin's comments, that she was familiar with the Kagonesti language, but that her sister Valursa was not.

** Elves live, on average, somewhat over 400 years. They mature more slowly than their human counterparts. An elf of 50 summers is roughly at the same stage of growth and maturity as a human of approximately 16 years. Genin's referral in the previous day's entry that she has seen 31 summers places her at a rough human equivalent of 11 years of age. This is, of course, only a general estimate. Elves mature at different rates, as can be seen in the example of Speaker Gilthas, who was only 16 at the time of his coronation, although some scholars have attributed his advanced maturity to his quarter-human blood. In any case, Genin's use of language is vastly superior to a human of 11 years.

slaves (call them what you will!) is barbaric. Our family keeps servants. They are free to go if they choose, and always have been. Father is very good about these things, however, and he spared me the disgrace of walking with Linnet in attendance. Linnet must remain behind to serve Valursa, the eldest. Such a curse that Kagonesti witch mouthed! I wonder what it meant. How Father kept from striking the impudent wench, I'll never know. He is so patient with the servants, it is perfectly scandalous. Mother hates it, and for once I agree with her. But then again, were he not patient with them, he might not also be patient with us. Gods know, we do test him so!

We arrived at the Speaker's residence quite early and found ourselves a good place near enough the front without causing a scandal among the greater nobles. It is a pity that we are not of the greater nobility. Really, we should be, there isn't any difference between our family and theirs, except for Mother, but that can happen even in the best of families, they say. The dance was more glorious that I had ever imagined. Gilthas arrived arrayed in robes of noble yellow. His hair was honey poured upon his shoulders in beauty and pride. I cannot describe it in mere words. He was a walking poem, Poesy's very child. I felt my heart stirred by such longing, such feeling. I felt words come unbidden into my heart, sweet verse, and I could scarcely contain myself for want of a pen and parchment to jot it down. So I repeated it to myself over and over until I returned home. Now they burn like a bowl filled with light in my soul. They are the first words I have writ that are

mature and worthy.* All others were but the prat-
tlings of a child.

NEXT DAY

Linnet says that she has heard that *she,* that Silvanesti witch, has been seen in the forest outside the
city, perhaps looking for her long-lost husband. It is
a shame she escaped, and with the aid of Tanis
Halfhuman and Dalamar. She and Tanis were companions in adventure, Father said. They met during
the War of the Lance.** How Dalamar became
involved, I am sure I don't know.

MONTHS LATER

I have been so lax, but there really isn't time, what
with my studies, to write. I have neglected my responsibility to the future, for as Father says, a diary is private, but a journal is written for future generations.
Mother grows worse by the day. She cries out in her
sleep of dragons. Father says that she is reliving the battle
in Qualinesti when our home was destroyed. How he
has managed all these years, I simply can't imagine.

Sosti has come home for a time, but Ardian is still
on border patrol. Sosti says that Ardian has been in
several battles, but he won't say with whom he is

---

* This poem is believed to be "Sonnet to the Sun."

** Dalamar did in fact assist Tanis Half-Elven (it is a derogatory term among elves
to call those of mixed elf lineage half-human) in his ill-fated attempt to stop his
son's assumption of the robes of the Speaker of the Suns. That Tanis was under
some spell of Dalamar's is doubtful. Of note: Genin's recording of Dalamar's name
is a severe breach of elven law. Such a mistake can be attributed only to her youth.
Tanis and Alhana Starbreeze met in Tarsis, where he and some of his companions
followed her to Silvanesti to search for her father Lorac. They helped free Lorac
from the evil dream that held him and the land in its magical sway.

fighting. He insists that I say nothing to the other families. I can't imagine why! If we are under attack, surely it can't or shouldn't be a secret.

Sosti took me aside and told me that were I not his sister, most certainly he would be smitten. He said that I had grown into a woman during his absence. I think I blushed. He is so wonderful!

WEEKS LATER

There is to be another grand ball tomorrow, and I hear that certain girls have been asked to dance for the king. I . . . I cannot write the words. I will die if he chooses another. Father must find a way to get me an invitation.

NEXT DAY

Mother said I am not old enough to go to the grand ball. The Spring Dawning dance was different, she says, because everyone was invited. I reminded her that I am older than the king. She . . . I cannot speak of it. I do not hate her for striking me, but I do not know if I shall ever forgive her calling me an impudent . . . my hand cannot be made to write the word, the same word we use in reference to the Silvanesti witch.

Father quickly took me aside and begged me to forgive Mother, for his sake. I told him that I would, and he wiped away my tears, and he took me into his strong arms and held me and wept. He wept on my shoulder. I did not think that fathers wept. He did not even cry when our home burned. I tried to be strong for him, but feeling his sobs I could not help but weep with him. He has suffered so terribly on our account, especially for Mother. She cannot help herself. Father then told me that although my birth had been difficult, I was not the cause of Mother's trouble. He said that she is a "sensitive" (I shall have to find out what that means) and that the upheaval of the time of my birth had already nearly driven her mad.

But she recovered. She did, and she was much better, until recently. She has always suffered from pains in her head and flashes of light, he said, but of late these have grown much worse. He said that as a young woman, I am old enough to learn these things. And then he said that Mother has been seeing things, things that are not there, and that she is afraid. They talk to her and tell her to do such terrible things, he says, and each day she grows a little weaker. She tells him what they say, and he tries to reassure her that the voices and the dark figures are not real, but she says that they are coming, they will soon be here, and when they do come . . .

Well, it is all her delusion, but it is frightening. I do feel so sorry for her now, but she should have known that I am her own daughter. I can't imagine that it could ever be so bad that she wouldn't know me.

But this is not the sorest blow I have been dealt this day. For Father then went on to tell me that I mustn't aim my bow so high. What do you mean, I asked him. Speaker Gilthas, he said. He said, certainly in a few years I should be allowed to attend the grand balls, but that our family is not of high enough station that I might ever hope to catch the king's eye. I will never be asked to dance for the king, he said. I must be strong, he said. There are gentle elves aplenty, he said, who will compose sonnets to my beauty someday. But not today. And not the king.

Weeks Later

Ardian has been taken captive! He is a prisoner, but we cannot learn of whom. I prayed when I heard the news, prayed as I have never done before. I shan't write here what I prayed, for if I do, it shan't come true. Prayers are like wishes, that way.

Several Days Later

No news yet of Ardian. Father and Sosti have been many times to the Knights' general to ask after him, but nothing can be learned.

Next Day

People are saying in the streets that an army of Knights of Solamnia is drawing near. Paladine grant that it be true! Linnet says that we shouldn't believe everything we hear. Rumors spread faster than fire and sow great sorrow wherever they burn.

The Knights have many of our people under guard.

Several Days Later

I went today myself to see our people who are held captive. I wanted to see if Ardian was there, because Sosti admits now that he was among the rebels. But the Dark Knights wouldn't let me near the enclosure.

But from a distance, I saw them, and it quite broke my heart. There they stood, milling about like cattle in a pen, in the mud, women and children with babes in arm, as well as men, warriors. There are Kagonesti there, too, but they did not seem so miserable as our own people—likely they are used to the filth.

Despite myself, tears sprang into my eyes to see them. A Knight saw me, a rough human man, and he began to laugh. He drew near, and I refused even to look at him or acknowledge his presence—my tears became my pride, but he stank so of leather and armor and sweat, I thought I might swoon. "Here now, here's a pretty maiden. Why do you cry? Mayhap your lover is caught there in our cage? Come, then, into the bushes and let me comfort you," he said, and he grabbed my arm.

Well, that got my blood up! No more swooning now. I clawed him quick at that, a great bloody welt across his eyes, for I had not cut my nails (Linnet had neglected them, bless her). He let go, and I jumped away, but then I stood my ground again. I was not about to let him frighten me away. I dare say he was in such a rage, he might have lopped my head right off. He drew his sword, but an officer called him down, and he slunk off like the cowardly fool he was. I said farewell to him with my spit. I must say it brightened his dark armor, gleaming there as it dripped from the skulls.

SEVERAL DAYS LATER

I have heard on the street that Sir Thomas, the leader of the Knights of Solamnia, is to link up and attack the Knights of Takhisis here on the morrow. They will be some 100,000 strong, and they have silver dragons, and copper, bronze, too, in addition to griffins. That should be quite enough to handle the Knights here! Knights say that most likely Ardian was killed. There was a terrible slaughter on the border. But I do not believe them. The Dark Knights are filled with lies. They lie to see us hurt.

SEVERAL DAYS LATER

It seems the talk of the Knights of Solamnia is only that—talk. So Father says. He says I mustn't encourage Madame Rumor, she is harlot enough already. He really is a jewel! But it is a shame. I would have liked to see some Knights rolled in the dust for once. Still no word of Ardian.

SOME WEEKS LATER

It has been a terribly hot summer. This morning, I took up my journal to catch up on details, but there hasn't been much to write about, except the weather, which has been abominable. There is still no word about Ardian, but Father begged me to quit going to the jail to look.

This morning, the room was so hot and stuffy that I went to the window to open it and let in a little air. While I was at the window, I must have left my journal lying open, for when I turned round, there stood Valursa reading it, and laughing! Laughing! I could have struck her impudent chin, were I not a lady. I asked her, "What are you laughing at, you silly *valurshin?*" And she said she wouldn't tell me until I told her what *valurshin* meant. So I told her. What does it matter to me? I was betraying nothing. She could have learned for herself simply by asking any servant, if ever she'd get her nose away from the looking glass. Well, she got her twigs all in a bundle, as the saying goes, and ran off to Mother. Mother, no less!

Well, Mother is Mother. She had had her fill of Kagonesti impudence, she said. She wanted Linnet dismissed, sent away. Let her grub for worms with all her other kin, she said. Father had no choice. Mother can be so obstinate, especially when she is having one of her spells, which come more and more often, it seems.

So Linnet is gone. It is remarkable how quickly she left and how little she took with her. I suppose she never quite gave up her barbarian ways. I shall miss her, I suppose. She hugged me close for a moment, then took her little wrap filled with her things (pitifully little, I take more with me just going to the market), and walked straight off into the forest. She didn't even take a path.

"Who will dress you now, you stupid girl?" I asked Valursa back in our room. I could see already that she was sorry for what she had done, but she has Mother's overweening pride. She turned her back on me, turned back to her only true love—her looking glass.

"Who will tug the knots from your rat's nest now?" I asked. If her middle name is Pride, then mine must be Spite, for I could not stop myself. I have been this way ever since the war. "Who will have the patience not to rip the hair from your head?"

"Oh, do shut up, Genin," she said as haughtily as she could muster. But I saw that she was near to tears, so I twisted and drove in to the hilt.

I said, "Do you think the next servant will deliver your scented missives to your lovers in the dark of night? Do you think she will hide your notes under the mattress, or bring you purgative draughts from the Kagonesti midwives?"

Her face, I thought, went white as though I had tapped her with a hammer and all her blood drained out the bung.* Her lip trembled. "What do you know about that?" she said in a whisper.

"Only that it is true, and that I have never said anything about it to anyone. It would kill Father, you know. And what Mother might do, I couldn't say. Most likely she would be beyond retrieval."

She rushed at me, and I thought she wanted to strangle me, but instead she fell to her knees and clasped my hands in hers. "Oh, Genin," she wept. "You mustn't. You mustn't tell. I am sorry. You are right. It would kill Father to know. It would destroy us all."

"You scandalous imp!" I said. "Now you *must* tell me. Who is he, then?"

But she did cry so, all I could do was hold her and stroke her pretty hair. Really, I only call it a rat's nest to be evil. She does have ever so lovely hair, much lovelier than mine.

Finally, she calmed enough to speak, but she would not let me go. She held my hand like a drowning woman. We sat together on the bed, closer than we had sat in many a long year. I had almost forgotten

---

* A keg, as of wine or beer, is tapped at its bung. However, this image foreshadows a more dramatic usage in the elegy "Gas!" which, ironically, was also written about Valursa.

how pretty she is. With her eyes full of tears, I loved her so, just then. I would have done anything for her.

"He is of low birth," she said at last.*

"Do you love him truly?" I asked.

"As true as true hearts may love," she sobbed prettily. "But that is not the worst. He is allied with the rebels. He fights against the Knights of Takhisis and the noble houses allied with them."

I hugged her close. "That is wonderful!" I cried. "Splendid! When Ardian and his band drives the Dark Knights from this land, then your love shall be a hero and you can marry him!"

"Do you think?" Valursa asked, daring not to believe me, I know.

"Of course. But you must be terribly frightened for him," I said. "And it is so wonderfully romantic. Do you think... do you think he might know of Ardian?"

She swallowed hard, her eyes gleaming. "Yes," she whispered. "Dear Ardian is alive! He fights at my love's side."

"You knew this and you didn't tell me?" I said, pushing her away. "How could you? Well, we must tell Father right away."

"No!" she cried, clutching at my legs. "You mustn't tell, because then he will know how I learned, and he mustn't find out about my love or about the work I have been doing. We are not supposed to know. Father and Sosti say that Ardian has been captured, because if it was known that one of our kin is helping the rebels, the Knights would come and take our

---

* In traditional elf society, a male may marry below his station, but never a woman. Among noble elves, not even the male may marry below his station.

house and throw Father and Sosti in prison. Father is to take the Oath tomorrow, for our sakes."

Well, I didn't know what to say first. That Father intended to take the Non-aggression Oath[*] fairly boiled my blood. At the same time, I was dying to know what kind of work Valursa had been doing for the rebellion.

WINTER—5 SC

It seems ages since last I wrote. The whole world has changed. I can't begin to list what all has happened, and if anyone were to actually read this, I am sure that they would already know what has happened. But for the sake of future generations, I shall attempt to reconstruct those last days, and what has gone since.

I found Mother nearly out of her mind with pain. Outside, it seemed whole armies were marching, and the air seemed to burn in my lungs. I could not understand it. Outside were screams, the sounds of battle, of people dying. At night sometimes, I awake to those sounds. This morning, when I pulled my old cloak about me with the first chill of winter, I could still smell the odor of burning flesh clinging to the fibers. It is in everything that we had then, and it won't wash out.

---

[*] The Non-aggression Oath was required by the Knights of Takhisis of all elves having dealings within Qualinost. Those who did not take it were not allowed to conduct business, either buying or selling. If a head of a house took the Oath, he or she was considered to have spoken for the entire family. Many took the Oath rather than starve or be forced into the woods for survival. However, once the Oath had been sworn, anyone found breaking the Oath by supporting or engaging in rebellious activities would be treated as a spy, rather than an opponent in war. Spies were usually hung, while captives of war were merely imprisoned.

The Knights came during the night, hunting rebels, they said. They gathered together many of the lesser families who could not account for the whereabouts of their missing relatives. The men, they marched away, and the women were cast adrift, robbed of their every treasure. Homes, some of them ancient houses, were put to the torch.

Of course, some tried to fight, they tried to resist, and there was terrible slaughter in the streets. Our home was destroyed in one battle. Mother, Valursa, and I escaped it before the flames engulfed us. But Father and Sosti were elsewhere trying to plead for the release of innocents taken in the raid. We were alone, the three of us, and I fear I am the child of my mother after all, because I became hysterical. I thought the shadow wights had returned. I had forgotten them, somehow, I don't know how I forgot them, they were so horrible. I suppose I was still in shock from the horrors I saw when the minions of Chaos entered Qualinost; the shadow wights and daemon warriors. Sosti told me that when a shadow wight destroys a man, it destroys him utterly. Even the memories of that person in other people's minds vanish. It is strange, because it seems to me now that I had a lover in those days before the Chaos War, a boy whom I loved ever so deeply. But it is like the memory of a dream. When I try to grasp it, it slips away. This had preyed upon my mind for some time, all through the year, and then I remembered my diary and my poetry book. I found them among the things I had salvaged from the fire. I looked for him here among these pages, I looked for him among the pages of my poetry journal, but though he is here, I don't remember him. He is lost to me now, lost to me forever.

There has been no word of Ardian all this year. Father knows now that we had word of Ardian's fate before the Night of Fire. He gave us such a look as still breaks my heart even to think of it. But now, we are as much in the dark as he. Valursa's love, poor dear, was hung as a rebel. But he died valiantly, they say, and Valursa is changed, but proud. She no longer hides her love for him and openly mourns his death.

Worst of all, perhaps, is that we are still under the dominion of the Knights of Takhisis. The Night of Fire changed nothing, except to rob us of many of our best and bravest, and to slaughter many who were innocent of any crime. Worst of all is that the raid was approved by Senator Palthainon. We had hoped, after the Chaos War and the death of Senator Rashas, that Speaker Gilthas might lead us to a new day. But he is a puppet still. Now, there truly is no hope of rescue, for the world is unmade. There are no heroes.

The only bright light in all this is that Mother is her old self again. She has been a source of inexhaustible strength to us all. When Father needed her most, she has been like a rock to him. Father has found work in the gardens of the king, but our fortunes are much reduced. After our house was destroyed, Valursa and I took it upon ourselves to beg, so we have not done so badly as some others. At least Father works for the Speaker now, so we are still near nobility. But we live in a rented room, all of us in one room, and no servants. There is no privacy, not that we need it any longer.

I almost destroyed this journal and all my poems. I could not bear to look upon the world I have lost, but neither could I part with that part of me, recorded in this book, that is no more. I said that Valursa is changed. I, too, am changed. I am not the child I was before. There are no children in Qualinesti anymore.

SOME TIME LATER—5 SC

The Knights are building a proper prison to house the brave rebels whom they continue to capture. The winter was especially cruel and hard on them in their outdoor enclosure. Many died for want of blankets and warm food. Valursa and I did what we could, begging for blankets and shoes, and food when we could get it. They were all so pitiful but so polite and thankful for every little thing we could do for them. There was no fighting among them for the meager provisions we brought, and many I am told died of cold after giving away their blankets to others more miserable than themselves.

SOME TIME LATER

There was an escape, the last night before they were to begin moving our people to the new prison. They had been tunneling under the enclosure for weeks, and nearly half escaped into the forest before the alarm was raised. A few were subsequently recaptured, mostly those weakened by disease or hunger who could not move quickly enough.

In retaliation, the Knights hung every elf who was captured. They hung them from the scaffolding surrounding the new prison, and made the other prisoners walk under that awful canopy to enter the place few if any of them will ever leave. I stood outside and wept openly. People tried to pull me away, to send me home for my own safety, lest the Knights think me a rebel. But I am a rebel, and to the Abyss with those who will not resist!

TWO DAYS LATER

They have left those poor bodies hanging for the third day now. Some are beginning to come apart! It is a disgrace. How could people, even humans, be such barbarians? I have heard it said in some company that there is no such thing as evil, that what we call evil is only differences in culture and circumstances, misunderstandings, that what may seem evil to me may be perfectly normal in another culture. What rubbish! Evil is evil no matter where you are or who you are or what you believe. If you do not believe evil is real, then look upon those bodies, let the wind blow over them and fill your nostrils with their smell, and then look at the Dark Knights in their skull armor standing there leering at those who pass by with noses covered and faces averted. Hear their laughter, and tell me they are not evil. There can be no reconciliation, no working together with them toward a common goal.

Today I went there and stood before the prison. One of the Knights approached me and said, "What are you doing here, you damned rebel? You'd better go home before you get in trouble."

I said, "I have come to honor these heroes."

"What heroes?" he asked, laughing. "I see only carrion."

"I, too, see carrion about me," I said. "Only it is still walking and talking. If they could raise their eyes to heaven, they would see heroes hanging above them, with swords of vengeance poised to strike."

He grew furious and raised his fist to strike me. I did not flinch. "I shall soon see children hanging from these scaffolds," he threatened.

So I gave him my best. I lifted my eyes and looked beyond him, and such a look of awe and wonder came over my face as I hoped would make him look. I pointed and said, my voice trembling with fear, "Look! They come!"

His face went white, and he spun, drawing his sword. I spit on his back and walked away. As I left, I heard his fellows laughing at him, and he shouted, "Don't let me catch you around here again, you little whelp."

Father went tonight to beg an audience with Marshal Medan, the Dark Knights' leader, to ask that our people be taken down and their bodies cremated. He has not returned home. I hope I haven't gotten him into any trouble.

NEXT DAY

They have taken them down. Father still has not come home. But apparently he succeeded.

SEVERAL DAYS LATER

They have brought in a new group of prisoners captured in skirmishes east of the city. Valursa and I are going to see what condition they are in. We have been knitting socks and begging for blankets to give to the prisoners. Our neighbors on the floor below us have managed to keep a servant, and she showed us how to knit. Valursa acquired the skill more easily than I, for I have little patience. But I am better than her at begging, for I have no pride when it comes to trying to help our soldiers, and I am persistent as a tick.

Still no word from Father.

NEXT DAY

The prisoners are a sad lot. Many are wounded and have not had their wounds treated. We went begging for medicine and bandages for them. They were otherwise pretty well supplied, except they had no boots, for the Knights had taken these. But they have no money to buy food, and the Knights have begun to require the prisoners to pay for their own food. It is criminal, but to whom can we appeal? There is no one. We must rely upon ourselves.

WEEKS LATER

Madame Rumor is at it again. There is talk that Porthios is still alive and gathering an army to relieve us. I have no faith in these tales, however. I have talked to people who saw Porthios fall.*

---

* In the battle with the forces of Chaos, Porthios and the dragon he rode into battle were caught in a blast of dragon fire. Porthios was last seen plummeting to the ground, trailing flames. Rumors of his surviving the fall began to appear at about this time, but Genin gives them little credence. In any case, it is remarkable that she mentions his name at all, considering her past opinion of him. Perhaps because he had led a rebellion against the Knights before the Chaos War, she felt more inclined to sympathy for him now. Certainly, she no longer considers him a dark elf.

Two Years Later—7 SC

Things have been more difficult than I could ever have dreamed. Father was in prison for eleven months because of what I had done, and during that time we were utterly, utterly ruined. We were turned out of our little room and were forced to take up residence with Uncle Dorthinion.* He is a true great soul, but he was already poor. Taking us four into his household completely drained his resources. Valursa married, just to take some of the burden off of the rest of us. Her husband is not a particularly bad person, but he is of pathetically low station. Valursa was quite a catch for him, but Mother approved (not without regret). He is proud of her and takes good care of her, but his family is miserable to her because she is of minor nobility.

Father was finally released from prison. That day was a joyful one, but also one deep with regret. I tried to apologize to him. Mother, poor dear, never held me to account for what happened to him, even though it was my fault. But he said to me, "Genin, I do not begrudge you my suffering. Would that there were more like you, and we might throw these black dogs off our backs!"

Mother was aghast. They were the first revolutionary words anyone had heard Father speak. He and Uncle Dorthinion then off together for a good long while, and no one knows what they spoke about. But when they returned, their faces

---

* Dorthinion was the brother of Genin's mother. As such, he could take in his sister's family without causing a scandal.

were set, and they walked side by side, as equals.[*]

A few months later, Sosti took his leave of us. He was going out to see what was passing in the world, he said, and he slipped away in the dead of night. The Dark Knights do not allow us free travel, and they certainly wouldn't let him just leave. Mother was beside herself with grief, but he went with Father's blessings. Send word, Father told him, if you discover anything that can help us.

So, for the past year Father has been working with Uncle Dorthinion, learning the craft of bookbinding. It puts bread on the table, but I can tell how Father misses the forest. Sometimes I will find him staring out toward the edge of the city, where the true forest begins, his head tilted to one side as though listening. And his breast is ever filled with sighs.

In all this time, there has been no word from Ardian. Mother speaks of him as though he were dead. "My youngest son was . . . ," she will sometimes say. It is hard to believe that he would have been gone all this time without sending word. I cannot believe he is dead. Not Ardian.

Meanwhile, I have spent my time as best I know how. I have begged for food, blankets, cloaks, boots, anything to help our brave prisoners. I have gone each time a new group is brought in, to see if Ardian is among them.

Today a thing has happened that I have longed for

---

[*] Dorthinion was of lower station than Genin's father. The comment about their walking as equals is of some importance. That they had come to some agreement to work together toward something is obvious. What exactly that was is revealed later.

this past year! Sosti has returned! He came in the dead of night. We keep him hidden during the day, for no one must know that he is here, or the Dark Knights will surely put him in prison. There has been no time to talk to him today, because we must act as though nothing is different. But you can see in Father's eyes his joy, when for so long now there has been so little to bring a smile to his beautiful face.

NEXT DAY

Last night we spoke late with Sosti and learned of all the wonders that he has seen. He was among humans most of the year that he was gone, traveling to Palanthas and Kalaman and Haven. He speaks strangely now, with an accent that is almost uncouth, but somehow charming, and he mixes into his sentences words I have never heard before. He says they are words from the dwarf language that cannot be translated into Elvish. He traveled much of the time in the company of a dwarf named Rexord, and it seems they have become great friends. But he dared not bring Rexord with him, not into Qualinesti, so he left him in Solace while he journeyed here to tell Father of his discovery.

There is a human woman named Goldmoon, one of the original Heroes of the Lance, and the one who first brought word of the gods' return. She sojourned here in Qualinost for a time* and brought hope to us

---

* Goldmoon brought word to the Qualinesti of the gods' return to Krynn. At first, most elves were reluctant to believe her. "Why should the gods announce themselves to a human?" most argued. Having long admired the Heroes, it is understandable that Genin's father would be excited by word of Goldmoon's discovery.

in those dark days. Now, she brings hope again to us. She has discovered a new form of healing magic, Sosti says. He has seen her power. She says the power derives from within the heart. It seems so very unlikely, but Father has hope. As long as he is hopeful, I shall try to be hopeful as well.

TWO DAYS LATER

The most remarkable thing has happened. Father has somehow had an audience with Speaker Gilthas and obtained his permission to go north and study under Goldmoon! The Dark Knight Marshal Medan was most unwilling to allow Father to leave, but Speaker Gilthas insisted! He has some backbone after all! (I really shouldn't have said that, but he has such promise, and if only he would lead us, we would follow him!) In any case, he insisted, because if what Goldmoon says is true then House Woodshaper might be reestablished and our powers once again be used to beautify our city. Hearing this, the marshal agreed. No one was more surprised than Father, except perhaps Senator Palthainon. Father is to leave in two weeks' time. Oh, I wish I could go with him! But there is too much still to do here.

TWO WEEKS LATER

Father is gone. I was so miserable all day that I could not bring myself to go begging for the prisoners. I remained inside all day. I could not even compose a poem in my sorrow. My pain is too deep. I do miss him so, more so than when he was in prison. At least then I could visit him daily. I don't know what the prisoners will think of me. I have never before missed a day, not even when I had the fever.*

ONE MONTH LATER

A letter arrived from Father. He has found Goldmoon but doesn't say where he is writing from. He says that the power is real, he has seen it work, and that Goldmoon has taken him and Sosti as pupils. He doesn't know when he will return.

FOUR MONTHS LATER—8 SC

The most remarkable thing happened today. While I was out begging for blankets, a woman stopped me in the street. She wore a deep hood and a heavy cloak against the cold, so that I could not see her face. Without saying a word, she dropped a pair of good winter boots of Kagonesti handicraft into my basket and continued on her way. At the road crossing, she paused and turned back, then lifted her hood away from her face. It was Linnet! She put her finger to her lips, then covered her head again and moved briskly away. I was stunned. I could not believe it.

By the time I had gotten home, I had forgotten about the boots. Only when Mother and I began sorting through the things I had begged did I remember them. I showed them to Mother, and inside them she found a letter addressed to me. I told Mother that I thought Linnet had dropped them into my basket, but she was rather skeptical. "Your memory of her

---

* In 6 SC, a fever swept through Qualinost during the month of Summer Home. Several dozen elves perished in the plague.

has faded into the faces of the thousands of other Kagonesti that you have seen since," she said.

In any case, there was still the letter. I opened it, and never in my life have I so truly fainted. I thought it was but a ploy taught to women to help us out of difficult situations. I have used it myself on several occasions. But that isn't important. Get to the point, Genin!

The letter was from Ardian! He is alive! Dear sweet gods, he is alive!

Uncle Dorthinion found Mother and me sprawled side by side on the floor. He said that when he first saw us, he thought that we had been struck dead. But he roused us with a little wine (we haven't had brandy in years), and read the letter to us. I can scarcely breathe for my bruised ribs, Mother held me so tight in her joy. I gave to her as well as I received, though. And I don't think I have another tear inside me, we cried so much!

The letter (as I write this, I clutch it to my heart), Ardian's dear letter, told us of his fate. He had been captured just after the Night of Fire, and sent north to a prison camp. There he languished for years, unable to write or get word to us, his heart breaking to know of our fate, for he had heard such terrible stories about the battle in Qualinesti. Finally, he escaped and returned to our homeland, but he could not enter the city. He hid in the forest for many weeks before finally being found by a band of Kagonesti, some of whom had been in his rebel band under Porthios (yes, Porthios! Ardian is filled with secrets) before the war. They gave him shelter and news, and in one of their villages he ran into beloved old Linnet.

Bless her. She told him how we had fared, though how she knew of us I cannot begin to guess. She told him that she could get a message to me, that I often wandered through all parts of the city begging for the prisoners (for his sake, really, for it was ever in my heart that, if he were being held prisoner in some other place, that someone like me might do likewise and take it upon herself to care for him). It would be simple enough to slip something to me, whereas approaching Uncle Dorthinion's dwelling would be far too risky. We are known still as rebels, mostly because of me. So he knew he could trust me.

He has been in contact with Father already. We have not had news from Father for some time, so it was welcome indeed to learn that he and Sosti are faring well.

I have read his letter a thousand times already, and as I look at his words, I can see his beautiful hand holding the pen and scratching them out. Oh, his handwriting is as horrid as it ever was, but I love it so I could scream! Tomorrow will never come, I think. I am going to visit Valursa and bring her the news.

NEXT DAY

Valursa was so stunned by my news that she went into labor! Twins! So rare, and such an omen of hope! I am an aunt twice over and all at once. It is glorious.

TWO DAYS LATER

Hope turns to fear. Today, a green dragon flew right over the city. I have never felt so sick with fear in my life and hope to never again. People say that green dragons have been seen battling in the remote parts of the forest, battling each other, but no one knows why.

A WEEK LATER

Another letter from Ardian, and this time with instructions on how to write back to him. Linnet will wait for me at the bakery near Uncle Dorthinion's shop. I mustn't talk to her, simply drop the letter into her basket. Mother is in a state! She absolutely forbade that I should go, then turned around wrote a letter for me to deliver!

NEXT DAY

Met Linnet at the bakery. Her eyes were fierce like an eagle's. She has gone back to the wild almost completely. I am glad to have her on my side, for she would make a dreadful enemy. But it was so wonderfully exciting to be clandestine. It is a thing I could get used to. I felt so alive! Taunting Knights is one thing, but this, this made my heart drum in my chest. It was better than falling in love.

9 SC

Father and Sosti have returned in the company of many others of our people who also went north to the Citadel of Light.* Their homecoming was quite beyond joyous. We were dancing in the realms of rapture!** Father and the other heads of household

---

* The Citadel of Light was founded on the Isle of Schallsea in 8 SC by Goldmoon, as a beacon of hope promised by the mystic powers she had discovered.

** See Kierloth's Parable—"His hands bound to the helm/ his soul went lofting/ dancing in the realm/of rapture."

are to meet with Speaker Gilthas tomorrow to demonstrate what they have learned. I have not seen Father so happy in many a long year. His steps spring with vigor.

During this period, the family fortunes began to greatly improve, although Genin makes little mention of it. In large part, she carried on much as she had done over the last few years. However, her involvement in the elves' rebellion gradually grew more involved. As she spent more and more time working, begging for the prisoners, and carrying messages, she was spared little time for, and had little interest in, her diary. What is more, large sections of the diary covering this period were either destroyed outright or were too damaged to decipher. By 10 SC, her interest in poetry had been rekindled, largely because of her involvement in the rebellion (see below).

10 SC

I have been meeting regularly with Linnet now for many months. What began as a simple correspondence between family members has grown into something of a conspiracy, with me at its hub! It is remarkable, altogether remarkable. During my daily rounds of begging, I also pick up and deliver letters to various households with family and friends involved in the rebellion. I am the link to a vast network of communication. I am sure that there are others like me, but I do not know who they are. What is important is that twenty-odd families like my own are able to maintain contact with their loved ones in the forest, and to pass on information gleaned about the Knights' movements. I do this with Father's blessings. He entrusts his missives to me as well! Surely, I am no longer a child, at least in his eyes. I do not know to what depth he is involved in the rebellion, but that he is involved is beyond doubt. Good for him! With such as him working for us, we cannot but succeed.

My little nephews, oh! I adore them. That I might one day have a child half so sweet as they. But until the evil stain is removed from my home-land, my heart must remain true to the rebellion, and no mundane love shall stir *me*. I have been to see the little darlings almost every day. I am sure Valursa has grown weary of me, always hanging about and trying to help. Things are not as they were between us. Where once she was bitter and selfish, now she is quiet and understanding and forebearing, much like Father. Gods! Does that mean I am like Mother?

DAYS LATER

Received a letter from Ardian today. He thinks my idea of a verse code is remarkable. He promises to present it to their leader and let me know. I have already begun to work out the code words, patterns, and meters based on the natural sequences to be found in nature. Linnet has brought me a collection of leaves and drawings of plants that are quite bewildering! If I can catalogue these, I think I shall go a long way to establishing a code that will prove infinite in its variety and impossible to break!

There is just one thing. I do not know who is the leader of the rebellion. I suspect, but oh! I shall not, I shall not even think it.

Delivered a letter to M__. Bad news. I do not envy her. That is why I refuse to give my heart to anyone but the rebellion—Father, the gods, and homeland!*

Several pages are missing here. One page remained, but it had been in large part burned. Dorthinion provided no clues as to the contents of these missing pages, but what is clear is that during this period, Valursa's husband leaves the picture. He may have died, but the textual evidence does not support this conclusion. Most likely, he was forced to flee into the forest to avoid arrest for rebellious activities.

12 SC

There is still talk that I shall be sent to Lemnost.** I'll resist every step of the way, if I am! But I don't believe. Father will keep the dogs at bay.

Tonight, I attended a small gathering at the home of Senator Q__. She was a gracious hostess, and so very liberal for a Senator. At this gathering, I was to deliver a verse message to H__, so I brought along my poetry journal. Well, it did get rather warm inside, especially the conversation! I stepped outside for a glance at the stars, and when I returned, I found several people passing around my poetry journal!

"Whose is it, do you suppose?" Senator Q__ asked.

---

* At forty-two, Genin had begun to attract admirers among her male contemporaries, the most notable Theonathas, her childhood paramour.

** Probably for her own safety.

I didn't dare speak up, not because there was anything in it that could possibly be revealing except to those who know my code. I stepped back out onto the balcony, and waited there for a moment until the conversation lulled, and then I returned, and as prettily as I could, asked, "Has anyone seen my journal?" Well, that stirred them up. It's not yours, is it, Genin? I had no idea you had such poetry in you! I thought you were only a stubborn patriot! Paladine knows all you Woodshapers have patriotism in your blood.

Of course it is mine, I said.

You must read, they said. They wouldn't let me rest until I had read them something. So I chose my "Heroes and Children," since H__ was in the room at the time, and this was the message I was to deliver to him. It went quite well, and everyone applauded politely, but one clapped more loudly than the rest. I searched round for this enthusiast, and found to my astonishment none other than Speaker Gilthas. He stood in the doorway with his attendants, and Senator Palthainon! Oh, the Senator is ever a dullard. This night was no different, and he obviously found my poem pointless and, at the worst, a waste of breath. But Speaker Gilthas enjoyed it. Did he! He approached, and I curtsied ever so deeply, flushing up to the tips of my ears.

"May I?" he asked.

"Yes, Speaker."

What could I do? He took my journal into his gentle white hand and opened it, scanned a few lines, then asked, "May I keep this for a time? I'd like to read it through."

I nearly fainted. To think how I worshiped him once, and to have him there now before me, asking leave to read my poems, and the first one about him! But I couldn't refuse. He is our Speaker.

He has it now. If I live through the night without dying of shame, I shall be surprised.

Genin did survive the night and within several days was called to an audience with the Speaker. Of her work, the Speaker said, "Here is a poet soon to take her place among our great Voices." In an aside to her, he said, "Your work is much admired and appreciated. I sense deeper meanings in many of your verses, meanings that speak to those with the ear to hear. Pray continue in your efforts. They do not go unnoticed." The import of his words were not fully understood at that time.

Much of the diary beyond this point has been lost, except for the last few pages. Many pages survived partially intact, but are largely unreadable except for dates and words along the inner margins. The outer pages were burnt, then soaked with water and other fluids, some of which appear to be blood.

From these hazy references may be gleaned something of the years between 12 SC and 39 SC, where the last entries detail the days leading up to Genin's arrest. A few entries have survived well enough that specific passages may be transcribed or inferred.

Between 12 SC and 17 SC, Genin's life went on much as it had before. The family's fortunes continued to rise, though Genin was never asked to dance for Speaker Gilthas at any of the parties. Her regard for the Speaker rose in those years, though the general population continued to think him weak and ineffectual.

Around 16 SC, the name Porthios begins to appear more often, but in what context cannot be determined. A revealing pair of words immediately precedes the first entries for 17 SC, which survived well enough to be transcribed below. These two momentous words are, "meet Porthios."

17 SC

Letter from Ardian today. I have permission to visit his camp and meet some of those for whom I have so longed toiled. Linnet will deliver me unto them tomorrow eve. Valursa has agreed to make my rounds and visit the prison, though she begrudges my trip, for Killaeras[*] is a member Ardian's regiment now. If, that is, I can escape my nephews! I think they are enamored of me. Ah, to have such beauties at my beck and call. I feel like a queen, sometimes.

Two Days Later

I shan't go. I am in no danger here. I shan't go. This is my city, my home! They can kidnap me and spirit me to Lemnost on griffin-back, but I'll claw my way back home. There is too much to do here.[**]

---

[*] Probably Valursa's husband, though this may be the name of a new love interest for her.

[**] The meaning of this passage is unclear. Most likely, she was under considerable pressure from the leaders of the rebellion to leave Qualinost for a time. Her activities, and especially her belligerence in regard to the resident Knights of Takhisis, have been documented in captured military reports.

Jeff Crook

The next four years are time of ever growing rebelliousness. Around 21 SC, Genin is finally sent away for her own safety. The entries for that year are datelined Lemnost, but of her activities there, little is known, for the pages are mostly unreadable. She returned to Qualinost in 22 SC, apparently because her mother had begun to relapse, and Valursa was with child again. But Genin had begun to change.

22 SC

Found Mother suffering from a headache this morning. I heard her cry out last night, but she claims no memory of it. I wish Valursa were here to help, but she has enough on her hands. I have no patience for Mother these days. I feel restless. My hands are ten idle digits forever wandering. I shall die for want of something meaningful to do. There is a feeling of change in the air. I smell it. The forest is stirring. I saw six crows flying west today, a bad omen.*

ONE MONTH LATER

I have asked Father to hire a nurse for Mother. I cannot help her. I have my own nightmares, mostly of dragons. It is all this talk of giant dragons, I cannot abide rumors.** They serve no purpose!

Valursa's child was born yesterday—a girl. They named her Valgenin. There is no joy in this child for me. I do not know what is wrong with me.

---

* A Kagonesti belief. This remark shows their growing influence, probably as a result of frequent contact.

** The great dragons, like Malys and Khellendros, were battling for territory all across Krynn. So far, Qualinesti had been spared.

One Week Later

I waited all morning at the bakery, but Linnet never appeared. It will give me good excuse to slip off into the forest for a time, to see what has become of her. The city stifles me. There are too many people here. It grows more difficult each day to beg for the prisoners. I am getting prideful, something I truly do not need. I should never have taken up the bow.* The pen is my true weapon, the pen and my natural boldness.

Three Days Later

Linnet has not been seen by anyone for three days. It is unlike her. But they cannot spare the scouts to carry out an extensive search. She will show up sometime, I am sure. What is curious is, the last time she was seen, she was headed for the city to meet me.

Eight Days Later

Linnet has vanished utterly. There are others as . . .

The remainder of this ill-boding page was destroyed, and we never learn Linnet's fate.

For the next two years, the elves continue their rebellion. Captured dispatches from the Knights of Neraka indicate that their activities slacken at this point, and the Knights report a strange restlessness in their own dragons. It is well known that even among

---

* Indicates that during her sojourn in Lemnost, Genin learned to shoot a bow. It is possible that she used it in anger at some point, but that is only conjecture. Certainly, something important has happened to change her.

non-rebellious elves traveling through the forest, dis-
appearances are not uncommon, but this was at first
attributed to abductions and internecine murders.
But in 25 SC, the culprit reveals herself in all her
majesty and fury—the huge green dragon Beryl
claims Qualinesti for her own. The Knights broker a
settlement with the dragon whereby they will rule the
elves in her name, and send her frequent tribute and
prisoners to sate her appetite.

Genin's feelings on this arrangement are not known,
but can easily be imagined. There is only one surviving
line of text from this period, dated around 26 SC. It
reads:

. . . while evil piles upon evil. We are as bad . . .

Another fragmentary text from this time period is also
suggestive, though its exact meaning cannot be con-
firmed. It is dated around 28 SC. It reads:

. . . Gilthanis [next few words are blurred] spoke
with him at length at the sacred tree of Anaya."

As the brother of Porthios, Gilthanis (if alive) would
be a contender for the throne of Qualinesti, a leader for
whom the rebellion had long been dreaming. But no
other documents speak of Gilthanis, and the period
between Beryl's arrival in 25 SC and the last entries
of 39 SC is only unique in that the rebellion neither
grew nor diminished. A status quo was maintained,
in which the Knights held the populated regions and

the roads, while the rebels ruled all the wild places except those areas in the immediate vicinity of Beryl's lair.

However, little of this may be gleaned from Genin's diary, for these years are missing entirely, ripped from the binding and lost to history. That she continued her efforts is without doubt, for her last surviving entries, dating from the last months of 39 SC and on into the year 40, pick up from where the previous intact pages leave off, except that some time during this period, Valursa took her children and joined her husband/lover in the forest. The first entry begins ominously in mid sentence, and is undated.

. . . killed him. I was not sorry. Ardian dragged the body off the road and gave me the spurs. I returned to the city before nightfall, and left the spurs with F__ to melt down for arrowheads. I spent the remainder of the night sewing a cloak for Ardian and listening to Father try to quiet Mother. I will speak no words of ill-omen, but if the gods (who are no more) were merciful . . .

NEXT DAY—WINTER COME—39 SC

As usual, I did not rest much last night. Whenever I close my eyes, the visions of destruction return, just as though they were images painted on the underside of my eyelids. But unlike tapestries or paintings, these images move, live, breathe, burn, and die. I wish the war would come, that

Beryl would attack and it could all be decided. Though I have seen but seventy-one summers, I am weary, weary as no elf should be when the first snow falls. It brings no joy to my heart any longer. I see snow and can only think of the misery it will bring to those who have no shelter.

Two Weeks Later

Spent three days in Ardian's camp with Valursa, Killaeras, the twins, and little Valgenin—she is not well. I see it in her eyes. She is a sensitive like Mother . . . and me. But she is so young . . . surely it will kill her if the tension is not broken somehow. The twins are learning to use the bow. They are quite good, better than me at short distances. When they are strong enough to pull a full-sized bow, they will be marvelous fighters. Killaeras is teaching me to combine sword with shield. I can handle the sword well enough, but the shield is a nuisance. I can't remember to use it, so it ends up being nothing more than a weight. Ardian liked the cloak. It looks good on him.

At the evening meal, I had words with Lithoquin, and it almost came to blows. I cannot abide mages, and since his sorcerous powers have begun to fail him (much like all the others), I never resist twisting this into his soul. I can't abide magic users. I once wanted to be one, but now I am glad I never learned the craft. I should have hated myself as well. Ha ha.

They say Palin Majere passed through our camp the second night of my stay. I didn't see him, and I'm glad of it. It is good that cooler heads than mine prevail. I should never have made an effective leader. I much prefer doing what I do.

SEVERAL MONTHS LATER

Sosti is to be married. He is marrying a loyalist bitch. I can't imagine why. I'll not attend the wedding, and I told Father so. He merely gave me that look of his, the one that makes you feel about as big as a worm. But I won't go. I'll claim a headache. It works for Mother, so why shouldn't it work for me?

NEXT DAY

Mother has passed. She died last night during the storm, but not from injuries. Her hair went white as snow just before she died.

It is for the best. I cannot write about it. Father is sad, but in his heart he is happy that she no longer suffers.

But I still suffer. It has not lessened for me. But I am younger. It won't kill me. The storm was for me a nightmare from which I shall never recover. Like Mother, I have a streak of white in my hair, won last night battling the horror within my own soul.

There is much to do in the city today. Others died violently last night, crushed beneath trees and fallen walls. At any rate, Sosti has postponed the wedding. That's a blessing.

LATER THE SAME DAY

It is to be a double funeral. Little Valgenin died within the same hour as Mother. That's two. It just leaves me. Poor Valursa! Poor us. We cannot attend both funerals, and they cannot bring Valgenin into the city without being arrested. Oh, gods! I hate the Dark Knights. I hate what they have done to us.

Two Days Later

Of course, Valursa and Ardian could not attend Mother's funeral, but I still I wish they could have been here. I was angry with them, and I don't know why. I don't understand myself any longer.

At the funeral, Father said that Mother's last words were of her children. It was very pretty and sad. He dared not speak the truth, that with her last tormented breath,* she sobbed, "Takhisis, my Dark Queen!" Father was aghast. He turned positively white, and cried, "Do not call upon her, my love. If you must call, call upon Paladine." But by then she was dead. I know what it is that she saw in those last fearful moments. Do I not see it every night?

Somehow, I do not believe she is gone. Sometimes, when I enter a room, I can smell her hair, just as though she were standing right before me. I close my eyes, and I can almost feel her touch upon my cheek, just as she touched me when I was a child. But now it gives me a chill. I can't stand to be in this house when it is dark.

---

* Foreshadows a similar scene in "Gas!"

ONE WEEK LATER

Ardian is heartbroken at Valgenin's death, even more than Mother's. He doted on her so. But things are moving now. Madame Rumor is flying through the streets of Qualinost. Leave? Abandon our beloved homeland? I can't believe it. Beryl attacking? Madame Rumor has never been more the whore. I give little merit to these rumors. Besides, so long as evil stains my homeland, I will never leave it.

Nevertheless, something is happening.

A Kagonesti maid stopped me in the street today. She whispered, "They are coming for you soon." I tried to wring more from her, but she wouldn't speak and I didn't want to cause a scene. I was within sight of the prison.

TWO DAYS LATER

It is dangerous for one such as I to keep a journal. Caution warns me to destroy it, but I cannot bring myself to throw away the last of that which I once was. I wonder if it would not be best to escape to the forest. Ardian will have me. I can shoot a bow.

No other journal entries are found beyond this point. Genin was arrested the following day for suspicion of treason, and her diary was confiscated. It appears that most of the damage to the diary was accomplished by Genin herself. The diary was used at her trial, but enough of it had been destroyed that little could be proven against her. She was not executed. She was imprisoned in the same place she had visited nearly

*every day for the past thirty-eight years, chained side
by side with those she had worked so hard to help. It was
well that she had done so, because for the previous ten
years, they had been burrowing an escape tunnel. Genin
spent fewer than three days in prison. However, only she
escaped. Before any of the others could enter the tunnel,
the Dark Knights surprised them, and their escape was
foiled.*

*Little is known about Genin's whereabouts today. Her
Uncle Dorthinion, who brought us these manuscripts,
refused to reveal more about her activities for fear that
the publication of this book might compromise her and
her rebellion. His only desire, he said, was to see that
history and literature were preserved. For that, he shall
long be remembered.*

*The last surviving documents relating to Genin are
her poems. In his last letter to us, Dorthinion told of a
night when he wandered near the eaves of Qualinost,
and there he met an elf horribly disfigured by fire, but
who was nonetheless alive. The man spoke no word,
simply handed Dorthinion a small bundle of papers
wrapped in a soiled green ribbon, and turned and
reentered the wood. As Dorthinion states, upon opening the bundle, he was stunned to find that it was
Genin's poetry journal, the very volume of blank pages
that her mother had given her for her Eleventh Day of
Life Gift. Its binding was gone, and many of the
papers were ruined. Only a few of her poems survived,
but some of these are among the most visually and
emotionally powerful verses that have emerged from*

these times. In the last two poems, we learn perhaps what Genin has been doing since her escape, as well as of the unfortunate demise of her sister. Still, there is hope that this poet, one of the great voices of a generation and a people, yet lives.

Jeff Crook

Sonnet to the Sun

In autumn raiment stood he to the sky,
His face a-gleam, his flowing golden curls
Like molten sunlight poured for trembling girls
To break their hearts and make them long to die.
Look once my way, and grace me with your eye   5
Gilthas Solostaran! Speaker! King!
Your very name has set my soul to sing.
Or if my voice should fail me, then to sigh
My simple words, to set your name on high
In no less beauty than a clutch of pearls   10
Or starlight caught upon the harper's string,
Or if the words should fail me, then to cry.
Arrayed in white, the grieving lover hurls
Her body at your feet, to kiss, and cling.

---

1 Composed in 2 SC in honor of Gilthas of House Solostaran after seeing him at the
Spring Dawning dance of that year. Revised in 12 SC after a change suggested by
Speaker Gilthas. Of this poem, Genin noted in her diary, "They are the first words
I have writ that are mature and worthy." The form is a Kierlothian sonnet, with a
rhyme scheme of abba/abba/acb/acb.

10 Originally written "In no less beauty than a stream that purls." The phrase
"clutch of pearls" was suggested in the margin by Speaker Gilthas. Genin adopted
his suggestion, crossing out "stream that purls."
Drafted according to the manuscript on the 21st day of Autumn Harvest, 2 SC.
Fair-copied later, with minor revision, in 8 SC.

[I TIPPED LOVE'S BOLT]

I tipped Love's bolt with kisses
   And nocked it to my heart's string,
Pulled full taut my soul's green bow,
   And gave my gentle thorn wing.

But gusts of Chance were veering.   5
   Grim Fate and a lowly birth
Had already shorn my hopes
   Before the arrow kissed the earth.

TITLE   Attributed to Dorthinion
3 See Merturan's "The Wildrunner"
          Pull full taut thy green bow
          And loose thy arrow singing
Begun in 9 SC, the manuscript was extensively revised in 10 SC, and again in the
month of Winter Deep in 39 SC.

Jeff Crook

TO A FORGOTTEN LOVE

Lines written to an imagined lover stolen away by
shadow wights

Marry me, thou sweet somber flower
Tarry thee here another hour
        and more
Daringly I sing your beauty, yet
Verily, thy lights are deeper set   5
        than a door.
Why how long thy nails have grown of late.
How I long to be thy wanton mate,
        thy whore.
Why do you not touch me as I would   10
Try to do, if trembling fingers could
        adore.
You grin, I see, your thin lips stretched,
And then I flee your visage wretched
        with gore.   15
Nine years now have you been dead
Mine fears fill me with dread
        of war.

TITLE   Lines written to an imagined lover stolen away by shadow wights
According to her diary, Genin came to suspect that she had had a sweetheart before
the Chaos War, but that the memory of him and all record of him was lost when she
was slain by shadow wights.

5 Lights: eyes.
6 See Kierloth's "To a Dead Love"
        Thy lights are set deep as doors
        Within thy castle wall.
7 Both an exclamation and a question. The fingernails and hair of the dead are said
to continue growing in the grave.
9 Indicative of Genin's growing restlessness in 39 SC.
16 Though she revised the poem in 39 SC, she kept the time set in the revision of 10 SC.
Drafted in 8 SC and extensively revised in the month of Winter Deep in 39 SC.

[FULL NINE SUMMERS]

Full nine summers hath surpassed
Since supposed treason stained a noble throne
While wondered I all aghast
Had treason stained a name where there was none?

Had some grievous madness come   5
To fool the wise with folly wrapped in verse
Wrought cold to seem like wisdom,
A bitter blight a blessing, a boon a curse?

Had noble Solostaran,
King, been cast to darkness, his soul still bright? 10
Has the star breeze child begun
His life turned from a home his own by right?

When I to my father turned
Cold truth in sadness sat upon his brow
With longing, yet his eyes burned   15
To see the truth turned up as with a plow

Could I but push my shoulder
Into the jingling traces and the hame,
And with a stouter heart, and bolder,
Set my steps to harrow out our shame.   20

TITLE Attribute to Dorthinion.
10 Refers to Porthios of House Solostaran.
11 *star breeze child* – Refers to Silvanoshei, the son born to Alhana Starbreeze and
Porthios. Because his parents were cast from the light, he was denied his royal
birthright as a prince to the thrones of both Qualinesti and Silvanesti. This
acknowledgement of his rights by a patriotic Qualinesti elf is remarkable.

Jeff Crook

[THICK NIGHT]

Thick night moves upon the hills
Wolves cry meetings in the wood
Frogs still at any movement
In the endless unmoving night.
Heaven's orbs cross a darkened sky   5
To announce the day.
Swans split Dawn's autumn canvas
Gray wings mute the wind's sound
And tug my soul to rise and fly
An arrow's course into the clouds   10
To course an ancient remembered path
To the winter nesting ground.

TITLE Attributed to Dorthinion.
Written in 11 SC, this is the first surviving example of Genin's coded verse
messages, the secret of which has never been revealed. Although the meaning of
this message is not known, it is known that animals, plants, heavenly objects,
directions, movement, and even the number of lines, are coded references to
military matters.

HEROES AND CHILDREN

The sky bent orange trees, leaves
Everywhere like locusts, buzzing
Birds
Dipped, rose, twisted, spiraled in happy
War   5
The people walked along, unnoticed,
Down the milling road to gather
Acorns, talk,
Scratch, stand, and worry together.
Children hide, dart, giggle and shush   10
And only the strong become
Heroes
But now sunset and dinner's smells
Bring dead emptiness
To the fall dusk. People   15
Sit about tables, fires, ashes
To stop
The whole city wraps
In brown and green and sable night
To sleep, or not, find comfort   20
In the body lying close
Or not.

TITLE Attributed to Dorthinion
Written in 12 SC, as stated in her diary, genin coded this message to be delivered to
a fellow rebel identified only as H__. However, the reading of this poem was the
occasion that brought Genin to Speaker Gilthas' notice. The coded references
themselves are obscure.
Drafted in 17 SC and revised in Lemnost in 22 SC.

Jeff Crook

[WINTER SONG]

Come Winter, sing of snow to mute the cries
Of Summer Flame so horror filled.
Come covering mantle white to blind our eyes
To blood of elves and dragons spilled.

So sang I while wandering lonely places: 5
Forget, alas, forget and weep
For loss, and loved ones lost. Their faces
Linger at the gray edge of sleep.

But clinging to Hope's grinding ledge
Has honed my grief unto a bitter edge.   10

Now sing I songs more keen than swords
To set round me impenetrable wards.

Come hoarfrost's bitter sting into our woe,
Mind us of what went before.
Not unto a blind complacency we go   15
Again, like lemmings to the shore.

TITLE Attributed to Dorthinion.
Written in 22 SC at Lemnost.

SONNET TO THE MAGE

Through leafy bower sought I Nature's breast
With weariness of war and all I'd seen
To throw me down among the fronds and rest.

I came upon a chapel fair and green
With somber acolytes in gray bark dressed   5
Like monks, who did upon each other lean

To serve as roof and spire and leafy crest,
And with their spreading branches form the beams
From which depended bats with eyes of red.

Deep by the largest bole I spied a mage   10
Come here to rest and heal, or so I thought.
But sooner learned I that his soul had fled.

I found his wisdom wise as any sage.
His mouth spoke only flies. We never fought.

---

1 See Kierloth's "A Leafy Bower."
Written in 39 SC, this poem, as well as surviving diary entries of the same period,
hint that Genin's rebellious activities have moved from peaceful to violent means.
Certainly this poem is indicative of a certain callousness towards death, while the
subject reinforces the statements in her diary concerning her dislike of mages.
In this poem, the first of her true war poems, Genin makes one last attempt to
recall a more innocent past. She reverts back to the Romantic form of the sonnet,
using a classic style, with a rhyme scheme of abab/abab/cde/cde. However, the
breaking of the lines from the classic sonnet form, and the progression of the poem
from classical nature images to that of the dead mage shows Genin's own
progression from innocence to grim realism. Her use of dark humor is
extraordinary for an elf, who normally revere life.

Jeff Crook

[NO HEART WAS EVER PIERCED]

No heart was ever pierced
  By any Love so deep
Than by this hungry spear's
  Keen prick.

      No sweet child's sleep   5
Was ever sweeter than this sleep
  Upon the stone,

      No kind
Words expressed in word or thought
  So fair   10

      As 'coming home.'
No silver net for maiden's hair
 Was wrought

Weaker than this
Mind, broken by what bitter war   15
Hath bought.

TITLE Attributed to Dorthinion.
This poem seems to be a response to Kierloth's famous poem, "A Heart Unmade by
Love." In that poem, Kierloth laments the loss and pain of a loved one slain in war,
and how the warrior fears to be left widowed should his wife be slain while he lies
abed with a wound.

12 In Genin's first surviving diary entry, she mentions wearing a silver net in her
hair to Gilthas's party.

[GAS!]

"Gas!" she cried.
"Beware! Green dragon's breath!"
And shoving me aside
She drank her bosom's fill of death.

"Lucky for you!" they said   5
But then
You should have seen the cart
They flung her in.
If you'd beheld her beating heart

And heard her breath boiling in her lungs,   10
Atop a pile of fellows once so fair:
A dozen others bleeding out their bungs—
Though dead, their humors sought the air.

And know that her last tortured thought
Was turned to mouth frail words, and plead   15
In voiceless utterance a message wrought
Meaningless by the madness of her need.

TITLE Attributed to Dorthinion.
This poem is dated 40 SC. Although Genin never mentiones Valursa by name, it is
believed that this poem tells of the death of her sister during the dragon's attack.
2 Unlike red dragons, who exhale fire, green dragons breathe out a poisonous
chlorine gas.
12 An image first explored by Genin in her diary. A keg is tapped at the bung.
13 Another remarkable use of dark humor through a pun upon itself. Revealing of
Genin's callousness towards death.
17 The dying woman's attempts to utter last words reflect Genin's experience at
her mother's death several years previous.

Bertrem's Note

My colleague Brother John has recently come into possession of the report produced below from Valter Liebert. The loreseeker has provided other materials to Brother John in the past, and from the high quality of the material here, one may hope the two continue their collaboration in the future.

Solace is, of course, a justly famous town in the annals of Ansalonian history. Seat of the Inn of the Last Home, it has been celebrated in song and story since the days of the War of the Lance. However, in these latter days it has, like so many places throughout the land, fallen upon hard times. The value of Liebert's report is precisely that it shows how even the most well known of places may suffer in times of war and upheaval.

Brother John has warned me that Liebert's report is sadly lacking in organization and thoroughness. He

John Grubber

flits like a bird from one flower to the next, sipping but never drinking too deeply. Perhaps, now that I consider the matter, this is precisely its value: it provides the reader with a broad overview of life in the town rather than a detailed examination of only one aspect.

Whatever the case, I am indebted to Brother John for cultivating his relationship with Liebert and for editing the report prior to handing it to me.

My friend, Brother John Grubber
of the Order of Aesthetics:

Greetings and well met! I hope this report reached
you in a timely manner. As you may have noticed, it
was not I who delivered it, but a courier I hired.
After completing my sojourn in Solace, I had to
return to Zaradene for further research, some of
which is included here, the remainder will be with
me when I return. I shall return to the library soon,
but there are other matters I must attend to first.
Regards,
Loreseeker Valter Liebert

ཉ ཉ ཉ ཉ ཉ

28th day of Paleswelt, 38 SC
Zaradene, Abanasinia

When first I landed in Abanasinia at Zaradene
some months ago, I took on the guise of Valter Bau-
mann, a Solamnic merchant with my mother's
maiden name. It seemed the simplest way to explain
away my accent to those I met. I have found people
are not as forthcoming when they know someone
will be scribing their thoughts and words, and I have
no desire to see the inside of a prison again, not after
the unfortunate incident in Solanthus last year. I
arrived in Solace close to dusk a week after landfall,
to find many of the streets and walkways empty.
Few people traveled to visit friends after dark, and
since the conquest of Haven to the east, I discovered
that few people travel at all. I found lodgings far

from the well-known Inn of the Last Home, taking a room in a boarding house near the tavern known to the locals as the Trough. From my seat in the Trough and taverns like it, I set about chronicling the lives of the people of Solace.

Far too many times in its history Solace has had to live up to its name, and provide shelter and a new start to those in need. As the dominions of the overlords spread, more and more people are without places to lay their heads, more and more have no food in their bellies. Solace has opened its arms to the needy survivors of Haven, the escapees from the camps of Sable, and any others hoping to find freedom.

A Note on the Structure of my Report

Having found so many emotions running through Solace and its citizens, I opted to choose a diary, events from my notes, or a relevant essay from my research that I felt typified each. I have also included selected quotations from Ansalon's literary history, as I think they best summarize the emotions I uncovered. I have also included a brief history of Solace and the region surrounding it, compiled before I went to the treetop city to familiarize myself and complete my disguise.
Valter Liebert

ಜಿ ಜಿ ಜಿ ಜಿ ಜಿ

The History and Archaeology of the Solace Region
(excerpted from *Abanasinian Archaeology* by Flinders Pitrye, 350 AC)

Pre-Cataclysm:

Prior to the hubris of the Kingpriest drawing down the wrath of the gods on a wicked world, the region where Solace now stands sat deep in the heart of the elven nation of Qualinesti. Detailed maps of the Pre-Cataclysmic lands are scarce, but according to the Qualinesti, the region was only moderately settled and of little value. It should be remembered though that they were pushed unwillingly out of the area, and elven pride being what it is, they likely dismiss the land as useless rather than admit defeat at the hands of ragged refugees.

Every year though, when the farmers plow their fields, or when a fisherman hauls in his nets, artifacts are found. The churning of the soil makes them difficult to date, but the longevity of the elven civilization and its slow rate of change alleviate this difficulty somewhat.

Post-Cataclysm:

The smiting of the earth by the heavens was the event that spurred the founding of Solace. As the lands fell and the seas rose, refugees from what was once Solamnia and Ergoth streamed south and west, the only directions they could go. Naturally the elves of Qualinesti were resistant to this, and conflict did erupt, but in the end the diasporic tide couldn't be stopped. The elves, facing overwhelming numbers and the devastation within their own kingdom, pulled their forces back to the very edges of what remained of their forests, and the land of Abanasinia was born.

Settlement Begins (1–100 AC):

As the elves retreated, the goblins and hobgoblins their patrols previously kept trapped in the mountains again descended on the land. Refugees died by the hundreds as the raiding hordes, already used to rough living, capitalized on the confusion by burning and attacking the hastily erected camps and unwalled villages. One group of refugees, realizing there was no way to beat the monsters in battle, sought to avoid them altogether by building their homes in the giant trees—Solace was born. Eventually the humans of Abanasinia organized themselves, driving back the monsters with the aid of the Qualinesti, and settled to form Gateway, Haven, and several other settlements. Throughout the countryside, villages sprang up around the ruins of elven structures, the poor peasants scraping out existence, unaware of the ancient structures or their significance. In some places, the slender ruins jut above the grasslands or out of a lake, where once there was forest surrounding them. The settlements of Abanasinia are built upon the bones of elven history.

The Plague Times (70–100 AC):

In an age without healers, disease is a settlement's greatest enemy. It stalks the streets with impunity, slaying weak and strong, young and old, male and female. While disease was present throughout Solace's history, on two occasions the plague has come to ravage the town, though there have always been people sick from various things. In a country town, sickness is a fact of life.

In 70 AC, the dragon fever swept through the town, killing few but crippling many with its crimson rash. The epidemic lasted for over a year, the victims slowly wasting away but only rarely dying. Instead they were left in an invalid state, weak and pale, not fit to work the fields, but rarely skilled enough in a trade to work in the town.

Only thirty years later, the Kholera came, after a season of heavy rains and flooding. For the only time in memory, it was possible to navigate the streets of Solace by small boats, so high did the waters of Crystalmir Lake rise. When they finally subsided weeks later, the citizens thought the worst of their troubles were over. They thought wrong. The dead livestock and plants rotted in the lakes and streams, fouling the wells of the unsuspecting populace. In Gateway and Solace several hundred people died, though many more had been ill.

Witch Burnings and Warlords (60–250 AC):

As the Cataclysm and the Ansalon of the past faded into memory, the survivors adapted to their new lands, though some decided they were entitled to more than others. Petty warlords appeared, carving out baronies and kingdoms, setting themselves in feudal luxury even though they often held little more than a few villages. These would-be monarchs warred against each other, hiring mercenaries and levying their serfs into service, all to increase their own holdings and prestige. Solace always remained a free town, its size and the fortifications used against the sporadic goblinoid raids presenting too large an obstacle for the petty despots to challenge. As with all tyrants, the warlords chose to fight those who would offer little resistance—small villages and isolated towns. In spite of numerous threats, Haven, Gateway, and Solace, though they had close ties with each other, remained essentially independent city-states, at least until the coming of the Seekers.

The Rise of the Seekers (240–350 AC):

The origins of this elaborate and influential cult are lost, though it is generally believed that their gods were more numerous than the old gods whom they replaced when they abandoned their children on Krynn. The religion was based in Haven, where their council hall was built, and they had temples to their pantheon throughout Abanasinia.

With their growing numbers and followers, the Seekers began to influence politics and city behaviors. Once this gap between religion and rule began to close, it was an easy task for the corrupt among the Seekers to manipulate for their own gain.

In some cases, the Seekers allied themselves with the petty barons of the region, hoping to further their own ends by gaining a martial ally. The tyrants knew this too but saw the Seekers and their followers as perfect tools to manipulate a populace in war or in peace and so accepted their duplicitous bargains.

The War of the Lance (348 AC):

The War of the Lance in Solace is well related, both in tavern tales and official histories. The town served as a slaving center for the Red Dragonarmy and was heavily damaged during the early part of the war in Abanasinia, but after the liberation of Pax Tharkas, little of note happened there. Peace reigned in Solace for several decades, until once again the lands erupted in turmoil.

The written sources I had to work with had little infor-
mation on Solace in the modern age. The following
information is gathered from my own research findings.
Liebert

The Chaos War (383 AC):

Solace itself was affected little by the Chaos War. The minions of the Father of All and Nothing were never directed against the treetop town. They did, however, assault Haven, ravaging it and destroying one of the famous six white towers. The militia of Solace aided the city guard of Haven in driving out the beasts and shadow wights, many giving their very existences in the process, their names lost even to their families.

Solace in the Fifth Age (0–35 SC):

The Age of Mortals began well for Solace, as it did for much of Ansalon. The damage of the Chaos War was slowly repaired, and people began to return to normal lives. The lands of Abanasinia were free for a time, before the coming of the great dragons. Five years after the Second Cataclysm, the dragon purges reached the subcontinent when Beryllinthranox the Green engaged other green dragons in battles for control of Qualinesti. Her supremacy was finally attained twenty years later when she was able to start expanding the great forests to her liking.

In 28 SC the discovery of sorcery and founding of the Academy expanded Solaces' population and brought many of the most learned people to her. Some sought to train as new mages, while others hoped to regain their lost powers. The hundreds of students swelled the economy, resulting in strange and exotic peripheral businesses appearing in the treetop city.

Liebert's note: The destruction of the Academy ten years later and the corresponding decline in Sorcerous powers has caused many of those same businesses and rooming houses to close again. The activities of the Knights of Neraka and Beryl's minions, the proverbial "wolves at the door," have played a most significant role in the tense confusion and fear that now grips the city.

ఌ ఌ ఌ ఌ ఌ

"…and so Soth wheeled on the road to Istar, turning towards the home fires;
their warmth to him poisoned;
turning his back on a destiny noble, fully embracing in fury a fate that maketh dark gods smile."
—Medeon, *The Fall of Istar,* Book XVI, lines 242–245

26th day of Fleurgreen, 38 SC
Solace, Abanasinia

In the near month that I have been in Solace, I have encountered many conflicting emotions and moods in

Solace and her people. Most of these tensions arose as a result of the arrival of the wealthy from Haven and then were heightened by the arrival of the refugees from the doomed city. While the actions of Beryl, the green dragon overlord, are the larger cause of events, the coming of the Havenites was the direct stimulus of much of what I encountered. Consequently, it is the fall of Haven to which I now turn.

In the taverns of Solace I encountered many survivors of the attack on Haven. Most had escaped serious injury, at least physically. Their eyes and ears however, have heard such things that the scars on their souls will likely never heal. One such man was Tavin Methgar, who was a bookkeeper in Haven when Beryl and her minions attacked. He took shelter at the time but was able to escape the city between the end of the initial attack and the arrival of Beryl's troops.

It has been over thirty years since Solace last saw the ravages of a dragon, so many of these refugees find little in the way of sympathy. Though many in Solace are old enough to remember the green dragon battle five years after the Chaos War, it has largely faded in memory as an event of history, the effects of which were able to be overcome. In this dark age, mercy is in short supply—the hatred for the corrupt Haven upper class is extended to all from that city, deserving or not. Small wonder then that I encountered Methgar in an alehouse, trying to drink away the demons that had taken his life, and nearly his sanity, away. He sat alone, rising only to order drinks, for even the barmaids shunned him.

The following is his story in his own words, left for me at the rooming house where I was staying.

Why you want to know this I don't know, and why I want to tell it escapes me too. What I do know is that I haven't slept through a full night since it happened, at least not without help.

I lived all my life in Haven, met and married my wife there, raised my family there. My whole life was within the city with its white towers. There had been seven, but one was destroyed in the First Cataclysm, and two more fell during the Chaos War. They were never rebuilt.

Haven was originally a Qualinesti city, destroyed during the First Cataclysm and resettled by human refugees in about 80 AC. Under the leadership of the warlord Garud, the homeless horde took refuge from the goblin marauders within the still-standing walls. The interior was covered in trees and woods, the people long gone and the buildings little more than ruins. Over the centuries, the city now known as Haven was rebuilt. Though the techniques of elven masons and architects are largely unknown to any but elves, much effort was spent in retaining and restoring as much of the unique flavor of the fortifications as possible. It is no surprise then that elves have a love-hate relationship with Haven, favoring it for its familiarity but viewing its residents as squatters and trespassers.

The day was sunny and the skies were clear as I walked to my employer's counting house. Without a second look I passed the old Highseekers Council-hall, which in my parents' time had been converted to a hospital and refugee hostel. The wretched poor and sick crowded its marble steps, fouling the air around them, and I hurried past, eyes averted lest they press me for alms. I gazed into the sky as I sauntered down the cobbled streets, seeing several birds high above the city, occasional sparkles dancing in the sky around them. I paid them no more heed as I was nearing my place of work.

I had just settled down and opened a ledger at my desk when I heard a patter on the slate roof. I glanced out, saw glittering chunks on the ground, and puzzled over the strange hail at this time of year. Again picking up my ledger, I was about to set pen to it when the first screams started. They were cries of terror and confusion coming from the streets all around the counting house and even from the alleys and their beggars.

The clattering grew louder. The screams continued and were added to by frantic horses in the streets. Looking out the window, I was horrified to see people running past, bloodied and raving. A man charged across a square towards the door of a tavern, only to have his reaching hand sliced from his arm by a glittering shard.

Glass.

Glass rained from the sky. When I looked at the ground more closely, it was littered with stones and metal chunks, like the refuse from a smithy. Bodies lay across each other, draining blood onto the cobblestones from dozens of wounds. Children, women, the elderly—no one was spared the horrific rain.

I stood paralyzed at my window for too long, watching as my fellow citizens were felled like wheat. Suddenly the clattering stopped, and I snapped to my senses. Flinging open the door, I ran into the street to the nearest victim, nearly slipping on the blood, gravel, and glass. Again I saw the birds in the sky, this time heading west, while another group approached from the east, as though following them. I looked closer. They were not birds—they were dragons.

The man on the ground was dead, his skull cracked. I threw my coat over his staring eyes, but I still see them haunting me. Other people were entering the street now, drawn by the screams and by their own curiosity. Seconds later, the ground shook, and I was knocked from my feet by a thunderous noise and gust of wind. As I lay on the ground I felt dust, wind and bits of debris pelt me, and when I turned over, all that was left of my counting house was a shattered, smoking, ruin. The council hall bells rang out an alarm, too late for some, and as they did, I felt the ground shudder again, this time more softly. More screams filled the afternoon air, followed by more ground-shaking thuds. I got to my feet and looked towards the nearest of Garud's Towers, at the East Gate, just in time to see a massive stone smash through it midway up its slender body. The upper half tumbled to the ground below. The cries of its occupants could be heard above the horrendous crash of its impact, which shattered the windows in the buildings around me, showering those of us in the street with glass. I ran again for cover, this time to a nearby archway, and surveyed the destruction around me.

As suddenly as they had begun, the bells stopped ringing and the stones stopped falling. Many emerged from buildings to help the wounded and gather the dead, to seek out families and friends amid the destruction. As long minutes passed, smoke rose above the city in a few places. I raced to my home, ignoring cries for help all around me. The minutes it took to reach my home felt like hours. Rounding the last corner, I fell to my knees in shock when I saw my house, or what was left of it, perched on the edge of a small crater formed by a rock and the collapsing catacombs and cisterns under the city. The entire side of the house was torn away, and I could see my family within, trapped on the second floor. I raced towards the house to help them but was held back by people when I tried to enter. They told me the house was too unstable, that we had to get a ladder to those within. As we worked with what broken timbers we could find, the bells started to ring again, and I chanced another look into the sky.

I barely remember much after that, so mad was I with fear. When I saw the dragons, the wave of nausea that hit me was so strong I soiled myself and collapsed to my knees, throwing up. People around me screamed and ran in every direction as the dragons bore down on the city. I begged them to help me save my family, but no one would listen. They all ran, ignoring me as I had ignored others when they needed me.

The beasts hurtled past me, very low in the sky: dragons of blue, red, and green. The wind from their passing almost knocked me down.

There was a sound of snapping timbers and screams from my family. The house shifted as it slid, then fell over, raising a cloud of dust and shaking the earth as it landed.

I knew they were dead. No one could survive such a thing. Still I climbed over the rubble, trying to dig them out with my bare hands. I still hear them, the screams of those dying all around me as I dug, but I ignored them. I pushed aside stone and wood until my hands bled, but I knew they were already dead. I heard no cries. There was no movement. I finally stopped my digging and began to weep.

The dragons bellowed in fury and rage, belching fire and lightning until the air was thick with smoke. Bells still rang, and cries still echoed as they continued their attack, continued destroying Haven, while I knelt amid the ruins of my life and cried like a child.

I had nothing. My family, my home, my work—all were gone. The shock of this numbed me, and I walked through the wrecked city. I don't know how long I traveled, but it was nighttime when I came to my senses, and the dragons had long since left.

The hoarse screams of panicking guards startled me. They were calling for reinforcements to the gates. Apparently draconians and other troops of the overlords were trying to break through the palisaded outer neighborhoods and gain entry to the city itself. Bells again began to ring, and many rushed to aid the people of the outer neighborhoods, citizens and guardsmen alike, leaving their rescue operations for more pressing tasks. Fighting was fierce at the eastern gates, and I quickly moved away from there, having seen enough death and destruction for one day. In truth, with my family dead and my home destroyed, I didn't care a whit about the people of Haven anymore.

I picked my way through the ruins of the market district, stopping to try and find food and a blanket among the darkened wreckage. As I rummaged, the fluttering snap of wings and the thud of dozens of feet filled the night around me. I spun around, only to find draconians settling to the ground in the square in front of me, though I was hidden from their view. I had no weapons, and I was no fighter, so in my cowardice, I dove under a merchant's wagon, hoping to avoid detection.

Under the wagon I hid, huddled on my knees, broken glass, stones, and chunks of metal digging into me. My heart raced, and fear clutched at me. The beasts hissed orders at each other and began to move about, and I waited for an eternity while they distanced themselves from my hiding place. Fate had placed me near a stable that had escaped major damage, and stealing inside, I quickly found a horse suited to my needs. As I saddled the mare, I heard more rustling wings and landing draconians. This was no mere raid—this was a full-scale invasion.

There was nothing left for me in Haven. I mounted the horse I had stolen and headed for the western gates, hoping to get past the draconians and escape the doomed city.

A few days later, I found myself in Solace, seeking out whatever work I could after the money from the horse's sale ran out. Any steel I earned went to pay for my room and the drink that keeps me sane. I have been here for months, but still my stomach knots when I hear bells ring or smell smoke. I wake every night to their screams. Every time I close my eyes, I see the buildings falling and the dragons wheeling in the sky. Every night I try and save my family, only to wake up in some wench's bed, the stench of ale in the air and my cowardice staring me in the face.

I have stayed away from the refugee camp, even though I have seen people whom I once knew in it. They don't recognize me. I don't even recognize myself anymore. I couldn't face them even if they did know me. I ran from them all when they needed help. I only thought of myself and my family—not of the people around me.

I found out later that things in Haven did not end as badly as I thought. The city wasn't destroyed completely, but it did fall to the green peril. If I had helped, maybe fewer people would've died, maybe more would've escaped. All these "'what ifs" and "'should haves" haunt me day and night.

I hope you never have to live through what I did. In truth, I wish I had died with my family, or at least fought for Haven. We may not have won, but it would have spared me this wretched life.

Tavin Methgar of Haven

笽 笽 笽 笽 笽

Liebert's note: Methgar was found, clean shaven, well dressed, and apparently sober, hanging by the neck from one of Solace's treewalks this morning. I regret that I did not tell him my true name or purpose in Solace. Perhaps his tragic fate could have been averted, but perhaps putting the words to page finally gave him some peace.

I am journeying to Gateway for about a month. It appears I underestimated the cost of living in Solace, and I must seek employment translating at the library there briefly, to secure enough steel for the remainder of my research. It works well with my disguise, as I have told my companions and informants that I must go to Gateway on business.

ᨦ ᨦ ᨦ ᨦ ᨦ

"Envy . . . taking root but not growing, nay, spreading like a blight upon ones' soul until that soul recognizes not the shell that is its prison."
Aesymar, *The Sesteriae*, Act II: 108, ca. 2600 PC

2nd day of Fireswelt, 38 SC
Solace, Abanasinia

Upon returning to Solace and securing more affordable and more permanent lodgings for my stay, I have spent several days exploring the town and its local businesses. I have set about finding informants again and gaining their confidence to aid in my research. In dark times such as these, the friendship of a man is apparently no more costly than a drink and a friendly ear, which works perfectly for me and my purposes. In short, I am being treated with all manner of viewpoints and opinions, which I shall endeavor to record.

The tales and tirades turned eventually from local problems to local heroes, Solace being the home of many of the Heroes of the Lance. I expected that when these tales were told, the somber mood of many of my newfound "friends" would dissipate in fond memories and wild heroic tales. I was very wrong. While some remembered the legendary residents, other regarded them with much scorn. A great deal of this venom was reserved for the late Caramon Majere, which honestly surprised me. The hatred some held for him was exemplified by a middle-aged woman who sat with us at the bar, who loudly cursed his memory and bade him a speedy journey to an infernal realm. Intrigued, I moved closer to her to find out more about her hatred.

Elya, as she introduced herself, was likely once an attractive woman, though years and rough living have marred her features. This woman's bitterness puzzled me, her words a mixture of half-drunken slurs and insults to him and his memory, and I prepared to move and leave her to her ramblings, until she started to talk about how it was all his fault that she was alone and penniless. Elya told her tale at my urging, despite the cries of protest from my companions, who had apparently heard it all before, perhaps a few too many times. Her story began months ago, before the fall of Haven, an event that seems to have been the source of many of Solaces' newfound problems. If her tale is to believed, she was once married, to Marten, a man of modest means, and had two sons by him. The husband and wife were young, both having been born in Solace the year after the Chaos War, long before the coming of the dragon overlord Beryl.

Their lives were happy, even after Beryl's arrival, for the dragon did not concern herself overmuch with the human cities. Indeed, according to other reports, Beryl seems to worry only about the elves infesting her realm and finding the Tower of High Sorcery in Wayreth.

Elya's troubles began when Caramon Majere began speaking out against Beryl and all the dragon overlords, urging people to stand against them and fight as he had in the past. Apparently his words were too convincing, for Elya's sons and husband joined a resistance group shortly before Haven's fall.

The group was poorly trained and led. Its members were arrested in a series of ambushes along the roads and trails between Solace, Gateway, and Haven. The Knights of Neraka, acting on Beryl's command, executed several members of the group in each city, leaving the remains in gibbets as a message for all who would raise sword against her. As it happened, Elya's family hung in Haven, where she couldn't mourn or bury them.

Death is a risk one takes for such activities, I tried to explain to her, but rather than see them as heroes, she saw them as victims of an old fool reliving his youth. It was easy for him to speak out against the dragons, she said. His wife was gone, his children grown or dead, he had nothing to lose, he had nothing to live for, and everyone around him knew it. Quieter men though, like her husband and sons, were often ridiculed and bullied as cowards and felt they had to prove themselves as men. They had joined the rebel group as an indirect result of Majere's stories—seeking the acceptance and admiration lavished on him since his youth. They were no soldiers, though, and Caramon Majere should have known that most people in Solace weren't. Perhaps preaching that people should take up the sword for their freedom is easy when you aren't the one who has to swing it. Not to besmirch the reputation of a legend, but almost everyone wants to be a hero, and not everyone can. The old warrior's stories seem to have inspired many who should have fought in other, more subtle ways, ways that would not have cost them their lives.

You are not a martyr if your name is forgotten—there are all kinds of heroes in the world, not just the ones that slay dragons and lead armies. She blames Majere and his inflammatory rhetoric for killing her family and reducing her to her current state, and perhaps the blame and hatred is somewhat well placed. We would do well to think about all the lessons we learn from our heroes.

≋ ≋ ≋ ≋ ≋

"Sleep and dream like children then, while long shadows creep out around you to make your night endless!" —Sir Lesityr uth Paarison, speaking to the Solamnic Knights High Council, on their unwillingness to dispatch a force to deal with the growing ogre hordes, *Annals of Solamnic History,* Vol. 723, no. 37, 1052 PC.

10th day of Fireswelt, 38 SC
Solace, Abanasinia

In their efforts to forget the darkness around them that seems grow with each passing day, citizens of Solace have turned to gaming. The arrival of the citizens of Haven, wealthy and poor, has brought new games and gambling houses to the treetop city, halls that are always full of young and old. In a slip of the tongue, Lord Warren's aide-de-camp, Devar Oppem, commented that it was a waste of valuable preparation time—when I pressed him for details, he became rather vague, speaking about the harvest and other winter preparation matters. I suspect that there is trouble brewing—trouble the citizens are either not aware of or refuse to take seriously.

The following are several games, long popular in Solace, as well as several games that arrived with the refugees from Haven. I have included rules and regional variants in hopes of preserving and sharing these enjoyable pastimes that have driven the residents of Solace to distraction and helped them forget the doom on their doorstep.

This may not be the best way for the residents to spend their time, but they do not seem to care—gambling and drinking help them forget the shadows of the past and the clouds on the horizon.

ꞩꞩ ꞩꞩ ꞩꞩ ꞩꞩ ꞩꞩ

Fortress

Description:

This game can be played with standard draughts or checkers pieces on an improvised nine-square by nine-square board. The central block of nine squares is the fortress, and each player's nine pieces represent his army. The goal is for a single player to capture the fortress according to the rules below, while preventing the opponent from doing the same.

Pieces and Setup:

One player has eight knights and one general. The other has eight ogres, the general being an ogre chieftain. The armies start in diagonally opposed corners of the board.

John Grubber

FORTRESS

Plans of Occupation

Movement

O: Ogre G: General

C: Chieftain K: Knight

94

Rules:

Pieces may only move forward or backward one square, diagonally in each turn. Only one piece can be moved per turn. Victory conditions are agreed to at the start of the game, specifically the pattern that must be obtained in order for the fortress to be captured. Regardless of conditions, the central square must be occupied by the general or chieftain, while the squares around him must be occupied by at least two soldiers in a set pattern. These typically include corner occupation (the fortress towers) or side occupation (the fortress walls). A player can still win if the set pattern is at least half filled, though the leader must always occupy the center square. Pieces are taken out of play by being captured or killed. Capture occurs when a single piece of one color is blocked diagonally in front and behind by opposing forces. The capture appears as a line of three pieces in diagonally adjacent squares. After capture the prisoner is sent to a square of the opponent's choice, where he may again begin to move on his next turn. A piece can be killed if it is surrounded in all four possible move directions. Killed pieces are removed from play.

Loss of the leader forfeits the game immediately, as the troops or horde have no one to direct them. Capture of the leader does not end the game however.

ᨦᨦ ᨦᨦ ᨦᨦ ᨦᨦ ᨦᨦ

Ogres

Description:

This is a simple game of the Fox and Geese family. The object is for the knight to evade or kill the ogres and for the ogres to trap the knight before he reaches the safety of the fortress.

Ogres Board
and Starting Layout

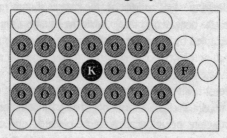

Movement

Ogre Killing

Pieces:

The board is a piece of parchment with thirty-nine circles drawn on it in seven rows of five circles each. The remaining four circles are placed in a triangle at one end of the board, adjacent to the second, third, and fourth circles of the last row of circles. The center circle of this pyramid is marked as the fortress. Twenty markers of one type and one marker of a different type are needed. These are the ogre horde and the single Solamnic Knight.

Rules:

Play begins with the knight in the center of the seven rows, on the third circle. Ogres are placed in all other circles around him, though none may be placed in the first or last circle of any of the seven columns.

The knight moves first, and his first move is always a kill, as he must break through the ogre battle lines. Killing is done by jumping over an occupied circle to an empty one. The dead ogre is then removed from the board. The pieces may only move one circle horizontally or vertically; diagonal moves are not typically allowed. Play ends when the knight reaches the fortress, or the ogres surround him or her at least two deep on each side, preventing jumps and hence, kills.

Some knight players take different strategies, opting to try to kill as many of the ogres as possible before eventually succumbing, while others make a mad dash for the fortress. The game can be scored as a straight win or loss, or the remaining ogres can be tallied against the dead ones and the victor so determined.

Variants:

The game can be played by teams on larger boards with several knights and even more ogres. The knights can start back to back, but each must have at least two avenues of escape to break through the ogre lines. Some versions of this game also include a dragon for the ogres, another unique piece that can move only diagonally and must move four circles at a time. The dragon can be killed in the same manner as the ogres, and its death is worth ten ogres if the game is being scored that way.

ㄣㄣㄣㄣㄣ

Jaggana, or Cutthroat

Description:

This game was brought from Haven, but according to its players at one of the local gambling houses, it originated in ancient Istar. According to research conducted in the Hoyel Library of Solanthus, the game was brought back to the civilized parts of the empire by members of the Order of the Divine Hammer, the Kingpriest's elite guard, when they returned from the Heathen Wars or postings on the northern frontier.

The name comes from the city of Jaggana, a haven for outlaws and criminals who chose exile there rather than execution or re-education at the hands of Istar's priests. Its other name, Cutthroat, comes from the tendency for the alliances in the game to last only so long as needed, as in the ancient city itself. It is a draughts-like game, but involves a great deal of strategy. For that reason, it is sometimes called Beggar's Khas.

Pieces:

The game uses a standard hexagonal khas* board, of ninety-one six-sided tiles in three different colors, but instead of the traditional khas pieces, it uses chips of three different colors, matching the tiles.

---

* Bertrem's note: The rules for Khas can be found in *More Leaves from the Inn of the Last Home.*

JAGGANA
(Cutthroat)

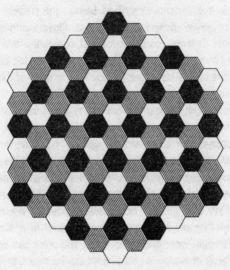

Movement

Piece Taking

Multiple
Piece Taking

John Grubber

Rules:

The game is typically for three players, though more are allowed in the variants described below. The players' pieces start in opposite corners of the board. Players arrange their nine pieces in three rows, the longest containing five pieces, one in a corner of the board and two on either side of it. The row in front of this has three pieces, and in front of this is the last remaining piece.

The player can move one piece one space in any of six directions. If another of his own pieces occupies the tile to be moved into, the player's piece passes through to one of the three tiles on the side opposite the originating side, but only if the desired tile is unoccupied. A player cannot attack through an occupied tile. If it is occupied by any of the players, another tile must be chosen. Only one tile may be passed through by a piece in a turn. If another player's piece is encountered in a tile to be moved through, there are two options. The piece can be taken and removed from play, or an alliance can be negotiated. If two players ally, their pieces can move through each other's tiles in accordance with the restrictions above for moving through friendly tiles.

Pieces can be taken only in jumps that originate on one side of the occupied tile, and terminate in one of the three tiles on the opposite side of the occupied tile. Multiple piece-taking jumps are possible if a player jumps into a tile that is unoccupied and finds an enemy piece in one of the three adjacent tiles opposite the entry tile. On the second jump, the enemy piece can be taken only if there is an empty tile on the side of the occupied tile that is directly opposite the tile from which the jump originated. The jumper's direction is in a straight line on the second jump; it cannot turn as it can on the first jump. Alliances are broken at the moving player's choosing, without warning, by the taking of a piece that was friendly.

When a piece reaches the corner tile of an opposing player, it becomes an "assassin." When this happens, a second piece is stacked on top of it, and it can move two tiles in any of the six directions available, though it is subject to the same restrictions for moving or attacking through occupied tiles as any other piece.

The game ends when one player remains.

Variants:

The game can be played with two, three, four, or six players. With two players, each player gets eleven pieces, and they start in the opposing north and south tiles. The starting layout is up to the players, but all pieces must be within three tiles of the boards' edge. With four players, each has nine pieces, and they start in the eastern and western corner tiles, leaving the northern and southern corner tiles empty. With six players, all corners are occupied, and each player gets seven pieces, arranged in two rows of three, with a single piece in front.

ཀ ཀ ཀ ཀ ཀ

"Eat, hoard, feast, and dine, but when those great gates groan under the weight of the desperate, remember, liege, an empty stomach has no ears."
—Kethos Praxea, Advisor to the Emperor during the siege of Daltigoth, 1791 PC.

28th day of Fireswelt, 38 SC
Solace, Abanasinia

During my stay in Solace, I spent a portion of each day wandering the town, using my meager funds to simulate the lifestyle of an inhabitant. In doing this, I hoped to gain the confidence of locals, that they would expose me to some of the more undesirable elements of Solace. Throughout my research, I heard many rumors of former Havenites running dens of debauchery and smoking-houses, secret havens filled with the elderly trying to forget, and the young seeking excitement.

My search was in vain though, for I could find no informants to direct me to them. It is likely such places exist, but such an underbelly is open only to the initiated—the Knights and constabulary would quickly shut down any such places if they did find them.

ཪ ཪ ཪ ཪ ཪ

"My thirst. It does take, but not give; yearn for, but not in longing; it is thee Nabaka, that I possess not by my right, but by my hunger."
the windows, Pesar—shield us from the light;
these deeds should be seen not even by the likes of us."
—Heregar of Istar, *Nabaka and Pesar,* Act III, Scene II: 130–135, ca. 540 PC

2nd day of Paleswelt, 38 SC
Solace, Abanasinia

I came to possess the following diary in a most interesting way. While walking through the town I chose a side street that ran alongside a house on the ground, somewhat of a rarity in the part of Solace in which I traveled. I learned later that it belonged to a merchant and his family, but on that day, I was merely passing by en route to the refugee shantytown to explore. As I walked, I could hear shouting and screaming, the sounds of a struggle within the house. Before I could react, a body hurtled out a window, knocking me to the ground. Looking around, I saw a girl of not more than twelve picking herself off the ground, eyes darting about as though she were looking for something. A door banged around the front of the house, and I heard voices, as did the girl. She threw a box at me, and asked me to hide it as she started to run down the street in the direction I came from. By the time I was on my feet, she was gone. I heard footsteps from around the corner, coming towards me, and quickly decided that I should be somewhere else. Secreting the small box under my cloak, I hurried off towards a nearby stairway, seeking refuge in the treewalks.

As I mounted the stairs, I saw two men hauling the girl towards a wagon while a third scanned the street around them. Given the rumors of thieves being among the refugees, I assumed the child was a cutpurse or a footpad under someone else's tutelage. If I had known then what was within the box or the fate that awaited the girl, I would have helped her myself, or at least alerted the law sooner. As it was, by the time I opened the box and sorted its contents, the wagon was long gone, rumbling towards the southern gate.

I recopied the relevant journal entries here before turning them over to the authorities. I only hope this child's tale does not have the ending I fear it will.

John Grubber

38 SC, 7th of Brookgreen
Father has been so sad since the fire. Gerison offered him a job, but he wouldn't take it. Mother was mad at first, but now it doesn't seem to bother her. She doesn't really talk to anybody anymore. She just sits by herself by the window. I cannot wait until winter is over, so I won't be stuck inside all the time. Thanks to the fire, we'll have nothing to sell and no money to buy at the Spring Dawning festival in a few weeks. It looks like it will be another year before I get anything for Children's Day, too. Father says he just cannot afford it.

38 SC, 27th of Brookgreen
Last night was the most incredible storm! It was terrifying. The whole house shook ! The trees outside were shaking, and the lightning flashed. The roof has some holes in it now, but Father is covering them with straw. He said he can't afford to fix them right now.

Some Plainsmen also came to see Father today. They lost their tents in the storm and wanted to buy new ones from him for traveling, and they wanted to find bright cloth for the festival of the Harrowing. He sent them away, saying he had nothing to sell since the fire.

They look strange, all painted and dark-skinned. They smelled too, like horses, but they were nice to me. One of them even gave me a pendant. It is made of a smooth blue rock tied in a leather thong. The Plainsman—his name is Starshadow—said it was a hopestone and that all the children of his people wear them. Father said I can't wear it, but I still do, just under my collar where he can't see it. Starshadow was very handsome. I hope he comes back soon.

38 SC, 18th of Yurthgreen
Wonderful news came today! Father's shop is saved! A woman from Haven, Lila Dillyn, will become father's partner if he rebuilds the shop and reopens it. She's a widow—her family died when Haven was attacked. She says I remind her of her own daughters and that she hopes we can be great friends! I like her. Father was so happy today, he and mother danced and sang all night with Lila.

38 SC, 10th of Holmswelt
Mother seems so much happier since the store reopened. It has given her something to do—now she sweeps the shop and does other little jobs, and has started talking to us again. Lila is wonderful. It's like having two mothers! She insists that I call her auntie, and she is always bringing us gifts or inviting Mother and I to lunches. I started talking about school, and she got very sad, and she told me about her own daughters, who would have been schoolmates of mine at the school for girls in Gateway. I feel bad for making her sad. I won't ask her about her daughters anymore.

38 SC, 21st of Holmswelt
Mother is sick. She hasn't slept in days and she is all gray and sweaty. She can't keep any food down, and

she keeps having attacks. I tried to help her, but Lila has come to our rescue again. She stays with Mother while I work with Father at the store. She is so wonderful. I don't know what we'd do without her. I hope Mother gets better soon, I feel bad being so happy while she is sick. All around town, everybody was sad today. Father says that Caramon Majere died. He was famous for fighting in some war a long time ago, I think.

38 SC, 26th of Holmswelt
Mother has gotten better, thanks to Lila. Today she was up and walking, but Lila has stayed by her side, even cooking her food until she is fully recovered. The store is doing very well now, and there are lots of things in it now, not like early in the summer, and people are always coming in to shop. Lila has suggested to Father that they hire some people from the camp outside the wall, to give them a chance to earn some money and to ease the workload on us. Father thought about it, and when we got home today she had already hired two men who used to be from Haven, and set them to fixing the roof of the house! She's wonderful! It's as if she can read Father's mind! I don't know how we got along without her. Mother is feeling much better. She said she went outside today. Lila took her for a walk while the men worked on the roof.

38 SC, 10th of Fireswelt
Mother is sick again. Lila says she had a "relapse." I think that means she got sick with the same thing again. She sent Father to Gateway three days ago to buy things for the store and for Mother, some healing

things I think. Lyo and Garak, the two men Lila hired, minded the store with me, while Father was gone. Someone said they saw Father here in Solace yesterday, but they must have been wrong—he's in Gateway.

38 SC, 12th of Fireswelt
Mother has gotten worse, Lila says that she may have the plague, but Father doesn't seem worried. Lila has moved in to help take care of her, so that Father can get plenty of rest to run the store. I hope Mother gets well soon. I never get to spend any time with her or Lila.

38 SC, 13th of Fireswelt
I helped Lila make Mother's food today. She put this powder into the broth, and she said it was to help Mother sleep. She has even sent for a healer, who prayed to the lost gods and tried to help Mother, but it didn't work—she's getting sicker.

38 SC, 17th of Fireswelt
Mother died last night. Father is distraught. Now it's just him and me and Lila. She was up with Father all night. He seemed better this morning.

38 SC, 21st of Fireswelt
I miss Mother so much. With the store doing so well, Father has said I might like to go to school in Gateway in a few weeks, rather than waiting until after the harvest season. Lila agreed with him, saying that the school is a much more fitting place for a young lady, not a dirty town like Solace. She says I will

never find a husband with all the farmers and wood-cutters around. She is so nice—always thinking of me. I think Mother would have wanted me to go to the school, and so does Lila. I will leave in a fort-night, even though school has already started. I miss Mother so much, I think of her always, but I try not to cry. Lila says that a proper lady must control her emotions and not let them control her. I know she means well, but it still hurts a lot. I guess it's not as bad as losing your own children though.

38 SC, 26th of Fireswelt
Father and I have taken ill in the same way as Mother. I don't know what to do. I am so scared. What if it's the plague come for us too? I'm so scared, I don't want to die like Mother did. Lila has moved back to her home, and the healer who tried to help Mother comes to visit us often. He says he should be able to help Father, since he was called early. Gantree tried different things, but Father doesn't feel any bet-ter. I can't go to school now! I must stay and help as best I can. I can't leave Father! I won't!

38 SC, 28th of Fireswelt
A miracle has happened! Father is getting better, and so am I! I will be able to go to school as planned! Mas-ter Gantree is going to Gateway and has offered to bring me to the school himself to save Father the cost of the trip. He says it's the least he can do after not being able to save Mother. Lila has hired a man from Haven to mind the house and help Father as he gets better. I will continue to get better while I am at school.

Lila says that sometimes, a change is as good as a rest.

38 SC, 30th of Fireswelt
I went into Father's room to get Mother's silk scarf before I left, the one she promised to me, and I overheard them talking! Father took up with Lila just after she came to Solace, while Mother was still alive! He had been bedding with her on all those trips to Gateway! That's why people had seen him in Solace—he never left! I am going to the magistrate. I have to tell them that Mother was murdered!

Liebert's note: Too late did I realize what I was reading. I went to the sheriff with journal, but we were too late. By the time we went to the house, someone had already marked it with a white plague 'x' to presumably keep the curious away. When we went inside, it was a shambles. Everything of value had been taken, and the store had been similarly robbed. I pressed the sheriff to send a search party, but he wasn't willing to send men out as the sun was near setting, and these lands are far from safe at night. I would have gone myself, but with no weapons and no training, I would have been lucky to make it through one night. I took it upon myself to gather more information about this story, but it seems all of its players have disappeared from the town, from the healer and the hired hands to the helpful Lila and the girl's father.

♔ ♔ ♔ ♔ ♔

"The faithful need no answers; the faithless accept none."

John Grubber

—Elistan, first Revered Son of Paladine at the
Tower of the High Clerist, 352 AC

6th day of Paleswelt, 38 SC
Solace, Abanasinia

As I wander through Solace in my merchant's guise,
I have many opportunities to observe her citizens.
Throughout the treetop town, robed clerics preach,
usually claiming spots outside taverns, gambling
houses or smoking dens. From these perches they
cry out against excess, warn of the punishments
awaiting the indulgent, and speak their teachings, all
in hopes of swaying the crowds to join them.

The temples of the old gods are still maintained in
many cities out of respect, and seasonal festivals held,
but each year attendance dwindles. The people of
Ansalon have, for the most part, accepted the departure of the old gods and have embraced Mysticism in
their place. Rumors still trickle in, though, of gods old
and new. Tales also speak of small armies, soldiers
with fanatical devotion, laying waste to towns and villages that will not accept their ways and beliefs. In my
own youth in Solamnia, I remember that less than ten
years after the Second Cataclysm, one such group, the
"Summoners," burned Kerodin, and slaughtered its
inhabitants. They were declared "wicked" by its
leader, for they would not submit or change their
ways. Kerodin was destroyed, as were several other
villages of Eastern Solamnia in a holy war to bring
back the gods. They attempted to attack Khellendros,
the Storm over Krynn, but in the end, their religious

crusade was not about who was right, but who was left. Holy armies such as these are not a thing of the past it would seem, for rumors have been whispered about the Knights of Neraka marching to war again. Though they have renamed themselves, they cannot distance themselves from their founder's dark vision.

As I enjoyed a solitary drink today, my companions drifted in from their day's work, and the talk of the evening turned to religion. Further research seems to show that the gods of old still mean different things to different people, and as long as the worship of them does not hinder life, continued veneration is likely to occur out of superstitious habit if nothing else.

Midway through the evening, a man calling himself a Mystic and bearing the symbol of the Citadel of Light joined us. According to him, the people of Krynn, by holding to the old ways, are not allowing Mysticism to spread and flourish. I, of course, disagreed, insisting on the value of retaining faith in the old gods and their philosophies, if only to spark discussion.

The Mystic, Pharie Selatan, chuckled when I described my continued faith in Shinare, but he could not argue with me when I explained why. It was best put by one of my shipmates, a smith and former priest of Reorx, who explained his continued veneration of the divine craftsman thus:

"The forge god gave us a world, and he gave me the skills to mold it. If he no longer gives me miracles to work in his name, does that mean I should forget his other gifts?"

Perhaps this idea of faith is a sound one—the teachings of the gods were their true gifts, not the abilities they gave their followers. I am not surprised to find that many people still honor the old gods, especially those of neutrality, even though the gods are gone and their priesthoods extinct.

Mysticism has proved a double-edged sword for Krynn. While miracles can once again be wrought, some people cannot accept themselves as centers of faith. They can accept the power, but not the responsibility. With no promise of reward and no name to perform deeds in, some people have sunk into despair. I was introduced to such a man at the Empty Cask, another tavern in Solace. Once a priest of Paladine, Phylippo Rylenda lost his powers after the Chaos War and his faith shortly after that. He now served drinks for a living, no longer believing the teachings of his god or even seeing a purpose for faith. He claimed to have Mystical potential but saw no point in using it for any but himself. His bitterness made me realize that perhaps not all who served the gods were ideal candidates for the priesthood. It also made me wonder how many other priests held the same bitter confusion in their hearts.

The following is an excerpt from *The Amulet and the Sword: Religion in Ansalon's History*, by Mercia Eliadum, a newly published book that explores the social dimensions of religion in the Age of Mortals.

FAITH AND WORSHIP IN A GODLESS AGE

The departure of the gods for the second time in Krynn's history was an event that shook the lives of the faithful to their cores. Having found true faith only a few short decades before, both priests and congregations were distraught to find that their heavenly parents had left them. Though the departure of the gods was an act of love and sacrifice, not all saw it that way. Some who had given their lives to worship and devotion were enraged, while others were lost and empty inside. Some saw the true message in the gods' departure, while others saw only potential for domination and power. There is a universal thirst to believe, and in the early days of the Fifth Age, the candles of faith were lit and held by hands both light and dark.

The discovery of Mysticism and the founding of the Citadel of Light did a great deal to combat these growing problems, but in areas where the Mystics are turned away at the borders, shadows loom and dark forces preside over an unwitting populace.

FAITH AND THE CATACLYSMS

At the time of the First Cataclysm, the gods brought their devout with them into the realms beyond, where they might live in the divine range for eternity. Those remaining on Krynn were more often than not faithless and wicked, deserving the fate that awaited them. The departure of the gods and true priests was traumatic, especially to the impious populace after the devastation of the Cataclysm, but only because they could no longer call upon the divine powers they had taken for granted for so long. The greedy turned to the gods only when they needed them, instead of giving them due homage, and were punished for it.

The Second Cataclysm has presented a different situation altogether. The gods are gone, but they did not take the faithful with them, nor was their departure marked by worldwide destruction. The population as a whole suffered less in the aftermath of the Second Cataclysm, and the priesthoods suffered in their place. Perhaps because they believed and had faith, the people of Ansalon have faced the Fifth Age much better than expected. The clergy, to a large extent, have not. Many of the followers feel betrayed, abandoned, and confused.

After the Second Cataclysm, new religions arose, dedicated to new gods, as they did after the First Cataclysm. Some flourished for a few years, then declined as their leaders were exposed as charlatans. With the discovery and spread of Mysticism, this trend changed. Now, a devious cult leader can deliver on his promise of miracles and can hold followers in thrall by more than words.

Some people are quite uncomfortable with the power of Mysticism, and rightfully so. In the past, mortals have been irresponsible with the powers they have been given, as was the Kingpriest. The Kingpriest, though, had the gods to answer to. With the power of Mysticism, there is no one to strip the powers of the users if they use them impiously. The fearful prophesy an age where new Kingpriests could rise and there would be no gods to stop them, so powerful would they be. Others foresee an age of wonders. As always though, the future is unwritten, and unknown to us.

WORSHIP PRACTICES

The religious practices of most have changed little in the Fifth Age. To many, it does not really matter that the gods left—what matters is that they were here at all. People still hope the gods will return, but have accepted that they will not. Consequently, some people still pay homage to their patrons, especially tradespeople and artists. After the discovery of Mysticism, there was often conflict between the powerless priests and the miracle-working Mystics, with more than one turning a populace against the other, driving them out. Some of the old clergy preyed on the people's fear of the new magic, branding Mystics as witches. Mystics, in turn, publicly attacked the priests, labeling them frauds if they used Mysticism in the name of the old gods, or powerless, outdated charlatans who were trying to hold onto the past instead of embracing the future. Goldmoon and the other masters of the Citadel of Light have tried to make peace between the factions, but the beliefs are not easily reconciled, and in some cases, blood once again has been spilled in the name of religion.

PRIESTHOODS

The candle of faith still burns within many of the old priests, who in the loss of their powers have gained much wisdom. Many focus on the teachings of their gods, realizing that miracle-working is not true faith. Consequently, while there are those who have become bitter at the loss of their divine gifts, other have found new ones in the ideas and messages of the gods' teachings and in doing so have made peace with the gods' departure.

After the discovery of Mysticism, some of the old gods' faithful learned the new magic and returned to their temples and priesthoods, sharing the teachings with their powerless brethren. While the Mystics have not stopped them, they are not pleased with the deceptive use of Mystical power in the name of departed gods, regardless of motive. When confronted by Mystics, the priests working Mystical miracles in their old gods' names have replied that this new magic was a part of the gods and of the world, and so while the gods may be gone, their power remains.

TRAINING AND ETHOS

It has become more and more difficult to attract people to the worship of the old gods, and even harder to persuade them to dedicate their lives to the priesthoods. The discovery and flourishing of Mysticism revived many priesthoods, but by 30 SC, the temples of the old gods stood silent, somber monuments to a past long gone.

Curiously, as literacy has again started to flourish in these relatively peaceful times, interest has been sparked in the old gods' scriptures and the messages they contain. The scriptures of the old gods changed little in the long history of Ansalon, though new supplementary works have been written, explaining the ancient texts to readers in this godless age.

ARTIFACTS AND ITEMS

Ansalon has a long history of organized religion, and in those millennia countless major and minor relics were created. In the Age of Mortals, these artifacts retain their powers as mage-created artifacts do, being useable as power sources in much the same method as wizards' items. These artifacts and relics are now more prized than ever by those who possess them, for new items cannot be created with any degree of permanence. In some cases the objects still possess arcane power. In others they never did, but people still cherish heirloom talismans and medallions of the old gods, regardless of their efficacy. The power of the symbol lies not in the magic of the symbol, the priests of the old gods said, but rather in the meaning behind the symbol, to its creator and its wielder.

The newness of Mysticism and the comparative rarity of highly powerful Mystics has resulted in a relative scarcity of Mystical artifacts. Those that do exist are similar in function to those of the old gods, but as their power is imbued by a mortal Mystic. Their effects is impermanent.

Liebert's note: In Solace and as I have traveled, I have taken note that the Mystics are losing their powers. I had intended to study this, but the Mystics I spoke to have been closed-lipped about it. With the destruction of the Academy of Sorcery several years ago, sorcerers have left the area as well, so I am unable to investigate similar speculations about them.

TEMPLES

The First Cataclysm destroyed many of the old gods' grandest temples, and the vengeful populace destroyed most of the remainder during the Age of Darkness. However, the return of the true gods during the War of the Lance also brought about a great flourishing in sacred architecture. Ruins were reclaimed, holy sites were rebuilt, and new temples were consecrated. Great temples were built for most of the gods, elaborate buildings to profess the populace's faith and to quietly ask forgiveness for the wickedness that had driven out the gods. The departure of the gods after the Second Cataclysm had little effect on the temples, as they had the means and congregation to maintain themselves. People still flocked to them in droves, to thank the gods for their sacrifice in the Chaos War. As the years passed, though, the sacrifice faded into history. In some cases, the populace was angry over the damage of the war , and mobs or the priests themselves damaged the buildings, seeking retribution for perceived abandonment, betrayal, and manipulation. Congregation sizes declined, and with them, donations and funds.

In some cases priests even abandoned their temples, fleeing in the night when faced with a hostile populace. In certain areas, entire towns are deserted, the people fleeing before the wrath of the overlords or some petty despot. In many of these places, Mystics have come and reclaimed the ruins using magic and their own hands to rebuild the structures as hospitals, hostels, and temples dedicated to the power of the heart. The Mystics build their own temples as well, but usually in more populated areas where they already have many followers.

Liebert's note: Solace is filled with old temples and shrines, many standing empty or converted by the Mystics, while others were sold by destitute churches as the old faiths disappeared. Built in the religious revival following the War of the Lance, they sit mainly on the ground, throughout the town. In some cases, there was so little support and aid available for the aging priests that the cellars, tombs, and storage crypts were left full when they were walled up. Rumors and tales of riches beneath the town have drawn many an adventurer to Solace. Disappointment or the local constabulary have seen just as many leave empty-handed.

The Temple of the Heart in Solace is not large, due mainly to the proximity of the Citadel of Light. It was built anew rather than converted, mainly out of a desire to distance the teachings of the citadel from the old religions, so that the new faith would not be seen as standing on the shoulders of the old. It is frequented by many people, though there are not regular services. Instead there are silent meditation and circles, where issues of faith, problems, and questions are discussed with others or contemplated alone. The Mystics of the temple also work extensively in the community, aiding people wherever they can. In times of late, however, they have been more vocal, urging others to help in public sermons and speeches. In light of recent widespread rumors about the weakening of Mystics, Sorcerers, and their powers, this change of behavior is most curious indeed.

෫෫ ෫෫ ෫෫ ෫෫ ෫෫

"My pride is well earned, sir—men fear me who fear not the gods."
—Revered son and Senator of Istar Arinna Trachin, responding with threats to the noble houses of Istar who refused to support the Heathen Wars, 27 PC

10th day of Paleswelt, 38 SC
Solace, Abanasinia

John Grubber

*I obtained the following information somewhat
duplicitously by pocketing a translated report from the
desk of Lord Warren's aide-de-camp while inquiring
about safe routes to travel east of Solace. I procured the
report while he looked through a chest of maps, and I
intended to return it, but circumstances prevented it. I
will leave it with a messenger and the instructions that it
is to be delivered two days after I depart Solace. I hope it
is returned. The veracity of its contents is unconfirmed by
the report. Any accurate details may now be out of date.
The writer, Aryste Dimachus, was unknown to the
Knights, although he apparently was a member of the
Kirath, the elves who battled the dream in Silvanesti
under Porthios, the exiled elven prince. The report, journal, and letter were all found amid his personal effects
when his body was hauled from the shallows of Crystalmir Lake and brought to the garrison. His presence
was a puzzle, until the small waterproof case was found in
the false bottom of his backpack. A letter, rife with typical
elven arrogance, was found within, intended for his lady-
wife, who was apparently a refugee in the camp at Solace.
The letter would never reach its recipient. According to the
Knights' commentary, which I have omitted but summa-
rized, it is generally suspected that Dimachus suffered an
accidental death while trying to reach Solace and spirit
his family away. Why the letter to his wife was with him
this close to Solace is unknown, unless he planned to have
it delivered by an agent who could move freely within the
town. It seems he was putting his family ahead of his
people, even in dire times such as these, hoping to get them
to safety before reporting to his superiors.*

Warren's staff did their best to locate the woman it

was intended for, but to no avail. Given the date of the missive and its contents, it can only be assumed she fled, fearing the worst, after such a long time without hearing from her beloved.

Fifteenth day of Spring Dawning, thirty-eight years after the second great cataclysm
To: General-in-exile Lautas, of Qualinesti
From: Aryste Dimachus

Milord, as suspected and feared, the green dragon Beryllinthranox is amassing an army of minions to attack the cities in and around her domain. At first puzzled as to how I would find out more details about Beryl's forces, I was eventually able to join the army, posing as a dark elf Mystic, offering my services to a human mercenary company in need of a healer. My naturally superior archery abilities far exceeded their own meager skills, and I soon found myself instructing the humans in archery as well as serving as their healer.

Over the span of almost three months I was able to learn much about the group and its eventual missions. At any given time, the dragon had the majority of the force searching the forest for the Tower of High Sorcery at Wayreth, and it was not uncommon for a party to return with half of its members missing. This constant eroding of her military might consistently angers the dragon. Though I have never seen her, I have heard tales of her wrath being visited upon messengers with unpleasant news. I think the wearing down of her troops has been a godsend for we elves, for it has kept her army's size in check, at least for the time being. I

have heard rumblings recently that her patience with
the Speaker of the Sun is finally at an end, and that
Qualinost is to suffer the same fate as the human city of
Haven. By the army's level of preparedness and supply,
I would guess that we have no more than a month with
which to make ready our defenses, all under the watch-
ful eyes of Beryl's human toadies, the Knights of Neraka. Our only saving grace in that eventual battle is that
the army of Beryl is bottom heavy, having few commanders and many troops, making it prone to disarray,
unlike our own well-structured forces.

Army is perhaps the wrong word to use in dis-
cussing Beryl's troops, for it is little more than a
horde. This is its greatest weakness. She seems
unwilling to use capable leaders, fearing they will
plot against her, and as a result, most of her troops
are unruly and poorly drilled.

The majority of her forces are of the most monstrous sort—draconians, ogres, goblins and their ilk,
and strange dragonmen referred to as "spawn."

The ogres are few in number, and strangely, seem
the most prone to desertion—a characteristic they
are not known for. This should not be considered a
praise of their courage, but rather a commentary on
their slow-wittedness. The thought of giving up a
chance to maraud and kill simply does not occur to
them. Rumors abound in the camp that many of the
ogres have migrated far to the east, even beyond the
realm of Onysablet the Black. I know not why, but
those goblins I was forced to deal with said some of
them had visions and dreams while they slept and
convinced their fellows to travel with them.

There are very few of the Nerakans' brute troops. The majority of these apparently have remained close to the lands held by Ariakan's successors or have returned to their homeland. The force I am attached to swears fealty to the dragon herself.

I discovered during the attack on Haven that Beryl's horde is a slow-moving group, due mainly to its lack of discipline. I was loathe to participate in the assault and, thankfully, was able to stay behind the lines healing the injured mercenaries rather than attack the hapless humans. When traveling, the human mercenaries ride separately behind the advancing force in case of ambush and because they do not fully trust their fellow soldiers. They make up the bulk of the cavalry and the archers, while monsters make up the majority of the footsoldiers in the horde.

Truly the worst part of this assignment was having to stand by while innocents, even though they were just humans, were cut down like wheat or thrown into irons.

Recommendations:

With Haven now in her grasp, I fear that the dragon's next target will be Solace or Gateway before she attacks Qualinost itself. I would recommend that we do not inform the humans should we find Solace is the target, for it will buy us time to prepare Qualinost for defense and evacuation. I have no doubt in my mind that, were the situations reversed, the humans would leave us to fend for ourselves, as they have in the past.

Aryste Dimachus

ᆰ ᆰ ᆰ ᆰ ᆰ

Liebert's note: The following letter was also found among Dimachus's personal belongings. The Knights had not translated it as yet, because it was a personal communiqué. I had it translated in Zaradene upon my return there.

Twelfth day of Spring Dawning, thirty-eight years after the second great cataclysm

My dearest Sephone,

All that we feared is coming to pass. After what I have seen, I thank E'li that you and the children fled Qualinesti when the dragon attacked.

You must not tell anyone of this letter, its contents, or your true identity, lest the dragon send her agents after you. I have no concern for myself now. I know that it is likely we will never again see each other. In fact, it is likely that I am already discovered as you read this.

I know that you have come to love your adopted home in Solace and have even found a place in your heart for the humans, but in this matter, you must not think of them as friends. They have thrown their lot in with the dragon, as in the past. Some of the fools actually think that they are valuable to the dragon, that they are more than just a tool for her to use and throw away. They are so short-sighted, I don't know how you can live among them.

You must leave Solace. Go quickly and go quietly my love, for Solace is to suffer the same fate as Haven.

Even now the dragon marshals her forces to march. She has hired humans by the thousands. Their willingness to commit such atrocities for a few steel sickens me, and I am glad it is you in that village, not I, for I doubt I could contain my contempt for the humans.

If you wish, you may inform other elves who have sought refuge in Solace, but tell none of the humans. We know how prone they are to rash actions and their love of material wealth. In their hysteria, they will cause a panic, hoarding supplies and blocking roads with their carts of furniture, livestock, and other things best left behind. All the commotion will surely draw the dragon's attention even faster, and the highways around Solace will be bathed in the blood of the refugees.

I think it best if you go north or east, to Crossing, or some other port, as we planned. Tell any who ask that you are bound for Schallsea to help in the rebuilding of the Citadel of Light. No one should question that. Sail to Ankatavaka and seek out my relatives there, I have been in contact with them, and they know that at some point you will come.

As before, the humans have become greedy, seeking to take what is not theirs. Is it not enough that they hold Qualinost in their clutches? I truly have begun to envy the Silvanesti for their isolation. As I look at the recent past of our people, at the exiles, the invasions, the wars and deaths, I think that opening relations with the humans decades ago was a mistake. We should have left them alone and kept them from our borders, leaving them to fight over their lands. We could have remained safely in our forests, away from their greed.

In truth, I pity the humans, it must be so torturous to see a race such as ours, of such grace and beauty and longevity, and know that one's own people will never reach such heights. I suppose that is why they war so frequently—they seek some small measure of immortality, whatever its price. It angers me though that we pay the price for their folly. They are the cause of all our problems, and this time, they will be the cause of their ultimate doom. The dragon herself will see to that.

My love, they are not worth trusting. You must leave Solace right away, but tell no one why. If they find out your reasons, there will be panic in the streets, and you won't escape before the dragon comes. Do not tell the Solamnics of this, for they will surely begin to mobilize the town and its defenses. Just like a human to think they could stand against the dragon where an elven army could not. Fools. If they start to prepare, the dragon herself will raze the town, rather than just letting her minions conquer it.

I will meet you in Ankatavaka in three months time, or in Caergoth two months after that.

May E'li guide your path back to me, my love,

Aryste

සෑ සෑ සෑ සෑ සෑ

11th day of Paleswelt, 38 SC
Solace, Abanasinia

This journal came into my possession after I saw a youth steal it from the saddlebag of a Solamnic Knight's horse in the southern streets of Solace. I gave chase when I saw the urchin as he ducked into an alley, but he was gone by the time I reached the alley myself. This journal was lying on the ground, as were a few other items taken from the saddlebag. I scooped them up, intending to return them to their owner, but by the time I made my way back to where the Knight's horse had been tied up, the Knight had already departed. It was only when I read the journal that I realized his destination. I copied out some of his entries and left this journal with the elven letters to be returned to the garrison once I leave Solace.

EXCERPTS FROM THE PERSONAL JOURNAL OF SIR SIGRID UTH DISIGAR, KNIGHT OF THE SWORD

Deepkolt, 22nd day, 38 SC
Cadothus Citadel, Werim, Northern Ergoth

I cannot wait to see my love, Katrina. It has been far too long. Captain Tripps in the general office says that my term of good service here has been noticed by some people of note, and that my next posting will probably be wherever I choose! I guess it's quite clear to everyone where I hope to sent—straight into her arms in Aleph! I should know within a fortnight at the longest, because Commander Selig wants to ship out those who will be leaving on the next supply ship, in three weeks' time. I have missed her so these past two years. I can't wait to ride up to her father's keep and shout her name across the moat so all can hear the name of my future bride! I must go now, though, to take a patrol into the mountains for a few days. There have been rumors of ogre activity, and I have been ordered to take a group to investigate.

Deepkolt, 26th day, 38 SC
Chukatal Ruins, Sentinel Mountains, Northern Ergoth
I hate patrols. I hate patrols that take us into ruins. I hate patrols that take us into ogre ruins. There is something so unnerving about them. It's like walking through an enormous crypt—all cold gray stone towering above you. I can understand now why we chose to leave it empty rather than occupy it. I would go mad if I were there any longer than a few nights. I cannot wait to leave. Just knowing that they were filled with the human slaves and their masters and then abandoned so long ago gives me chills this night.

Deepkolt, 29th day, 38 SC
Chukatal Ruins, Sentinel Mountains, Northern Ergoth
Last night, our third in the ruins, we were attacked by a band of ogres. In their incompetence, the green Knights I was sent with must have fallen asleep at their posts, because the ogres came right into our campsite. Eight members of the patrol died, almost half our number, and we had to flee at first light. All this day, I have replayed the events in my mind. None of the sentries died or were even

attacked. The cowards must have run or hidden or else the ogres would have never gotten through. I designed that sentry rotation and chose the sites myself! It was perfect for our position. I will be sure to have the lot of them reprimanded when we reach the garrison!

Brookgreen, 5th day, 38 SC
Cadothus Citadel, Werim, Northern Ergoth

Somehow, the incompetence of my patrol has been blamed on me! My record, flawless until now, is tarnished. The blood of the dead is on my hands, or at least that is what the commander says. I know it was not my fault, that if I had been sent with proper Knights who could follow orders, and not a bunch of cowards and farmers, none of this would have happened. To make matters worse, because of this, I am not being sent to Sancrist, I am being sent to Solace, in Abanasinia, for "instruction under the commander" there. Lies! Treachery! I am not being sent for training—this is just another example of the Knighthood's attempts to punish and thwart me. And Abanasinia! They may as well ship me to Icewall! I also hear that this commander is Ergothian! By the lost gods, what is this Knighthood turning into? In my father's time, perhaps two of the members of my patrol would have been admitted to the Knighthood, and no Ergothian would ever have been made a commander of true Solamnics! At least I won't have to live among these Ergothians anymore. They sicken me with their barbaric arena games and their corrupt "justice" system. I won't miss this cursed city.

Brookgreen, 23rd day, 38 SC
On board the Seafire, *three days out of Gwynned*

I hate sea travel. Every day I am on this cursed scow, I am taken one day farther from Katrina. I would not blame her now for not waiting. My posting for "training," as the commander called it, is for two years. Two years! I will be past twenty-eight when, or if, I see Katrina again! I have a mind to leave the Knighthood and go to her now, but it would kill Father, and he would disown me for certain. Katrina's father would never give her to me either—how could an outcast be worthy of her? He would think I am after his lands. No, I will wait this out. I will hold through this frontier posting. And when this is all over, I hope I never have to set foot on a ship again.

Brookgreen, 28th day, 38 SC
On board the Seafire, *eight days out of Gwynned*

I never want to set foot on a ship again. Yesterday came a storm the likes of which neither I nor the captain had ever seen! The ship lost the bowsprit and one of the masts, but the captain assures me that we will be able to limp on to Zaradene safely. I did what I could while the storm raged, manning a bilge as the ship tossed about like a cork. We lost four crewmen overboard. I couldn't think of a worse way to die, alone in the dark, cold sea. I shiver just thinking about it. I will have to help out with ship's duties until we make landfall, since we are so shorthanded.

Fleurgreen, 15th day, 38 SC
Long Ridge, Abanasinia

In Zaradene, where *Seafire* docked for repairs, I
met several other Knights being stationed in Solace,
and we resolved to travel together. The company is
good most of the time. Sir Kallen is endlessly cheer-
ful. He is only recently knighted and has never been
posted so far from home. He sees this as some grand
adventure. A childish fop like him will never be
more than a Knight of the Crown. Jaryd uth Lystan,
on the other hand, is a fellow Knight of the Sword
and of the same mind as I. He sees this posting for
the punishment it truly is. At our current rate of
progress, I will only have to put up with Sir *Perky* for
four more days before we reach Solace. Although,
knowing my luck, this backwoods posting has
shared quarters for junior and senior Knights, and
he will be bunked next to me. That torture, if not
this entire posting, will be enough to make me throw
my lot in with the Nerakans!

Fleurgreen, 21st day, 38 SC
Solace

Today we reached the fabled treetop city of
Solace. I was not impressed. Granted, I have not
toured the town, but from what I have seen, this is
going to be a long two years. The garrison leaves
much to be desired. It is like stepping back in time—
all palisade and guard towers, not a stone fortification to be found. I highly doubt it would hold against
a concerted assault. The barracks are as I suspected—a hall of bunks with no separate quarters
for the senior Knights. Only the commander himself
has his own lodgings, filled, not suprisingly, with

Ergothian "art." It's as if he's mocking us Solamnics, waving mementos from his home while our nation sits under the heel of Khellendros the Blue. It's going to be a long two years.

Fleurgreen, 26th day, 38 SC
Solace

Another exciting day in Solace, a day of walking to the tomb, standing on guard duty, and driving away kender before walking through the refugee camp and back to the garrison. A man was found hanging from one of the treewalks this morning. People said he had fled Haven when it was attacked, but I did not learn anything more about him. Not that I care—only a coward would do such a thing. He certainly wasn't a Solamnic to do such an honorless thing.

Holmswelt, 15th day, 38 SC
Solace

Though I have passed through it before, I was treated to my first patrol in refugee camp today. It is a hive of wretches the likes of which I have never seen! Everywhere filthy children run, and dogs bark. Flies buzz about the place incessantly. By the time the shift ended and my relief arrived I was near mad from the droning wings. The grimy children paw endlessly at me, their grubby hands smearing my armor and clothes. It is infuriating. I'll have to polish my armor every day to avoid it rusting! The place is a firetrap, full of ramshackle huts and shanties, in no semblance of order at all. If I had my way, we'd burn the lot of it and build proper barracks for the refugees. As I patrolled I encountered a young woman, Marta Lobrie, several times. She seemed pleasant enough, but far too obsessed with bettering the lot of the refugees. I think we should be helping them with supplies, and sending them on their way, especially since more arrive every day. By my father's gods, if they let them all stay, the shanty-town will be bigger than Solace soon. No, they should be urged on to the coastal lands. At least there they could find work rather than being a burden on the people of Solace.

Holmswelt, 21st day, 38 SC
Solace

The people of Solace have started asking questions, given the rumors of war in the north and across the sea in Silvanesti. Travelers and new refugees aren't helping the situation. The commander has given us strict orders to deny any word of us pulling out, though I think it would be a good idea, given that there are so few of us left. I think we should pull back to Sancrist and Northern Ergoth, and wait out whatever is happening there. I personally don't like idea of Beryl being as close as she is. It's only a matter of time before she isn't happy with Haven and decides she wants Solace and Gateway to add to her holdings. Caramon Majere, famed hero of the lance, died today. Much of the town has been in mourning because of it. For an outsider, he was a man of Knightly honor. He will be missed, it seems.

Fireswelt, 10th day, 38 SC
Solace

I am growing accustomed to the summer heat in Solace, though I long for the windy coasts of Sancrist more than ever, and every day I miss Katrina more. I can not wait for this posting to end. So eager am I to leave that I volunteered to scout in the territory of Beryl the Green in hopes that a few dangerous assignments would raise my prestige to the point of getting me out of here. No such luck though. The commander himself informed me that I was here for two years, whether I liked it or not. Damn Ergothian! Who does he think he is? Some outlander commanding Solamnics! The Knighthood must be in dire straits indeed if their filth can enter the ranks. Three Knights were sent to Sancrist today. That makes five in the past two weeks. I don't know what the Ergothian has planned, but it wouldn't surprise me if his traitor blood intended to weaken us before the dragon attacks.

Paleswelt, 1st day, 38 SC
Solace

Little has happened in Solace of late, though there was a brief bit of excitement as I noticed a hysterical young girl being thrust into a barred wagon. Only seconds before, I saw her jump out through a window and flatten some poor merchant as she ran. She said something to him, and gave him something in their mere seconds of contact, but she was up and running again even before he even stood up. It's none of my business, though. That's what Solace has a sheriff for.

The treewalks in Solace are interesting, I must

say, they would be quite useful in fending off invaders, though I suspect they must be very susceptible to fire. These farmers cannot think of everything. It's not as though they have any training beyond a peasant militia. That's why our honor guard for the tomb has been expanded in recent years. At least until times of late.

Paleswelt, 3rd day, 38 SC
Solace

As I walked to the tomb for today's patrol, I noticed that the house the girl was pulled from yesterday has a white **X** painted on the door. Apparently one of the Mystics has been doing plague rounds again. The girl was probably being taken to the plague colony between Solace and Gateway. I hear rumors about how the Mystics at the Temple of the Heart haven't had much luck with the fevers that have appeared in Solace lately. Not that I'd ask a Mystic. Those witches and charlatans never speak the truth. Maybe now the people will see them for what they are.

Paleswelt, 5th day, 38 SC
Solace

The sheriff raised the hue and cry. Apparently someone entered the plague house to take out the bodies and didn't find any, but the house had been ransacked, and so had its owner's shop. A body was found in the bush south of Solace today too, wrapped in curtains from the house. It was the girl's father, the owner of the shop. The Mystics apparently knew nothing about the plague house. They claim none of their people marked the door. A man came forward today too. I recognized him as the man the girl knocked down. He gave a package to the sheriff—her diary it seems. There is a dark side to the little town after all. The girl was evidently not sick and not being brought to the plague colony.

Paleswelt, 6th day, 38 SC
Solace

Things have taken an interesting turn here in Solace. An elf's body was found floating in Crystalmir Lake. It looks as if the poor bastard drowned. What he's doing here I don't know—he should be in Qualinesti. Maybe if the elves put up a fight once in a while instead of rolling over like they always do, they wouldn't be run out of their lands every few decades. They found a pack nearby, empty of everything, as if it had been searched. The sheriff and his men want to write it off as a simple robbery, but when the commander had the pack searched we found a compartment in the bottom, with two letters inside. After reading the contents, it is the commander's opinion that this death was no random act. It has been ordered that this information does not leave the compound, though.

Paleswelt, 9th day, 38 SC
Solace

It has been almost a week since the girl was hauled away in the wagon, but the sheriff has asked the town for donations to hire a bounty hunter to find her, or at least the people who did this. I doubt they'll find her, though. The trail has long since grown cold. Besides, she could be almost in New Swamp by now. People say that's where all the missing people go. They say that Sable has slaves brought in by wagon and riverboat to the camps at her island. Rumors of war continue to filter in from the east. Some even say that Sanction itself has fallen. Given the size of the Solamnic force that defended the city, I find that hard to believe. The Knights even had the help of the Legion of Steel, whatever good that band of brigands would be. All this talk of armies concerns me, and I have requested that I be sent home to Sancrist. I don't expect it to be granted, least of all by some Ergothian cur, but it is worth asking. I found out that I have been asked to take a patrol out into the countryside. I have to go into the town to purchase supplies tomorrow. It's sickening! A garrison without enough supplies for a long patrol! Things wouldn't be this way if a true Solamnic was in charge!

꿨 꿨 꿨 꿨 꿨

"Dine my traitorous friend, sup, sup, but be not sated; your hunger is not of the gut, but of the soul, and is a craving this world whole cannot fill. My empire will never be enough for you."
—Emperor Quevalin XI, as he lies dying of poisoned wine, speaking to Macqui Hellman, general of the Imperial Guard, from Lothana Usriel, *Quevalin XI*, Act VI, Scene II: 263–265, ca. 780 PC

John Grubber

15th day of Paleswelt, 38 SC
Solace, Abanasinia

Prior to my arrival, I spent much time versing myself in the history of Solace. From my earliest days in town, though, I noticed many wagons and carts rumbling about, marked with coats of arms and sigils that were unfamiliar to my research. It was only later, in my tavern "research," that I learned about these new factions in the treetop town.

From tavern tables and bar stools throughout the town I learned that these unfamiliar marks of ownership came from Haven, a nearby town full of wealthy merchants. The green dragon Beryllinthranox and her minions only recently conquered Haven, and many of her citizens, on both sides of the law, fled the city in the weeks and months preceding the attack. While some went to other realms, taking their fortunes with them, some migrated to Solace, and set up their organizations here.

These new mercantile houses, guilds, crime families, and brotherhoods have integrated themselves into Solace's social fabric, whether they are welcome or not. Some have flung open their doors for new members, while others capitalized on the move as a way to thin their ranks.

Initially the refugees were welcomed, but once they started to open businesses, things changed. The people of Solace began to find themselves strong-armed by the hirelings and henchman of these wealthy migrants, encouraged to give them deals and preferential treatment. At present, the economic strata in Solace are very divided. Some profiteers threw their lots in with the

Haven merchants and all their corruption, while others have tried to stand against the criminal elements. To the careful observer, the town is polarized, and it is evident when one sees the veiled contempt with which the new wagons and businesses are viewed by passersby.

The people of Solace are unhappy with this new situation, but since some have allied with the avaricious migrants, no one really knows whom to trust. It is a situation that the greedy groups are skilled at fostering and exploiting.

ᤕ ᤕ ᤕ ᤕ ᤕ

The Solace Refugee Camp,
Exerpted from a Report to the Town Councilors

Turbulent times have changed the makeup of Solace's population. Though the majority of the buildings are still in the trees, many structures of stone and wood are built on the ground. Some of these are temples, halls, and smithies, the bulk of them concentrated around the southern entrance of the town, on the road that leads to Gateway and Haven. It is here that the refugees from Haven and other conquered lands have made their temporary homes. Their shanties and wagons crowd both sides of the road. The citizens of Solace are willing to help but would rather keep all of the refugees together than have huts and shacks spring up all through the town.

Next to the eastern palisade are the ruins of the two barracks built a few years ago to house the refugees. These burned down under somewhat suspicious circumstances, but no one has been accused. Rumors of people in high places being responsible have spread, but those who voice such opinions have disappeared soon after. Consequently, even the sheriff has attributed the fires to accidental causes. The homeless have been arriving sporadically since the conquests of the great dragons, though since the recent attack on Haven, the trickle has become a flood.

Many of the longest-residing refugees have, over the years, turned their simple shacks into stone crofts, low buildings with thatch roofs. These sit close to the western palisade, forming a class system even amongst the poorest of Solace's citizens. Those fleeing the recent capture of Haven and other cities of Abanasinia have not all been so prosperous. Lean-tos, shacks, wagons, hovels, and tents all crowd together in a labyrinth that houses more than three thousand people. Building supplies have been donated by many groups, and even the distant Plainsfolk have given tents so that the refugees may survive the coming winter cold.

The ramshackle buildings are clustered around several new permanent structures, built by the authorities of Solace to try to maintain some element of order amidst the growing chaos of poverty. These wood-and-brick buildings serve many roles, from a relief center where food and other supplies are given out, to a temple and hospital where the sick go and those with faith may worship. Few people visit the chapels in the halls, though, instead going to the Temple of the Heart or the decaying temples of the old gods when worshiping. The late Caramon Majere was overseeing a construction project out past the tomb that would have provided housing for all the refugees and more, but it is far from complete, and without his leadership, it may never be.

Every day, the mazelike lanes of the camp are crowded with people, some seeking work, others food, while most wait hopefully for word of loved ones in the weekly posted lists of arrivals and departures. News is rare, good news even rarer. After a few weeks, most simply give up and move on, passing their dwelling on to a friend in need if not abandoning it or taking it with them.

Even the sheriff makes use of the buildings, stationing several of his constables in them to hopefully deter poverty-spurred criminal activity. Thievery runs rampant in the shantytown, everything from pocket picking to murder—anything that will earn the perpetrator a few steel for his next pleasure. The more organized criminal element of the refugee town is controlled from outside it by the wealthy who migrated from Haven before the dragons' attack. As the situation in Solace grows more bleak, more and more people turn to crime, if only to feed their families.

The camp is permeated by a sense of dread, a fear that Solace will suffer the same fate as Haven, should Beryl see fit to expand again. Consequently, many of the residents are short-term, staying only long enough to get supplies, then continuing east to seek safety on the coast of the New Sea. This tension has spread in to the general populace, for the people of Solace know that when refugees fill the roads, soldiers are likely not far behind.

Most of the displaced are human, though some hill

dwarves and elves are among them. Generally women and children occupy the camp, their sons, husbands, fathers, and brothers having decided to stand against tyranny, buying their families' freedom with their own lives. It is far too high a price, for many of the refugees spend their time wallowing in despair or indulgence. Solace does not have enough work for all the newcomers, and as a result, they pass the hours in much the same way as Solace's citizens, indulging in drink and gambling, or worse, spending whatever meager coin they have. The atmosphere is all at once festive yet tragic, as the camp dwellers joyfully ignore the coming danger, embracing distractions to forget the present.

Through all the turmoil though, there is a stubborn sense of determination, a flame that burns bright in the hearts of most, that not even Beryl can extinguish. Many leave the camps, vowing to return and help when they can, to give back to those who helped them in their time of need. They leave, and others take their place in a cycle they all pray ends soon.

ꠥ ꠥ ꠥ ꠥ ꠥ

28th day of Paleswelt, 38 SC
Solace, Abanasinia

"The sins of old cast long shadows—and today we step out of them."
—Athacyn Laurier, priest of Kiri-Jolith, at the consecration of the new Great Temple of Kiri-Jolith in Kalaman, 358 AC

Solace is not alone in welcoming refugees. Reports indicate that throughout the free realms people have opened their doors and purses, finally looking beyond themselves and offering help to those in need. I think that it is actions such as these—the building of a camp, the donation of food and clothes—that will eventually free us all. It is the spirit of cooperation found in these lands that the dragons and their minions do not and cannot possess. The lesson of the old gods that "evil turns upon itself" is a well taught one, and in time it will come to pass that the tyrants will fall—even dragons are not all-powerful.

Though my friends complained about the beggars and the missionaries frequently seeking donations, I never once saw them keep their purses closed. They grow weary not of helping others but of the need to help. As was once said, "The lives of tyrants are only as long as the patience of those they oppress." The people of Solace and the free realms are nearing their limits I believe, and there will soon come a time when they will rise up in a fury and throw off the boots on their necks. Through all the confusion and distractions with which they fill their days, I saw in the people of Solace a growing grim resolve, a rod of iron that the dragons strengthen with their brutality. Soon there will be nothing left for the people to lose. There will be nothing left to be taken from them, and they will act. The true Age of Mortals will begin when this Time of Tyrants ends—and if the reports from across the land are true, that day is not far off.

It may appear that I have painted a rather dismal picture of life in the treetop city by focusing on so many negative themes. My intention in writing about this most famous of small towns was not to extol its virtues, however, but rather to show the undercurrents that run through it and through every community. Solace is by no means an unpleasant place, as I hope I have shown by mentioning some of the better traits for which it is known, attributes such as faith, charity, and hope.

My purpose in coming to Solace was to chronicle the lives of the common people in extraordinary times. Sadly, though, times of war and strife are all too ordinary in our world. This unpleasant side of life is often not reported by chroniclers, who seek to raise peoples' spirits rather than remind them of the awful truth. This noble goal does have a sinister side, though—for by ignoring the dark forces at work in our societies we let them control us. It is far better, in my opinion, to expose the ugliness within all of us to the harsh light of skepticism so that it can be acknowledged, then combated. As the Legion of Steel so often tries to show us, in this age of darkness, all we have is each other. If we let the dark sides of our souls win us over, what matter is the great dragons or their armies? We are already defeated. I hope my cautionary exploration of a seemingly average small town will serve as a waking-call to those who read it—if we are to survive, we must work together.

The people of Solace have been battered in their history, but they have never been broken. War has come to them, cloaked in fire and steel, more often than they care to remember. But remember they do—you can see the past in the eyes of the old, a haunted time they long to forget, but the present will not allow them to.

The complacence of many of Solace's residents is especially common in the young. I see this in my own children as well. They have grown up in an age of tyranny and helplessness, an age with no gods and fewer heroes. Small wonder then that they turn on each other and while away the hours on distractions—it is more pleasant than contemplating the truth of the situation, and easier, too, than taking a stand against the tides of darkness. The time for such a stand has not yet come, but it will.

My work in Solace is done.

Valter Liebert

Bertrem's Note

As I began the task of compiling these notes on Ansalon in an age of war, I was reminded that one of the benefits of old age is that one often rediscovers friends with whom one has lost touch. It is a bit like opening a present: One is never sure of the contents until they have been taken out into the light of day.

Sister Mary Herbert, having solicited from Dumarian, head librarian at the Library of Sanction, information about the Lords of Doom and the siege of Sanction, I have now discovered the charms of a friendship I thought dead.

Indebted as I am to the sister for her discovery, I cannot help but wonder if this is wise. Too often, old friends are like fine wine that has soured in the cask. Our recollection of its bouquet is better than the actual taste. I fear that if Dumarian and I were to sit down to a meal together, we might well find ourselves with little or nothing to talk about.

But this is a morbid reflection! I have every confidence that when the dark clouds lift, Dumarian and I will be able to share a glass of wine and reminisce to our hearts' content about our long journey among books and papers.

Dumarian and his agents have managed to collect a series of extraordinary vignettes of life in Sanction under siege. Unquestionably the jewel of this collection is the long diary excerpt of Sergeant Hartbrooke, a guard in the service of Lord Hogan Bight of Sanction. It is rare, in my experience, to come across a document that gives so vivid a picture of war from the inside. Dumarian is to be congratulated for acquiring this valuable document, and Sister Herbert is to be commended for persuading him to allow me to add it to my book.

This 2nd day of Sirrimont
38 SC

My dear friend Bertrem,

What a delight to hear from you after so many years. How long has it been . . . ? Fifteen, twenty years since I last saw you in Palanthas? I am pleased to read that you are well and immersed, as always, in the work you love.

I read the copy of your first guide with avid interest and send my thanks and appreciation for such an entertaining and informative book. I must say I am pleased to see someone decided to accept the challenge of compiling the vast and colorful social habits and lifestyles of our varied peoples.

With that in mind, I am happy to assist you in any way I can with your request for your second guide. Sanction has undergone many changes in the past one hundred years, but few have been so frightening, so sweeping as the events that have overwhelmed our city the past few years. The winds of change roar about us like a cyclone and still have not yet settled to silence. If Sanction vanishes under the weight of her doom, it would be a shame to allow the history of this unique city to vanish with her people, her buildings, her traditions. Fortunately, I am in a unique position to help both you and my city. As the Head Librarian and Collector of Manuscripts and Journals for the Hogan Bight Library of Sanction, I have gathered a goodly collection of books, tomes, letters, scrolls, manuscripts, journals, cookbooks, herbals, and memoirs written by the citizens of Sanction. With Lord Bight's permission, I am sending you a representative sampling of our collection. That way, if our city is destroyed by the Knights of Neraka, the great dragons, the Lords of Doom, or the gods themselves, at least Sanction will have told its own tale of the War of Souls.

With deep respect,
Dumarian, Head Librarian

THE LORDS OF DOOM

To: The Office of Research and Observation
   Department of Ruins, Antiquities, and Geologic Formations

Subject: The Lords of Doom volcanoes
   1. Mount Grishnor
   2. Mount Thunderhorn
   3. Mount Ashkir

As requested by his honor, Dumarian, Head Librarian of the Hogan Bight Library of the city of Sanction, this report is to detail the findings of the Geologic Survey Team sent by the Office of R and O to perform a detailed study of the three active volcanoes in the closest proximity to Sanction. The mission of the team was to study each volcano for the following:

1. Signs of new volcanic activity
2. Observable changes that have occurred since the last geologic report dated fifty years previous
3. Signs of renewing life in the older volcanic areas

The team consisted of Stroud Feldspear, Assistant Librarian, Research and Observation; four hill dwarves skilled in mountain climbing, geologic survey, and identification of indigenous life forms characteristic of mountainous regions and active volcanoes in particular; four mercenaries hired from the Black Knife Mercenary Guild to protect the team from possible interaction with Knights of Neraka; and five gully dwarves to carry gear and be on hand in the event the team ran afoul of rocs, skyfishers, giant insects, minotaur lizards, fire dragons, draconians, stray goblins, mountain lions, or other predators.

The survey team set out the first week of Bran and stayed in the field three weeks. An expense report has been filed with the Library Clerk. Death notices were sent to the appropriate authorities.

Stroud Feldspear, Assistant Librarian, Rsearch and Observation

Dated this 6th day of Corij, 37 SC

Mount Grishnor

Mount Grishnor was measured at 4200 feet, a gain of two hundred feet from the previous measurements. This volcano is the most sporadic of the three peaks. Its eruptions tend to come in fits and starts, explosive tantrums that fade as quickly as they begin. The lava dome that formed and burst on the northeastern side of the slope is an example of this erratic behavior. Most of the output is in the form of ash and pumice and the occasional flow of lava from the western and eastern lips of the crater.

The crater itself is a bowl-like depression a quarter of a mile across and nearly 150 feet deep. It sits at the north end of a high razorback ridge nearly a mile long. Steam rises from the vents and fissures deep within its interior where the earth flows, hisses, and smokes. (This survey team did not attempt to enter the crater due to the numerous vents belching noxious gases and the delicate nature of the crust edging the many fissures.)

Lava, when it does flow, exits the crater from two channels carved out of the soft stone by years of erosion and some adjustments by Lord Bight. Some flows down a channel to help fill the lava moat surrounding Sanction. Some, left on its own, flows sluggishly—like cooled day-old pudding, one of the gully dwarves suggested. (He was willing to try it, but we still needed a bearer and talked him out of it.) The hot lava moves down the northwestern slope of the volcano, then curves to the south and enters the waters of Sanction Harbor. There it hisses and steams as it hits the cold water, sometimes exploding in showers of cooled lava that rain down like hail on the lava plain.

We estimate the volcano has produced several miles of new land in just the past ten years. Added to this is the lava pouring from the lava moat at both the north and south ends of the harbor, and we estimate the port will be closed off within a hundred years if the flow of lava continues at its present rate.

While studying the lava river north of Grishnor's

crest, we looked for the Chaos-spawned fire dragons mentioned in earlier reports. Only two were spotted lounging in the fiery lava pits. Even from a distance these creatures were magnificent. Their skin was red and orange lava flecked with black and their breath was the steam of eruptions. They swam and sported and engaged in aggressive biting and mock battles. We theorized the two were a pair preparing to mate, but since both dragons looked active, this team did not attempt to approach them to observe the actual act. Previous reports describe the fire dragon's inherently aggressive and chaotic nature and its tendency to attack everything in sight.

From Mount Grishnor we worked our way down the slopes, past North Pass and the camp of the Dark Knights. Fortunately they were too busy cleaning up and rebuilding from a destructive mudflow caused by a recent storm. They did not notice us and we were able to slip around the camp and continue our studies.

Although the entire landscape is under threat from the three active volcanoes and much of it is still barren, we observed several positive changes on the mountains' slopes where lava has not flowed for many years. A survey from fifty years ago stated the three peaks were totally barren of life, that blown ash, pyroclastic surges, and uncontrolled lava flows had ravaged the upper slopes and rendered much of the area lifeless. We no longer found this to be true, particularly on the middle slopes edging the Vale. Here shrubs such as vine maples and huckleberries have sprouted. Seedlings of silver fir, alder, and cottonwood grow in protected areas. The wind has carried in seeds of tall fireweed and blue lupine to sprout prodigiously along the flanks of the mountains. We also spotted gophers, deer mice, a black viper, a pack of three giant scorpions (these made off with one of the gully dwarves), wild pigs and goats, several varieties of songbirds, and numerous insects.

From Mount Grishnor we traveled for four days through the rugged valleys and ridges leading up to the second, most eastern volcano, Mount Thunderhorn. We spent one night at Wizard's Brew Springs, one of the numerous thermal pools and springs that dot the Khalkist Mountains in this region. From there we traveled into the Doom range to examine the aqueducts that carry water from a reservoir deep in the mountains. To our dismay, but not our surprise, we learned the Knights of Neraka have already found the aqueducts. A patrol of Knights was camped near the arched waterway a few miles from its source at Diamond Lake. As Lord Bight requested if such a contingency should be discovered, we followed the aqueduct to an isolated and unguarded section of archways and destroyed the channel, thus preventing the possible poisoning of the city's water supply. The new cisterns should prove adequate for temporary use.

Mount Thunderhorn

This volcano, measured at about 4,400 feet, is the largest and most active of the three peaks. Located to the northeast of Sanction, its massive presence towers over the Vale like a menacing giant crowned by a perpetual wreath of smoke and steam.

Probably the most notable change on the mountain's face is the removal of the dragon-headed temple of Takhisis. As everyone in Sanction knows, Lord Bight obliterated the temple from the ground level to the subterranean tunnels the first years he ruled the city. He used the building stones in the lava moat, thus completely erasing all signs of the foundation from the mountain's face. There are no other ruins on Mount Thunderhorn.

The survey team approached the mountain from the southwest in order to take advantage of the relative safety provided by the city fortifications at the foot of the mountain. Unfortunately, this proximity to the guard lines allowed our mercenaries to slip out of camp one night and indulge in a binge of drinking and card playing with the sentries in one of the earthen redoubts. They made so much noise they attracted the attention of the duty officer. I believe the sentries were sent to dig out latrines and our mercenaries were returned to us trussed and gagged. I untied them and made them comfortable. I knew their punishment would be begin the next day when they would be forced to the climb four thousand feet of volcano with massive hangovers.

The following day the survey team proceeded up the flank of the mountain to a point about halfway to where the cave of Firestorm opened into the bowels of the volcano. We hoped to find signs of the bronze dragon rumored to live in the mountain. This dragon saved the city three years ago, and factions in Sanction would pay a great deal to have him come back. To our disappointment, the cave was abandoned and empty. There were no dragon scales or dragon hoard or tracks of anyone other than Lord Bight. Perhaps another team should be sent to the far side of the mountain to look for the dragon there.

From the cave the team climbed up into the dead zone of the volcano and made camp on the edge of the ash plain. Six miles across, Thunderhorn's ash plain is an eroded ash and lava cap hundreds of feet thick. As soon as the camp was established, the team then proceeded up the towering cone to the crater itself. The crater is fairly shallow, about eight hundred feet deep. Across its cindered slopes swirling with foul, acrid gases we could barely make out three active vents, constantly shaking the earth and spewing forth their brilliant orange-golden lava.

The sounds were horrendous: a roaring, rumbling thunder that shook the fragile ground underfoot and reverberated through our bones. The heat, too, was beyond intense. The very air burned our lungs and skin. We could only tolerate the lip of the crater for a few seconds at a time. Strong winds blew constantly around the crater, carrying bits of grit and clouds of gas.

We each took a turn to look down into the mouth of Thunderhorn. When it was my turn I took a deep breath, leaned against the wind, braced myself at the crater's edge and looked inside. Six hundred feet below, the nearest vent opened like a massive worm burrow that tunneled straight down into the basaltic rock. Bright yellow streaks of sulphur colored its mouth like vomit. Deep within glowed the fiery eye of molten lava.

The mountain has been in continuous eruption for years, its output varying from massive flows to small streams. This year the output has been steady. From the second vent, the lava bursts with a hideous roaring sound through a fissure-turned conduit. Magma pours from this vent in a great, brilliant, white-hot curtain of fire that flows into a lake and out of the caldera through several notches in the rim. The lava spills in molten ribbons down the steep sides of the volcano and into the moat that rings the city. The third vent, while not so spectacular, bubbles and boils and also spills its orange magma into the lava lake.

No life was observed in or near the crater, and after only a short period of observation, the team returned to its camp.

After a long miserable night in our camp, we decided to move on. An acid rain had fallen during the night and damaged or destroyed much of the exposed metal, including the mercenaries' shields, spear points, and metal embossed accoutrements, our shovels, pitons, hammers, spikes, and cooking pans, and the gully dwarves' helmets, which were mostly scrap metal anyway. We had to dispose of much of our gear. The team members were not happy and tempers grew hot from lack of sleep, intense headaches, sore muscles, and the annoyance of ruined equipment.

We lost the second gully dwarf when he went to hurl the ruined helmets into the crater, got engrossed by the view, and forgot to let go. At least there was less for the other three to carry.

The walk down Thunderhorn's steep slope was harrowing to say the least. No matter which route the team chose we had to traverse parts of the mountain's slopes that were gouged with deep, dangerous erosion gullies. We decided to follow the channel cut out of the mountain that funneled much of the lava downhill into the moat created by Lord Bight. This side of the mountain, while steep and slippery with crumbled lava, was at least protected somewhat from the wind and poisonous bursts of gases. Sunshine gleamed on the black tilting slopes, and winds eased to a mild breeze.

Staying west of the channel the team was able to climb down the mountain with little incident and bypass the second Dark Knight camp in the Zhakar Valley near Beckard's Cut. A unanimous decision was made to spend that night in the eastern guard camp to replenish our supplies and gully dwarves.

In the morning, once again, my colleagues and I had to track down the mercenaries at a tavern and drag them out to fulfill their contractual duties. For future reference, I do not recommend using the Black Knife Mercenary Guild for mountainous expeditions. The soldiers were sorely lacking in rock- and rope-climbing skills and in any rudimentary appreciation of the volcanic forces we were studying.

After some discussion, it was decided to terminate the contract and allow the mercenaries to return to the city. The third volcano was far from the Dark Knight camps and could be reached by following the lava channel around the southern edge of the city. This choice gave us ample time to study the lava moat and ensure its efficacy.

Mount Ashkir

After the climb to the blast furnace of Mount Thunderhorn's crater, the hike up Mount Ashkir was a pleasant stroll in the hills. The quietest of the three volcanoes, Ashkir rises approximately 4,000 feet and stands at the southern end of Sanction Vale. Its cone is relatively smooth and even and is unmarred by valleys, ravines, erosion, or volcanic anomalies.

Although Ashkir is still active, it is quiet much of the time and its occasional lava outbursts are routed away from Sanction either through a channel into the moat or under the mountain through pre-existing lava rivers.

On our 3,500–foot climb to Ashkir's crater, we followed a narrow trail through several zones of flora and fauna that represent the layers of damage and regrowth on the mountain's side. The first zone, closest to the valley floor, is the richest and most diverse. Here the farmers of the Vale have cultivated almost every square inch of the available rich volcanic soil in terraces, orchards, and patchwork gardens. Trees grow in the gullies, and the grass is thick and nutritious. The second zone has suffered more damage through the years and is slower to recover. Here the trees are few and the grass is sparser. Sheep and goats graze in these upper meadows and produce the milk for Sanction's signature cheeses. Next comes a wide zone to the tip of the peak where the slopes have been blasted by the hurricane force winds of pyroclastic flows. The last flow was noted nearly twenty years ago and devastated a wide area of the volcano's upper reaches. This area has been considered a dead zone for years, but this team discovered a number of active life forms, including small plants, sapling trees, fireweed, ground squirrels, birds, and many insects growing and thriving in the barren volcanic ash.

One of the gully dwarfs disturbed a pack of minotaur lizards and was unfortunate enough to be snatched up by one. The dwarfs and I set about us with our walking staffs and were able to drive off the creatures. Fortunately for the gully dwarf, the lizard did not like the taste and actually spit it out. I make note of this because in our experience, minotaur lizards are not usually so discriminating.

Shortly after the lizard incident, we reached the dead zone of the volcano and the crater. The view from the rim was breathtaking both toward the bay and the city, but our focus was on the crater. We walked halfway around the rim, hoping the inactivity of the volcano would last another day or two. The crater steamed and smoked in the afternoon sun. A lava dome rose about a hundred feet from the crater floor. It had an uneven surface and a small crater of its own through which blue vapors curled lazily to the sky. We could hear rocks tumbling down the slopes of the dome and the occasional small explosion rocked the area. Beneath our feet the ground trembled slightly from the movement of magma far underground.

After a brief meal, I decided to descend to the crater floor nearly four hundred feet below. No one else chose to go with me. I used ropes to lower myself past the steepest areas, then I carefully climbed down to the crater floor. As I approached the ground level, I noted a gradual increase in the noises from the growing dome surrounded by hundreds of active, whistling, hissing steam vents. The sound grew louder and more fearsome and I quickly began to hear many different pitches like the uproar of an orchestra of wind instruments all whistling and roaring at once.

The crater floor was a very strange, barren, gray, and apparently lifeless place. Rock falls slid, rumbling down around me. Clouds of gases and steam rose from vents and swirled on the wind. The floor was a sea of extremely rough lava with many ridges and depressions. Some ways away I saw a chunk of rock the size of a small house. Curious, I made my way toward the rock over the razor-sharp edges of loose lava, stumbling and climbing over small depressions.

The rock, which had been blown from inside the mountain, was a new part of the mountain's surface. I looked closer at the boulder and was astounded to see a greenish patch. I found small blobs of pale green algae growing on the surface. Walking around the rock, I saw a seven-spot ladybug warming on the sun side of the rock. A wasp laid its eggs close by. Even in this steam and gas laden air there were flies buzzing about the rock and my head. Already this new piece of earth held life.

When I completed my observations, I was not looking forward to the difficult climb out. Then I noticed a goat dropping whitely visible against the black backdrop of lava and saw another one twenty paces farther on. I followed them, thinking these pellets could be sign of a goat trail, and soon I saw a third and a fourth and more that led me through the rough landscape back up the lip of the crater. It took me an hour to climb down into the crater and reach the rock and only thirty minutes to follow the goat trail back up. I just can't decide why a goat would bother to go down into a volcanic crater.

The team spent one night on the peak then trekked down the mountain to the one ruin left on Ashkir, the Temple of Duergast. This black temple was once used for the worship of the goddess Takhisis, but it was abandoned years ago and has fallen into decay and rubble. The main altar room still stands and is presently being used as a sheep fold. We made sketches, took measurements, and made notes of the placement of the altar and various ceremonial decorations for the library but did not spend much time there. The ruin is not stable enough to rebuild and in our opinion does not warrant the effort and expense to excavate. The sheep are welcome to it.

This concludes the survey of the Lords of Doom. It is our belief that while the volcanoes remain active and probably will be troublesome in the next few years, they will not erupt with devastating consequences for a while at least. Lord Bight's magic has kept them under control for years and so far has proved sufficient to keep them in line. Even if his magic fails completely, we think the residual effects of his spells will hold off any major eruptions for months. Beyond that, we do not care to speculate.

Included with this report please find a portfolio of sketches, a list of various plants and animals observed on the three mountains, a recommendation for the maintenance of the lava moat, and an expense report. Three of the gully dwarves survived and demanded a tip. Please note the change in fees to be paid to the Black Knife Mercenary Guild.

Submitted by:
Stroud Feldspear, Assistant Librarian

LETTERS OF A KNIGHT AND HIS LADY, BEGINNING THE SECOND MONTH OF SOLAMNIC OCCUPATION, 38 SC

My dearest Madam,

I do not know who you are. I saw you walking in a garden this afternoon as I marched along Captain's Way to report for duty, and my heart was instantly smitten. Oh, madam, in your face I saw beauty, kindness, cheer, and warmth. Please allow me to visit and formally introduce myself.

Yours,

Sir Thomas deGracy, Knight of the Rose

Dear Sir Knight,

Before my father left on his ship, the *Fairway*, he took my hands in his, looked deep into my eyes, and gave me this advice: "Should any young man approach you with pleas and importunities while I am gone, just say 'no.'" Therefore, kind sir, I must refuse your gentle request.

Aubria Capellin

My lord, Sir deGracy,

My daughter has shown me your gracious request for an introduction and her own kind refusal. Please understand that our Aubria adores her father and tries to obey his every wish. My husband is a kind and loving man and is usually very reasonable, except when his only daughter's reputation and future are at stake. He prefers to be present during meetings between any eligible man and his daughter and, thus far, has yet to find one to meet his exacting standards.

I, on the other hand, am more practical and must constantly keep in mind the inherent danger and the long absences necessary to my husband's current status as a blockade runner.

Since I, too, hail from Solamnia, I am desirous to meet you and hear the latest news from home. I would like to invite you to our home to pay a call during our teatime in the late afternoon. I know your schedule may be pressing, so chose a day that suits your needs. I await your response.

Cordially,

Madame Clairanne Capellin

My most exquisite, darling Aubria,

Your mother is a queen among women. What a

delightful and understanding parent you have. I enjoyed most heartily our afternoon together.

But, oh, Aubria, I am a changed man. No longer are the Oath and Measure the be-all and end-all of my life. You have become the light of my existence, a pearl beyond price, the dearest being in my poor benighted life. Please, my dearest, my darling, say that you hold me in equal regard. Tell me I am your love, your hero, your heart. Say you will be mine.

Yours eternally,

Sir Thomas

Dear Sir Knight,

I, too, enjoyed our brief time together. Your stories of Solamnia and growing up in the Knighthood were fascinating, and I particularly liked your descriptions of your life here in Sanction. Living in a city under siege has been an experience that has grown quite tiresome to us, yet your viewpoint was refreshing and honest. I am pleased that the Knights of Solamnia are here, and it is my hope that you will help bring this dreadful siege to an end.

Beyond that I cannot say more. My father's advice holds my tongue.

Aubria

Oh, sweet Aubria,

Heart of my heart, how noble and wise was your father. He obviously cares deeply for you, his only girl, to have given you such sage advice, and you are wise to follow it as a devoted daughter should.

But what of me? Believe me when I say I cannot escape from your captivation. Like a heavy beautiful dream, I am bewitched. I stand my guard on the city walls and think of you. Everywhere I look I see you in the world around me. I see the shining gray of your eyes on a misty morning when the dew hangs glistening on the stone of the ramparts. I see the glorious red-gold of your hair in the strands of fire that roll down Mt. Thunderhorn. Your lips are as red as the banners of the Guard; your skin is as white as the snow on the distant mountains.

I treasure our evening visits together and for nothing in this world would I trade our walks together in your garden. For those brief times I would face a horde of Dark Knights and slay them with my bare hands. When we walk among the flowers, not even close to one another, yet I feel no gap between us. Then, I am just your shadow. For me to be there, it needs you.

To no one, ever, have I spoken words with such compulsion, such intensity. These feelings, these joys are only for you, dearest Aubria. Say that you may love me in the same way. Tell me your heart is mine.

Your loving Thomas

Dear Thomas,

Forgive me for taking so long to answer your missive. It arrived in the midst of a wild day when my mother and I were busy helping the Seafarer's Guild prepare for the arrival of a small convoy of freighters that slipped through the Dark Knights' blockade. Whenever some of our ships run the blockade, the guild greets the men with willing hands to make repairs and unload the cargo and offer whatever help they might require. The women bring hot food, medical aid if needed, and sometimes news from families. It is always hectic, and unfortunately someone set aside your letter in a pile of paperwork. Mother finally found it two days ago and gave it to me.

I have read your letter until every word is burned delightfully into my memory. I cherish your attention, your feelings for me, your devotion. Even in bed at night, my thoughts fly to you, and I pray into my pillow that you will be delivered through another day of siege and war. I cannot imagine my days without you in them.

But my brave Knight, our future is so uncertain. Our city is still under siege, and the Knights are doing little to change that. What is to happen to us? My father said several times before he left that if Sanction is still under siege when he returns, he may try to slip my mother and me out of the city on his ship. And what if the siege is broken? Will you return to Solamnia with nothing but a sweet memory of us walking in the garden? I have little left now but two parents who love me and an honor that is still untarnished. I will not give that up for only a few declarations of love spoken in the heat of war.

I am my father's girl, and I must say no.

Love, Aubria

Dearest Aubria,

In your steadfast devotion, you have wounded me deeply and struck a chord that resonates in my soul. Honor is the heart of any Solamnic Knight and an ideal we treasure above all worldly things. I would never think to cloud your mind with insincerity or impinge on your self-worth in any way. You are my breath, my light, and the power that binds me to this place. In only five months I have come to love this city as my own and if it is your wish that I stay here with you, I will move the stars and the mountains to remain. The siege will be over soon. Even now our captains make their plans, and when the Knights attack, the foul minions of Neraka will vanish from Sanction's gates forever.

You say you feel devotion to me and cherish our time together. Is there nothing more? Is there no love stirring your thoughts, no passion for me that warms your soul when we are together? Perhaps there is another love in your life, someone I do not know. There are many Knights in this town who would woo you. Do you find another more suitable than I?

Yours in love,

Thomas

Dearest Thomas,

No, there is no other. There is only confusion
and apprehension and the desire to obey the spirit
of my father's wishes. I never thought to fall in love
with a Knight or leave Sanction for strange lands. Is
there a love between us strong enough to endure the
future?

Love, Aubria

Ah, sweet Aubria,

To my mind, yes. Love is a conqueror who strikes
without regard to time or place or circumstances. I
never thought to come to this intriguing city and find
such a harsh master. If I submit to my master faithfully, it gives me joy. It intoxicates me and envelops me
in a longing for you that time will never destroy. But if
I turn my back to it, it strikes me with fear and isolation. I am cold to my soul and struck to the heart with
a restlessness beyond endurance. I cannot lose you.

Is this what you would condemn me to? Would you
force me to turn away from my love for you and condemn
myself to a life of emptiness and bitter grief? Do you
truly, in your innermost heart, wish me to leave you be?

Yours in life,

Thomas

Mary Herbert

Dearest Thomas,

As an obedient daughter, I answer, no.

Your Aubria

P.S. Thank you for the flowers

Aubria, my love.

If you speak true what is in your heart, then can *you* let me go? Will you grow old alone, having turned your dutiful back on a man who loves you with a passion beyond reproach? Will you take your father's advice to the cold bed of spinsterhood and leave me standing alone before a priest at the Temple of the Heart with my hopes in ashes and our love forever denied?

Thomas

Oh, no, Thomas. No. I cannot bear to deny you so.

If you truly have a priest ready and your vows waiting to be said, there is nowhere I would rather be than by your side.

Your Aubria

To: Captain Hugo Capellin
Dated the 14th day Argon

Dearest Husband,

Captain Novorny of the *Sea Fair* told me you have
been delayed in New Port. He gave me your letters
and assures me the *Fairway* did not suffer heavy
damage after the storm in the New Sea and that
repairs to the ship should be completed soon.

That is good news. Perhaps the delay will give you
time to understand what has occurred here in Sanction. You now have a new son-in-law. Do not for one
instant believe that Aubria disobeyed you or that we
tried to disregard your feelings on the subject of her
future. Her husband is a fine, well-regarded Knight
of good family who courted her properly as a gentle-
man should. Since we had received no word from
you in six months, we feared for your safety and
rather than let the love that blossomed between
Aubria and her Knight grow too impatient, I allowed
them to marry. I accept your blame, but I do not
regret my decision. They are deliriously happy—as
we were in our youth, you may remember!

For a while we despaired that the Solamnic
Knights were going to do anything useful about the
siege, but two weeks ago they tried to attack the Dark
Knights in a well-planned, all-out attack. Unfortunately something went dreadfully wrong, and the
attempt to drive off the Knights of Neraka failed.
Aubria's husband fought valiantly in the battle by
all telling, yet even he, who was in the thickest

fighting, could not tell us exactly what went wrong.

Our people are mourning their dead and trying not to despair. The Solamnics do not intend to leave the city, but I don't think even their commanders know what they will do now. One good thing, the blockade has loosened somewhat around the harbor, Captain Novorny says. You should be able to slip back into the city without too much difficulty.

Please hurry home. I miss you and we have a great deal to talk about.

All my love to you, my husband.

Yours,
Clairanne

A Conversation Recorded by an Observer at the Spur and Comb, an Establishment Known for its Cock Fights, Bad Beer, and Dark Corners

Valeria: The answer is no. Not now. Not in a few days. Not ever if I have my way. I don't care that there is no one else to milk the goats, or bake the bread, or scrub the floors, or weed the garden, or pick the olives, or wash your clothes, or do any one of the dozens of chores I have performed for you since our mother died last spring.

To be honest, it is my firm opinion that you worked her to death, and I have no intention of allowing the same fate to befall me. If you want a slave, buy one. If you want workers, hire some. Or—if you can find some pathetic female to whom menial drudgery is a way of life—get a wife. But I am sick unto death of that farm, its stinking goats, and you. Even this city in the midst of the siege is better than your scrap of dirt on the side of a volcano.

Putorian: Of all the ungrateful, hard-hearted, obstinate brats, Valeria, you take the prize. How could you dishonor our mother's memory with such accusations and irresponsible behavior? You have abandoned your home, your family—

Valeria: Abandoned! You're a fine one to talk, you who disappeared without a word or a letter or a message, for how long? . . . Three years? Then you show up last year, move back in, and take over like some land-hungry despot.

Putorian: *And* your heritage—for what? For the debaucheries, drunken orgies, and loose living of the city.

Valeria: Debaucheries! Oh, please! Do you have any idea what is going on in this city? Surely you have not buried yourself so completely in that dirt patch of a farm that you cannot see. Sanction is my home, and at the moment it is in desperate need of anyone it can get. We're at war, brother dear. Or did you miss that? The Knights of Neraka have us almost completely surrounded. They bombard the city day and night and block the roads and harbor. If we do not fight, the Dark Knights will take over and Sanction will sink back into the darkness.

Putorian: Who is this "we"? Surely you are not involved in the defense of Sanction. Not you.

Valeria: I am very involved! And proud of it. I am training to join the women's company of the city militia. We will fight side by side with the men. In fact, I have become quite good with the crossbow. All those years of shooting at rats and wolves with my bow paid off. We stand guard on the walls and help with the wounded. My unit even earned a commendation last week from Lord Bight.

Putorian: You fight with the men? You, the one who can't bear to be in the same room with spiders? The same girl who retires to her bed and moans at the slightest ache? Surely not.

Valeria: We all grow up some time, Putorian.

Putorian: That's what I'm afraid of. I want you back at the farm tomorrow. The farm is isolated from the fighting and safe enough. You would do well to come home before your reputation—and anything else—are totally ruined.

Valeria: Brother, you make me laugh. How long did it take you to find me? Three, four weeks? You weren't trying very hard, and if this city is as bad as you think, my "reputation" would already be burned to the ground.

Now I said no and I meant no. In spite of the fear, the constant shortages, the nightly bombardments, and the deaths I am busy, productive, and happier than I've been in years.

As for my reputation, I met a city guardsman the other day, and if all goes as I hope, my so-called reputation will be completely and irretrievably abandoned. Consider me a lost cause and go home.

Putorian: Not without you. This city has been under siege for well over a year now. The Knights of Neraka are not going to give up. Not after that debacle with the failed attempt to break their lines. Why do you want to stay in a city doomed to fall?

Valeria: Why do you stay on your hilltop farm when the Dark Knights have killed almost every farmer in the Vale who didn't flee? Any day some patrol could find that farm of yours and kill everything on it. Yet you love that land and you stay. I do not. I love this city, its shops and crazy taverns and crooked streets and fountains. Sanction may be short on rations and full of Knights of Solamnia, but at least I have found a place where I am appreciated and free to seek my own destiny. I want to stay here, Putorian, and fight for its freedom. You can go milk a goat.

Putorian: Fine. I give you about a week more before this all palls and you come running home. And when you do, stop by Galthic's Feed Store. We need a pound of salt, twine, and a jug of his finest lavender goat dip.

Valeria: Get your own goat dip, brother. I've got sentry duty.

Observer's note:

At this point the conversation ends abruptly when Valeria laughs and strolls out of the tavern. Legionnaire Putorian and this observer are satisfied with the reactions of Valeria Kusa to this interview and it is our recommendation she be approached for a place in the Legion of Steel. Her brother is pleased with her initiative and maturity, and he and I both agree that she has a strong, adaptable personality that is well suited to hardship, hard work, and covert adventure. Other observers have reported the same thing. Of course, until she has accepted a position in the Legion and undergone the basic training, she is not to know of her brother's rank and duties.

Legionnaire Putorian plans to return to his watcher's outpost on the farm tonight.

EXCERPTS FROM THE JOURNAL OF CAMBREN HARTBROOKE, SERGEANT, 2ND COMPANY OF THE GOVERNOR'S GUARDS

10th day of Corij, 36 SC

Sweetest Marli,

The days are growing longer now, but the nights

still seem dreary and empty. Only two years have passed since you left me, yet those years, stricken with sadness and fraught with danger, have slogged by like ten times their number. Not a day in those tiresome years went by that I did not think of you.

Now your birthday approaches, Midsummer Day, a day of pleasure and festivities, of sun warmed blossoms, ripe fruit, and spring mead, and of the smell of newly cut hay. Something stirs within me and warms the bleak shadows of my thoughts. Perhaps it is the sunbeam that breaks through my shuttered window every day at this time and dances like a sprite across my desk. Perhaps it is the heady fragrance of the honeysuckle with its flame-orange flowers that you planted by the gate. It was for the hummingbirds, you said. But dearest, it is I who has drawn more sustenance from those fiery-tipped vines than any bird.

Whatever the spell that has released my thoughts, I find myself thinking more about you. I talk to you in the empty hours of the night; I sing to you in our garden. To release some of this restless urge to communicate with you, I have decided to keep this journal and dedicate it to you. Then, if I rant and rave with my pen or scratch endless stories to someone who is not here, no one will think me mad. Perhaps in time there will be consolation in the writing.

15th day of Corij, 36 SC

To be honest, my dear, I don't remember very much about the year after you left. It is, and probably always will be, a blur in my mind. Wherever you have gone, you might remember the beginning of the plague that struck our city that hot, horrible summer of 34 SC—the sickness we called the Sailor's Scourge—and wherever you have gone, you did not go alone. Our city was devastated by the Dark Knights' poisonous plague; thousands died before the healers and Lord Bight devised a way to conquer the sickness.

Once the healers brought the disease under control, I admit I gave up my command and came home to die. Exhaustion, fever, grief—all took their toll. But our neighbor, Amania, found me unconscious on the ground in our garden, brought me into the house, and cared for me until I recovered.

Of course, you remember Amania. She would bake honey cakes for us and talk to you over the fence by the hour. She lost her husband to the plague, and her beautiful little daughter. After you left, she transferred her caring instincts to me. I would have died but for her. Sometimes I have wondered if she helped me or hindered me.

By the time I regained my strength, the city had buried its dead, and Lord Bight and the city elders could take stock of the actual damage done to Sanction. It was not a pleasant task. As soon as my commander, Captain Janklin, heard I had recovered, he immediately implored me to return to my original position. At first I refused him. I could barely hold myself together, keep a coherent thought, or speak to anyone above a murmur. How could he expect me to take charge of my old squad in the 2nd Company of Governor's Guards again?

Then he came to see me. And sweet Marli, when I looked into the captain's face, I saw much of what must have been in my own: lines of fatigue, shadows of sadness, the pallor of strain. I could not in good faith refuse him a second time. I had given my oath to protect the lord governor with my life if need be, and I had meant every word. Lord Bight can be difficult, harsh, arrogant, or self-absorbed at times, and sometimes all at once, yet he is the only hope this city has. I am and always will be his liege man.

Amania was pleased that I went back to the governor's palace. She thought the hard work would do me good. She was right.

The first day I returned to my duties, Captain Janklin gave me the reports gathered so far on the status of Sanction. By the absent gods, Marli, it was appalling. We will probably never know exactly how many people died in Sanction from the Sailor's Scourge, for we never had an exact count of the sailors, refugees, visitors, and traveling merchants who were in the city at the time, but the final counting of deaths that were registered numbered nearly six thousand. The City Guards who patrolled the city streets, the healers who helped the sick, and the refugees in their crowded camp were hit the hardest. Of the companies of the City Guard, nearly all suffered casualties of more than half their numbers.

The city lost three council members, five Guild Masters, the Harbormaster, and almost all of the mystic healers from the Temple of the Heart. The merchant community was decimated, as was the fishing guild. Perhaps the only two groups who did not suffer major losses were Lord Bight's servants and guards who were somewhat isolated in the palace and those farmers in the Vale who did not enter the city during the crisis.

Believe it or not, Marli, the real crisis came on a single day when the plague was at its height and Sanction had to face both an attack by a fleet of Dark Knight ships and a minor eruption of Mt. Thunderhorn (that was quite a day, one I still can't think about without intense sadness and great joy). Missiles from the Dark Knights' ships started several fires that burned five warehouses, two apartments, and a tavern. Fortunately, they were thwarted by a bronze dragon who appeared out of the volcanic peaks and destroyed their fleet before they could wreak any more havoc. The volcano caused some minor damage to the lava moat and the outer fortifications on the east side of the city, but its energy was brought under control by Lord Bight.

An assassin tried to kill the lord governor that day, too, and it was only because of the bravery and sacrifice of two of our own that he survived. But, Marli, you will never believe who the assassin turned out to be. Our commander, Ian Durne. All those years we knew him; all those days we worked with him, bled with him, fought with him, and no one ever guessed he was a Dark Knight. All of us are still troubled by his betrayal. Lord Bight will never speak of it.

It was the city council's opinion that most of the destruction inflicted on Sanction itself was superficial and could in time be repaired. It was the population that suffered the greatest devastation not only in numerical losses but in emotional stress, decreased security, financial loss, and in a future clouded in uncertainty.

Thankfully, we still had Lord Bight.

21st day of Corij
Midyear's Day

Happy Birthday, my dearest. In honor of your day, Amania and I took your favorite wine and honey cakes to the garden this afternoon and sat beneath the birch tree by the pond. Because I am so busy, she had taken over care of the garden in your honor and it thrives beneath her touch. Knowing how I can grow nothing but weeds, you would be pleased to see how well the flowers and herbs you loved respond to her attention.

Tonight, I sit in my study alone with my thoughts of you. You would be twenty-nine today and in my memories, you are still as slim and beautiful as the day I met you ten years ago when Sanction flourished in its peaceful prosperity—peaceful at least compared to now.

But this is your birthday. I will not depress you or myself with more gruesome details of Sanction's days after the plague. Instead, I will use this entry to tell about a few of Lord Bight's efforts to heal the wounds and improve the morale of the city.

As soon as the burial details were finished and the dead lay in peace, Lord Bight suggested to the city council that a memorial of some sort would be in order. Particularly, he wished to honor the two

Governor's Guards and his healer, Mica the dwarf, who died while trying to save Sanction and its governor. The council agreed wholeheartedly. However, deciding on a location and a fitting memorial was not so easy. The controversy raged for weeks. In the meantime, the City Guards quietly asked for and received permission to include the bronze dragon on their uniform to honor his timely intervention. A small, unobtrusive bronze-colored dragon shape was added to the right front chest of their scarlet uniforms. A bronze smith volunteered his time and materials as a gift to the Guards and added a relief of a winged dragon to the great West Gate on the city wall.

Meanwhile, the arguments raged among the city elders for the memorial until at last Lord Bight stepped in. He looked over their designs and suggestions and chose one that seemed appropriate to him. His only condition was *he* would design a statue to his two Guards and the healer.

We had the ceremony to dedicate the memorial late in the winter about seven months after the disaster. The whole city turned out on the cold, windy evening and gathered at the waterside to view the new memorial. People crowded onto the wharves, the long pier, and every boat and ship in the harbor. There was not a clear space left. For several months we had watched the construction of the new causeway and the tower upon it, but few knew exactly what it would do, if anything. Was it a citadel? Or a lighthouse? Or just a tower meant to honor the dead? Whatever Lord Bight planned, he kept it secret until the last moment. While the people watched, the city council and the lord governor marched down the causeway that now stretched out into the harbor. As horns trumpeted across the water, the dignitaries came to a halt beside the tower and together pulled off a huge sail that covered its top.

The edifice is beautiful, Marli. You would truly appreciate the elegant simplicity of its curved walls, the glowing white of its polished granite, even the stability of its foundation. It is strong enough to be used as a citadel and it will be manned perpetually by an honor squad of the City Guard. But its true value and beauty lies in its crown, for atop the gleaming walls, within a room of steel and glass, sits a polished lamp of crystal.

When the speeches and music had ended, Lord Bight entered the tower and climbed the stairs alone. A moment later a bright white light lanced out across the evening gloom and lit the harbor entrance with its starlike glow. The light shines perpetually, Marli, as a reminder to all of us who remain behind of the people we loved and lost and of those who gave their lives unselfishly to help this city. The memorial was a huge success.

In a smaller ceremony with the Governor's Guards the next day, Lord Bight unveiled a statue he had designed and had commissioned. The statue had been placed along the road to the palace at the edge of the woods close to the place where Mica died. It was a bronze set of figures: Mica the dwarf with Lynn of Gateway and Shanron, the two women who gave their lives defending Lord Bight. The sculptures were well done and, from what little I saw of Lynn

and Shanron, close to life. They stood on a rocky
incline as if climbing Mount Thunderhorn: Mica at
the base, then Shanron carrying her sword, and
Lynn at the crest.

Strangely, Lynn's figure carried an owl on her out-
stretched arm. I didn't remember any connection with an
owl, but Lord Bight seemed to know. He stood for a long
while, an odd look on his face, and stared only at her.

That was last year, yet even now he never goes by
that statue without glancing her way.

4th day Argon, 36 SC

My love,

The days are long this time of year and we have
been extremely busy. Do you remember how you
used to complain when I came home late, dirty, and
weary in the summer days? I wish you were here
now to click your tongue at me and fuss while I eat
my cold supper. Lord Bight has been working us, and
himself, very hard to rebuild the City Guards and
improve the Governor's Guards.

I told you the City Guards were decimated by the
plague to about half their former numbers. In most
cities this would be a cause for concern, but in Sanction
it is a problem vital to our survival. As I have griped for
years, the Knights of Takhisis—Chaos take their
souls—have besieged our city in an effort to wrest it
out of Lord Bight's hands. Up until the year 34 SC, they
satisfied themselves with minor attacks against the

defenses and petty raids into the Vale. Lord Bight managed to keep them at bay with the moat of lava encircling the city, a massive city wall, and a network of fortifications along the eastern half of the valley.

After their plans for the plague, the assassination of Lord Bight, and the invasion of sea forces failed, the Dark Knights fell back to reconsider and gave us a desperately needed respite. Ramparts and moats of lava are all well and good, but they are useless without the men and the mobile cavalry to defend them. Somehow we had to recruit and train reinforcements from a population already sadly reduced and in need of replacements in every vocation from baking to weaving. Many men of eligible age volunteered, but it was not enough.

To make matters worse, last year the Dark Knights began a systematic offensive along the overland route, the Hundred Mile Road, to dislodge groups of ogres and their villages that happen to be in the way. It is the belief of our spies and informers that the Dark Knights are setting up supply bases in preparation for a new major offensive against this city. Already they are reinforcing their camps in the Zhakar Valley to the east and the smaller North Pass.

The city council, that vaporish group of old men and dithering fools, is frantic. But for once I find myself in agreement with their fears. We are understaffed, undermanned, and Sanction's economy is still staggering under the blow dealt to it the summer of the plague. The Knights of Solamnia have sent several delegations to Lord Bight with offers of support and aid, but so far he has refused them. He prefers to govern his own without interference from outside sources. For what it's worth I think he is right.

And yet I can't help but wonder in the dark hours of these late summer nights if the time is coming when the choice to choose will be taken from us.

13th day Argon
36 SC

Dear Marli,

Something odd happened today. I've told you before of Lord Bight's visits to the Lords of Doom. He goes with one or two of his guards to the three volcanoes that surround Sanction and with his power to wield magic, he keeps the volcanic eruptions under control. For years now he has only needed occasional journeys to the peaks to deal with minor problems and to keep the flow of lava regulated. I don't presume to know how he does it; I am only grateful that he can.

Today, an early morning earthquake rumbled down from Mount Grishnor to the north and shook the Temple of the Heart, the refugee camp, the palace, and the northern suburbs. Several larger buildings tumbled down and cracks developed in the city wall. Lord Bight decided to check the volcano and survey its cone for new activity.

I was not on the roster for this day, but my friend Morgan was and he told me later what happened. After a long climb up Mount Grishnor, they soon saw what caused the earthquake in Sanction. On the northeastern slope of the cone, a lava dome had formed. It was on the far side of the volcano out of sight of the city and therefore posed little danger to us. It had burst, breaking loose from the slope, and its rock, dust, and ash had crashed down the mountainside toward the North Pass in a thick, stormlike mass that moved across the ground, creating a barren zone that was fan-shaped and edged with a rim of shattered boulders and young trees. Far below Morgan said they could see where the edge of the avalanche had brushed through the camp of the Dark Knights that blocked the pass. He was sorry to say the landslide did not wipe them out completely, but maybe it disconcerted them enough to make them move further back into the mountains.

Lord Bight studied the collapsed dome for a long time. There was little left of the dome but its edges and deep within its vents, the faintest glow of new lava. The governor did not look pleased, but he rolled up his sleeves and, ordering Morgan to stay on the rim, he strode into the crater.

Morgan did not see him work his magic. None of us ever has. Lord Bight takes a bodyguard only to satisfy his men, not really for his own safety. Dark Knights we can handle, but the explosive and often deadly whims of a volcano are beyond our power. So we go and we escort him to his destination and we guard his back, but we have never seen his magic.

Morgan said he waited about three hours, which was unusual. Lord Bight rarely takes more than hour or two to work his incantations. After a while he

grew frantic with worry and contemplated going
down into the crater to find the lord governor, when
at last he saw him stagger into sight.

Morgan helped him down the mountain and
took him back to the palace where his healer took
one look at him and sent the governor to bed. It
was a measure of Lord Bight's fatigue that he did
not argue. Lord Bight is a powerful man; the
magic he wields wearies him, but I have never
seen him to this point of utter exhaustion. He
could barely move his feet. His face was deathly
white and his skin was shrunken around his eye
sockets and mouth. His golden eyes looked
haunted. While our thoughts begged to ask what
happened, we could not broach the mantle of
secrecy he always wears. Nor did he try to tell us.

Everyone did ask Morgan what happened, but he
could not explain. He did not see anything occur.

And now that I have had time to think about it,
that simple fact scares me more than anything else.
The steams and vents did not disappear, the dome's
fissure did not close. The volcano seemed unchanged
by Lord Bight's power. Now the fear preys in my
mind, Marli. What happened down in that crater?

18th day of Argon
36 SC

Dearest Marli,

It's been five days since Lord Bight went to Mount

Grishnor, and in that time he has recovered his strength and built quite a bastion of anger. Whatever happened to him down in that crater, I can see in his eyes that he cannot believe it. There have been more mild rumblings from the volcano, almost like distant laughter—if I may be so fanciful—and every time the lord governor hears it, his eyes glow like molten bronze. He plans to return to the mountain tomorrow and try again. I wish I could go, but once again it is someone else's turn to accompany him. I am training recruits tomorrow.

20th day Argon
36 SC

Well Marli,

The absent gods be praised, Lord Bight's magic worked its will on the mountain yesterday and calmed the stirring danger. He came back from the peak, weary and relieved, the light of victory in his face. But I know the man well, Marli, and deep in his eyes I thought I glimpsed a disturbed shadow I have never seen before. He is worried, and that thought is disturbing indeed. Today he went to visit the Priestess Asharia at the Temple of the Heart. He was closeted with her for several hours in a private conversation. Whatever they said to one another did not seem to reassure Lord Bight. I hope he is not ill.

Mary Herbert

1st day Sirrimont
36 SC

Dear Marli,

Today was the hottest day of the summer thus far and for once it was not particularly busy. The city stirred early to work its business before the hottest hours of the day, so by noon most people retreated to the shade for some idling in the intense heat. The Guards were no exception. Training schedules have been changed for both the City and the Governor's Guards, so the men do not have to exert themselves in the furnace of Sanction's noon. Years ago we tried working the men through the hot daylight hours— only once. After we lost three men to heat prostration and dozens of other to dehydration, we altered the summer training and have done so ever since. Only city patrols and sentry duties remain constant.

After my duties at the palace, I returned to our little house, to the blessed shade and peace of your garden. Amania has hung a hammock for me in the grove of birch and there I sleep and dream of you, my beloved.

8th day Sirrimont
36 SC

Dear Marli,

There have been more tremors today. Sanction's

buildings, most built of brick and supported by diagonal wooden beams, survived the shaking unscathed. The city wall will need more minor repairs and the clock in the Merchant Guild's tower will need to be recalibrated and reset. The only real scare came at noon perhaps ten minutes after the worst shock when a large wave swept into the harbor and wreaked havoc among the ships and docks. Four smaller boats were literally washed into the streets. The long pier held firm to its pilings, but the smaller northern pier broke loose and smashed into the wharf. A number of ships were damaged, several were sunk, and no one knows yet how many sailors and dockhands drowned.

Lord Bight released several of his squads of Guards to help the City Guards with the rescue and clean-up effort. When we arrived at the waterfront, we found the townspeople hard at the task of setting right yet another disaster.

I firmly believe, Marli, that Sanction is one of the most resilient cities on Krynn. Somehow, despite volcanoes, earthquakes, floods, sieges, plagues, and attacks, Sanction manages to survive.

I asked Captain Janklin later if he knew what caused the wave. I'd heard several tales in town from people who blamed the Dark Knights, the black dragon Sable, even the new giant breed of ogres, the titans, that have appeared in Kern. His explanation was simpler, if not so fanciful. He told me what Lord Bight had explained to him, that the earth had shifted somewhere beneath New Sea and that shifting had caused the great wave. Having lived on the lap of volcanoes most of my life, I can believe his words. All the powers and all the wonders performed by the creatures of this world do not compare to the natural energies and mysteries of the earth we live on.

Selfishly, however, I wish Krynn would go entertain some other place with her geologic shows.

9th day Sirrimont
36 SC

Marli,

There is no water today. The earthquake of yesterday damaged the aqueducts coming from the mountains. In view of the fragility of the waterways and the increasing activity of the Knights of Takhisis, Lord Bight has ordered the construction of four large cisterns within the city limits to store water in case of future emergencies. He still has the services of the dwarf engineers who built the aqueduct and the memorial lighthouse, so construction should begin soon. He also gave permission for two new mines to be opened on Mount Ashkir. The operators are mining pumice now and hope to delve deeper for gem stones and ores. In return for the land and mineral rights, they are to deliver gypsum and volcanic ash to the construction sites for the cement mixers. The gypsum is mixed with clay for bricks; the volcanic ash, when added to lime and water, makes a very tolerable cement which is used to line the aqueducts and cisterns.

There is some balance in this crazy world, even in the eruptive violence of volcanoes. They give and they take away.

15th day Sirrimont
36 SC

Marli, my love.

I do miss you, especially today. Last year Lord Bight designated this day as Sanction's Festival of Bones in memory of those who died in the plague and in the battle to save the city. Instead of a city-wide memorial, though, this day is to be kept in the time-honored tradition of individual celebrations of life. All over the city, people remember a loved one or a family or a friend or a group of friends by reenacting or engaging in some activity or event that was special to that person (or persons). For that I am intensely grateful. Last year I could not bear to face the day or the meaning of it, but Time in its infinite, mindless march has numbed the pain of the gaping hole in my heart. Today I celebrate you: your vivacity, your generosity, your boundless love and caring, and your talent for growing things.

With the city council's permission, I had one of the abandoned houses near ours torn down and on the empty lot, I have had a garden planted in your honor that will be for our neighborhood to enjoy. Amania has worked very hard to propagate cuttings from your plants and to gather donations from other gardeners around us. The result has been all I could have wished for. Lord Bight donated several golden raintrees and acacias from his personal garden. Kathias down the street built a fishpond in thanks for all the loaves of cinnamon bread you used to give him. We placed benches in the shade of the trees, a fountain by the fishpond, and paths for children to explore. Marli, if only you could be here to see this place!

I wanted Amania to be with me today to open the garden—she has worked so hard on its completion— but she hired a boat and sailed into the bay to throw a wreath into the sea her husband loved so much. Instead, Kathias and several other friends and neighbors helped me open the gates and bury a shank bone to symbolize the Festival and the act of remembrance.

Tomorrow perhaps I will take Amania to Marli's Garden and treat her to a picnic.

13th day Reorxmont
36 SC

My sweet wife,

Please forgive me that it has been so long since my last note to you. Shortly after the Festival of Bones, Lord Bight put out a call to all able-bodied men between the ages of sixteen and thirty-six to report to the eastern Guard Training Camp for military training. His goal is to create a militia for the defense of the city.

Years ago, before the plague, this plan would not have been successful. Too many people were working hard, making a success, becoming prosperous in the freedom Sanction offered. Since the plague, however, too many things have changed. We have been reminded how vulnerable our freedom truly is and how fragile the health of this city can be. Reports come in daily of the movements of the Dark Knights and their growing desire to control our port.

Even more disturbing, we have heard more rumors and disquieting tales of the failure of the new-found magic. I have been told wizards all over Ansalon have been losing their ability to wield magic for almost a year now. Even our own mystics at the Temple of the Heart finally admit that their healing powers are not as effective. Yet no one seems to understand this terrible phenomenon. Is it also affecting the dragons? What a bizarre twist that would be.

Unfortunately for Sanction, this strange dwindling of magic could bring disaster. I think I understand now what happened to Lord Bight last spring. Although he will not admit to a lessening of his powers—probably for fear of terrifying the populace—he is doing much to prepare for the worst. Forming a citywide militia is one of his ideas. The call was answered with great enthusiasm and willingness by most of the men in the city. The women, though not specifically called, responded, too. Enough women joined the ranks to form a company of their own.

They are training to fight fires, retrieve wounded, and shoot the short bows used by the City Guards. Their accuracy at target practice is commendable. Amania joined, much to my surprise, and she has become the best shot in the city.

And that, my love, is why I have not kept up with this journal in a while. Between my hours serving Lord Bight, I am also organizing and training the recruits. As soon as their initial training period is over, they will be allowed to return to their usual work and will be required to attend militia duties once a month or as needed. This way, Sanction has a large base of reserves should she ever be attacked again.

22nd day Reorxmont
Harvest Come

Dear Marli,

The militia training is going well and the hot weather has broken at last. Autumn in Sanction has always been my favorite time of year. The heat and humidity have passed away for another season; the city's business hours have returned to normal. A few autumn rains have settled the dust and washed clean the streets. The nights are now cool enough to sleep indoors.

The farmers of the Vale, bless their enterprising and stubborn souls, have begun harvesting their crops of olives, hops, grapes, apples, cotton, and beans. The new batch of autumn cider is being pressed and sold by the keg at the Souk Bazaar. I plan to lay in a stock for our cellar. The cider is sweet this year and rich in flavor. If the grapes are half as good, this year's wine should be excellent. The Souk Bazaar will be open late tonight for the farmers to hold a Harvest celebration. I imagine the taverns and inns around the bazaar will be open late as well.

Amania asked me to accompany her tonight to the celebration to check out the crops and the latest goods from the merchant ships that arrived yesterday and today. She says I have been working too hard and since today is my day off, I should do something relaxing.

I tried to say no. Our training and guard schedules have been switched back to the usual rotations. I stand guard at the Palace from dawn to noon, work at the guards' training camp from midafternoon to three hours past sunset, and escort Lord Bight whenever necessary. Some days it is a grueling routine. Yet all of us work hard, the lord governor the most, and there is still more to do to bring this city back to a state of readiness. If the Knights of Takhisis knew how weak our garrison really was, they would attack tomorrow.

On second thought, Amania is right. This is my day off. I want to buy some cider before it is gone, and besides one night of shopping and strolling with a pretty friend is not going to ruin my day of rest. Should I invite her to dinner, as well?

Mary Herbert

29th day Reorxmont

Well, Marli, it finally happened. Lord Bight has chosen a new commander for the City Guards. He has held the position himself for two years now— I think because he did not want to trust another man with such a position of authority after the debacle with Ian Durne. Now, however, the work load is too great. He cannot do everything, as much as he tries, and he must put someone else in charge of the City Guards.

Hamner Gethrik is a good man, one I have known for years, and he will do well. The Guards themselves were pleased with the selection. As for us, I doubt Lord Bight will turn us over to a new commander. The Governor's Guards are too close to the lord governor to trust to someone unknown, and the captains of the four companies are working well together to balance the duties. Never again do we want a Dark Knight so close to Lord Bight.

Observer's note: I left out a number of passages here that dealt mostly with Sergeant Hartbrooke's personal memories from the months of Hiddumont and H'rarmont. Those months were fairly quiet in Sanction, so I have chosen to move forward to the significant events of 37 SC.

Yule, 21st day of Phoenix

Dearest Marli,

What a day this has been, even for Sanction and our ever-busy lord governor. The hour is late and the fire burns low, letting the winter chill ease into the house. But I have a cup of spiced wine still warm from the poker and a mind too full of thought to sleep quite yet. Perhaps the fire will last a little while longer and keep my ink warm. Sanction woke this morning, this first day of winter, to a light snowfall. It did not last long, of course, the days are still too mild for a heavy freeze, but for a few hours in the stillness of the morning, the houses and trees sat blanketed with a coverlet of crystal white. Snow swirled through the streets and piled in drifts of powdered flakes. The children were delighted. They ran and played in the falling snow. A few brave ones tried coasting down Dray's Hill on trays until one kender lad got going so fast he slid into the road nearly under the hooves of a brewer's team pulling a beer wagon. Scared the horses and driver so much, the man called the City Guard and had them chase the sliders off to another hill farther from the city.

Before long the snowfall stopped, the sun came out, and the snow turned into a dirty, muddy slush. Smoke from hundreds of kitchens, public bakeries, cook houses, and burning Yule logs filled the clearing skies and powdered the pristine snow with a fine residue of soot. The snowfall fell thicker in the higher vales and peaks of the mountains, and today

the volcanic range hunkered against the frigid blue
sky, its towering iron ramparts crowned with ice and
cloaked in snow and mist.

From the heights of the fortification towers, we
could see the smoke rising from the camps of the
Dark Knights in the passes. I can only wish them
empty bellies and hearty cases of frostbite this
cold night.

Yesterday, another delegation of Solamnic
Knights arrived to discuss yet another treaty with
Lord Bight. Because of the holiday, he put them off
for a few days by inviting them instead to a feast
today and, in fine Solamnic tradition, a hunt tomorrow. Usually, I'm told, the Solamnic Knights hunt
boar at Yule. There are no boar in the immediate
vicinity of the city or the volcanoes, so we will have
to improvise. Lord Bight suggested to their emissary
that they hunt the wild sheep that live on the high
mountain slopes. The Knight agreed, but he did not
look impressed. I could see his thoughts in his eyes.
A sheep? Why would anyone hunt a silly sheep? I
suspect they will be in for a surprise. Our mountain
rams grow larger, tougher, and meaner than any
sheep these Knights know, and you cannot chase
one with a horse. The hunt should be interesting to
watch.

Today was another matter. Lord Bight enter-
tained his visitors in generous style at the palace
with a huge feast and a gathering of Sanction's
finest and brightest citizens. The main hall was
filled with tables set with golden dishes, delicate
glass ware, and lamps that glowed with a golden

light. Greenery and swags of fragrant herbs decorated the walls, and a huge Yule log burned in the fireplace. Platters of geese stuffed with garlic, fruit, and herbs, chickens roasted in honey, fish fillets in a sweet and sour sauce, bowls of venison stew and lamb curry, fresh bread, puddings, turnovers, and pies covered the sideboards, all accompanied by Lord Bight's private stock of Sanction's finest wines. The vision of wealth and largess impressed even the Solamnics.

The feast began early in the afternoon, and I was ordered to stand with the honor guard by the large double doors leading into the hall. I was present when the Solamnics and their entourage arrived. There were three high-ranking Knights in the group: two Knights of the Rose and a Knight of the Sword (a master cleric), as well as two Shield Knights. We had not seen them before this day nor did we know their names until they introduced themselves with due respect to the lord governor.

There was nothing unusual about that. We often did not meet delegations until the day of the proposed meeting. But even if we had known their names, nothing would have prepared us for the surprise that walked into our midst. One of the Knights, the Rose Knight, was a woman—Linsha Majere, to be exact. Her name alone caused a buzz among our people. A Majere, daughter of Palin, granddaughter of Caramon, and the only woman to ever reach the rank of Rose Knight. Then we saw her face and the entire contingent of the old Governor's Guards (those of us that survived the plague and the past two years) froze in our places in utter astonishment.

Marli, it was amazing. The woman was the mirror image of Lynn of Gateway, the Governor's Guard who died protecting Lord Bight. They could have been twins. Linsha's hair was longer, and her carriage was more graceful and poised. Her smile was warmer than Lynn's, and when she saw us staring at her in an obvious boorish manner, her smile brightened like the sun and she saluted us in genuine regard. Then she swept by us and entered the hall.

I don't know how Lord Bight reacted. I would have given a year's pay to see his face when she entered the room. Captain Janklin told me later he had never seen the lord governor speechless before.

I wish you had been there, my dearest. You would have enjoyed the dance, the feast, and the festivities, and most of all you would have appreciated the pleasure that warmed Lord Bight's face when he escorted the Rose Knight to her waiting carriage later that evening. I had not seen him look so relaxed in months.

Perhaps later, in the privacy of our bed, you could have told me if the niggling little thought in the back of my mind was crazy or inspired. It came to me at that moment in the front entrance while I watched the Rose Knight in her red gown that perhaps we had seen her before. It was no secret to us that the Solamnics maintained a Clandestine Circle in Sanction. What if this Linsha Majere had once worn the uniform of the Guards and called herself Lynn? If we could be fooled by a Dark Knight, why not a Solamnic Knight?

30th day of Phoenix,
36 SC

Marli,

The Solamnic Knights have come and gone, once again without satisfaction. Lord Bight spent every day of their visit in the company of Linsha Majere, but if she tried to convince him to accept a treaty, she had to leave disappointed. The lord governor is still determined to hold the city alone.

As relieved as he was to have this delegation depart, I don't think he was pleased to see the Lady Knight go. He has been short-tempered and unpleasantly snappish these past few days.

This year is finally winding to an end. Good riddance. May this new year see the end of the Dark Knights and a bright renewal for Sanction.

5th day of Mishamont,
37 SC

Dear Marli,

We received disturbing news today from one of our more enterprising Khurish merchants who just returned from Neraka. No one seems to know yet what the significance will be for Sanction, but the news is the talk of the city. It seems a week ago, the Dark Knights' governor-general, the Lord of the Night, Mirielle Abrena succumbed to "tainted meat," a euphemism for poison if I've ever heard one. Her funeral was to be held two days ago in the city she helped rebuild, Neraka. We must wait to hear who her successor will be and how this change of leadership will affect the Knights' plans for Sanction.

10th day of Mishamont
37 SC

Marli,

The word has come. The Lord of the Skull Knights, Morham Targonne, the Adjudicator of the Dark Knights, has claimed his rights as successor to Abrena. Lord Bight commented dryly that probably indicated Targonne served the tainted meat. Such a dishonorable act wouldn't surprise me. What we have heard about Targonne has been less than complimentary: a bloodless, cunning, manipulating clerk who did not have the stomach to face his commander in a challenge face to face.

So what does this mean for Sanction? Unfortunately, we really do not know. Targonne is an unknown equation. Will he continue the push to capture our port, simply continue the blockade in the passes, or back off us completely? Speculation runs rampant in the city and rumors fly faster than locusts.

At least the merchants are not staying away. The port is always busy and the Souk Bazaar is almost filled to capacity again. The spring harvest looks good. There is still a shortage of labor, and many houses and businesses still stand empty. But Sanction is beginning to show her recovery.

I just hope the Dark Knights look elsewhere for a city to capture.

21st day of Mishamont
Spring Dawning 37 SC

Dearest wife,

I never thought the Knights of Takhisis would give me a laugh, but this day they have done it. We just learned their clerk of a commander has moved his headquarters from Neraka to Jelek. That part I can understand. Jelek is a prosperous, thriving town that has miraculously—or cunningly—avoided the depredations of the great dragons. Some spies tell us the seat of the Targonne family business empire is there (which explains a great deal). Neraka, on the other hand, is a foul dump of a settlement a little too close to the ruins of that haunted old temple of theirs.

Along with his capitol, Targonne has also decided to drop the decades-old pretense of faith in a departed goddess and change the Dark Knights' name. Did he call them the Knights of Jelek after his new headquarters? No. He is changing the name to the Knights of Neraka. Why Neraka, if he didn't like it well enough to stay there? Then again, what difference does it make? A Dark Knight by any name is a treacherous, black-hearted child of evil.

We've heard, too, that many of General Abrena's followers have followed her into death. I'm pleased to think she will be so well attended in the afterlife.

30th day Mishamont
37 SC

Marli,

The winds are sweeping winter from the hills and meadows. The sun is shining and the air is warm. Snowdrops and lupine are blooming in the fields. Most of the snow is gone from the passes and the roads through the mountains will soon be open to wains and heavy traffic. We shall see if the Dark Knights intend to follow through with their offensive against the city.

Your garden is growing well under Amania's gentle hand. She tells me everything survived the winter and is putting out new shoots and buds. She found some rose bushes for sale in the Souk Bazaar and I bought them for her.

She also tells me she is being approached by several suitors. Her time of mourning was over a year ago but it has only been this year that I have noticed she is wearing colors again, dressing her hair, and using the blush that looks so becoming to her cheeks. I am pleased for her but I am uncomfortable at the thought of Amania in the company of ardent men. She is still so vulnerable.

7th day of Chislmont
37 SC

Dear Marli,

We had more earthquakes today and for the first time in years an ash fall from Mount Thunderhorn dusted the city. Lord Bight fumed like one of the volcanoes and stormed off to deal with the problem. He must have had difficulties because it was hours before the ash stopped falling and the mountain settled down.

One of the guards who accompanied Lord Bight came racing back in the clearing twilight, yelling for a horse and an escort. We saddled quickly and rode up the mountain to the edge of a large cave (the old lair of the red dragon, Firestorm) where Lord Bight had collapsed. Without a word among us, we put him on his horse and took him back to the palace.

The healers say he will recover. What I and all of Sanction want to know is, will the magic recover before the volcanoes erupt out of control and destroy everything we have built?

The other news today is a little more positive. Thanks to a tip by an undercover Legionnaire, the City Guards captured an entire cell of Dark Knight spies. Their hideout was raided late this evening and the entire place turned upside down. The

Guards found code books, plans of the city fortifications, Guard schedules and lists, a list of names
of people targeted for assassination, and several
messages from a Dark Knight commander inform-
ing the undercover knights to prepare for Opera-
tion Downdraft, whatever that is. Commander
Gethrik was very pleased by this coup, and well he
should be. We owe the Legion of Steel a debt of gratitude whether Lord Bight will admit it or not.

I wish this was the end of it, but we know the
Knights who too recently called themselves Knights
of Takhisis. They are like cockroaches. Where you
see one or two, there are dozens in hiding.

16th day Bran
37 SC

My dear,

Here it is only the fifth month of the year. It is a
beautiful spring of warm winds and gentle rains.
The volcanoes have been quiet of late and the town
appears to be prospering. And yet those of us
around Lord Bight see already the clouds of evil
gathering.

My hopes that the Knights of Neraka would leave
us alone are fizzling into ashes. As the passes and
mountain roads open and become passable, more
and more Dark Knights are pouring into the region
east of Sanction. Our spies report the fortified camps
at both passes are expanding and new troops arrive

daily, particularly at the camp at Beckard's Cut. Black ships have been spotted in the Bay. They're not attacking yet, but they harass the fishermen and track the merchant ships to the very edge of the harbor before they turn away and sail out of sight. Caravans from the east have been stopped and searched and, unless the caravan master is stubborn and willing to bribe, the caravan is turned back. Dark Knights also raid the outlying farms and attack anyone who ventures too far from the city. We have tried to rout them. The City Guard has sent out mounted lancers to drive the Knights back, and Lord Bight has taken his Guards into the hills to capture raiding parties. To little avail. The Dark Knights fade away into the rugged mountains before us and as soon as we return to the city, they slink back more daring and numerous than before.

The city council and the Guild leaders are deeply worried. They want Lord Bight to sweep into the hills and put an end to the Dark Knights. A nice wish. It is too bad we cannot do it. The desire is there; the manpower is not. Even with the city militia, we have barely enough soldiers to guard the walls. A major offensive into the passes is out of the question.

28th day of Bran
37 SC

Of all the unmitigated gall! Those stone-faced, black-hearted, greedy whoresons of Neraka dared enter the lord governor's chambers and insulted him in front of his Guards, the Governor's Council, and half the palace staff.

Forgive me, Marli, I know you never liked my bursts of temper, but I am still so angry at their rude presence and bald contempt that even now I cannot write without a shaking hand. The intensity of my animosity toward them has surprised even me. I know in the first year after your death I ranted and raved my hatred of the Dark Knights for their reprehensible attacks on this city and their plague that took you away, yet I had thought my animosity had abated somewhat in the passage of time and was tucked safely away in a dim and cobwebbed part of my mind. It seems I was wrong. All it took was the sight of a Dark Knight facing my lord like a strutting martinet and demanding the surrender of the city, and I felt the hate rise up in me like a geyser ready to blow.

The delegation from Jelek arrived two days ago, bearing letters and greetings from the Lord of the Tainted Meat himself, Morham Targonne. Lord Bight did not want to see them at all, but they refused to leave and demanded an audience with the lord governor immediately. He managed to hold them off until today when he finally agreed to speak to them. He would not allow them to darken the doors of his palace, so he met them instead in his public chambers at the offices of the city council, bringing with him the entire contingent of Governor's Guards.

You know that building, Marli, the large one near the Guard's Headquarters. It is built like a fortress and a luxurious one at that. There is a new fountain in the courtyard and the Hogan Bight Library of Sanction has been added on the north end. Five new columns decorate the front door and several marble statues were donated for the foyer. It is not some rustic log hall. Yet the Dark Knights treated it as such. Perhaps they were annoyed that they were not invited to the palace, or perhaps bad manners is merely their nature.

They arrived early for the meeting and came in full armor as if they planned to attend a council of war. There were three ranking Knights and a full Talon of Knights of the Lily. Until the appointed time of the meeting, they sat on their black horses in front of the entrance, scaring off citizens and making the City Guard nervous. They ignored the councilors' efforts to welcome them. Only when the bell rang the time on the Merchant Guild's clock did they condescend to dismount and, still fully armed, entered the building to meet Lord Bight. Of course the Governor's Guards at the door to the public chambers did not let them cross the threshold with so much as a fingernail file. The leader of the Dark Knights, a Skull Knight by the name of Sir Ambross Burnside finally agreed to lay aside his weapons and the other two Knights followed suit. The Talon stood at attention at the hallway in front of the Guards and spent the entire meeting staring coldly at the governor's men. Morgan told me later he could only see their eyes glaring out of the slits of their helmets. They stood so still he wondered if they were truly men or some form of animated corpses.

Meanwhile, Sir Burnside strode into the public hall and approached Lord Bight. He did not bow or offer any gesture of respect. He simply tossed a packet of papers on the floor at Lord Bight's feet and said, "My lord sends his greetings." The contempt in his posture and voice was so obvious, he gave a whole new meaning to the word "sneer."

The elders and the magistrate, the scribes, and others who came to witness the meeting murmured angrily, but Lord Bight did not move a muscle; nor did Captain Janklin and I, standing at attention behind the governor. We had been ordered to remain still unless the Dark Knights directly threatened the governor. It was probably a good thing that we had been so ordered, because never had I wanted so badly to rearrange an expression on another man's face. One of the city councilors hurried forward, picked up the papers, and with a bow handed them to Lord Bight. Leaving the Dark Knights standing, the governor read the papers from beginning to end. I could see they did not please him because a dark red flush crept up the back of his neck into his hairline and a muscle began to twitch on the side of his jaw. With the same gesture of contempt, he tossed them fluttering to the floor at Sir Burnside's feet.

"No," was all he said.

Sir Burnside fastened his basilisk eyes on our governor. "Lord of the Night Targonne wants this city, and he will have it," the Knight snarled. "You have this one chance to surrender the city to me and leave it unharmed."

"The Dark Knights had their chance with Sanction years ago and lost it," Lord Bight said with the deadly quiet of a wary dragon. "Tell your lord to look elsewhere."

"You will regret this. We will take this city with or without you and when we do, you will rue your answer with every pile of corpses you see on the way to your execution."

"When, Sir Burnside?" one of the elders said. "I think the word should be 'if.' We will not give up this city without a fight." Of all people, it was Lutran Debone who spoke. Lutran, the oldest, fussiest, and—to me—most timorous of the city council.

I should know better. The man was and still is the head of the city council. He has a tortoise's longevity and the ability to survive the shifting sands of Sanction's changing fortunes, and he has been here almost as long as Lord Bight. That he has managed to stay as a city leader under Lord Bight for so many years should say something for his tenacity and thick hide.

The Dark Knight leveled a stare at him that would have etched steel. "Silence, doddering old fool!" he hissed.

I'm not exaggerating, Marli, the man hissed like a serpent. He was vile. I could feel my rage and hate for him and everything he represented rise up my throat like gorge.

The lord governor rose slowly to his feet. He had worn his great broadsword to the meeting, and as he glared down at the Knights, he coolly placed a hand on its hilt. Our entire line of Guards warily moved forward to protect his flanks.

"You have my answer. Take it and go," he ordered in a tone meant to be obeyed.

Knight Officer Burnside made an insulting gesture

usually seen only in the lowest gutters and slums. One of his men scooped up the papers and stuffed them into a pouch.

"I shall look forward to seeing you in the near future," Burnside said to Lord Bight. "I hope I am given the opportunity to dismember you very slowly." He began to laugh, a hard, brittle sound, and turned on his heel and marched out of the room.

It took everything I had within me not to rush forward and attack them on the steps of the building. Instead I gave a roar of rage and threw my dagger at the door so hard its blade embedded in the wood. The others jumped and exclaimed among themselves; Lord Bight merely turned to look at me and said, "My thoughts exactly."

The Dark Knights did not wait to attempt further negotiations. They rode down to their ship and left tonight on the evening tide.

By the absent gods, I do not want war for Sanction, but if it must come, I hope Knight Officer Burnside is in the vanguard so I have the pleasure of removing his sneer with my sword.

12th day of Corij
37 SC

Dear Marli,

I thought I had just sharpened my pen and scribbled a few words and now a year has already passed. You have been gone three years now, and while the acid pain of your death has eased, the loneliness grows worse. Our house gathers shadows without you to light it with happiness. I bury my mind in work and labor until my body is exhausted, and yet I cannot shake the sadness that clings to me like cobwebs.

Please don't get me wrong, my darling. My heart still cherishes your love and guards my feelings for you like the energy that holds body to soul. But . . . did you know there would be a "but"? . . . I cannot keep going like this much longer. The incident with the Dark Knights showed me my emotions are still seething beneath the surface of my scars. There must be a change before I fail my duty or my lord or my honor. I feel I am standing on the fragile edge of a volcano's rim, peering down into the malevolent red eye of a vent. Below me lies collapse, ruin, despair. If I let go I will never fight my way out of it. Several friends have told me more than once that it is time to put aside my grief and move on. For a long time I did not want to believe them. Now I must face the fact that the sadness is eating away at me. I do not believe, even in the most selfish secrets of my thoughts, that you would want me to be like this. Somehow, I must find a way to back away from the edge and find again my path in the sun.

21st day Corij
Midsummer

Happy Birthday, Sweet Marli,

Please forgive my outburst of the other night. It was the result of too much wine and a long, depressing day full of mishaps, misunderstandings, and a stupid fall from my horse. I guess I was feeling sorry for myself when I came home to an empty house full of too many memories and too much grief. Amania says I need to air out the house. She is coming over soon to help me do just that. I'm not sure what she has in mind but for the first time in days, my curiosity is aroused and I find myself looking forward to her arrival.

I hope you understand, my dearest wife, if I fall for another. No one will ever fill your place, but there is room in the human heart for more than one love. I don't know how Amania feels about me—what do I have to offer someone like her? My hair is graying, my heart is worn, my joints crack in the morning. I am a warrior but a tired one and our future here in Sanction is looking bleak.

And yet . . . she is willing to come. We will air the house and celebrate your birthday and see perhaps if our feelings find a mutual regard.

Sleep well, my dearest.

15th day Argon
37 SC

Marli,

Today we celebrated again the Festival of Bones. Amania agreed to join me today in our celebrations of our loved ones, and the day was a joy. We spent the morning in your garden pruning and watering and talking about you. In the afternoon we flew kites and remembered her beautiful daughter. The day was one of healing for me. Some of the strange, clinging sadness is gone and I can find desire in Amania's arms.

1st day of Sirrimont
37 SC

What we have feared has happened at last. Early this morning as the sun rose over the mountains, the Knights of Neraka launched their attack against us. Rank after rank of armored men marched out of the two passes and filled the valley beyond the lava moat. They swiftly overwhelmed the outposts and attempted to capture the few remaining bridges over the lava. But the bridges had been set for destruction weeks ago, and the guards, warned by the outpost sentries, managed to collapse the narrow bridges and escape back to the fortifications. We worry for the farmers in the Vale who are now trapped beyond the moat. Unfortunately there is little we can do for them now. If they decide to abandon their farms, they can escape to the bay and be picked up by the Harbormaster's marine sentries.

With the bridges out of their hands, the Dark Knights resorted to aerial attacks. They fired swaths of arrows into our earthen fortifications. Engineers set up lines of catapults just out of our arrow range and hurled missiles into the defenders. It did not take them long to find the range, and soon their stones fell with deadly accuracy.

I and some of the other guards watched the attack from the eastern guard tower. Our defenders endured the barrage well and held their ground.

By noon many of the enemy pulled back to their camps in the passes, but too many others made camps just beyond the lava moat in two long strings from the North Pass to the northern flank of Mount Thunderhorn and from the south edge of the volcano along the eastern defenses to the northern flank of Mount Ashkir. It is apparent to us they are planning to stay. The catapults have not ceased their endless barrage and we can see activity that indicates the Dark Knights are bringing in pieces of what looks like larger siege equipment.

No one is happy about this attack. With Lord Bight's magic dwindling by the day, we must count on our courage and determination to hold the walls. Yet, I am relieved the battle has finally come and resolved the terrible suspense.

10th day Sirrimont
37 SC

Dear Marli,

The siege continues.

I fear I will be writing that for many days to come. The Dark Knights are in no hurry to broach our defenses. They have settled in for a long siege. Already they have cut off all roads to Sanction, shutting out the merchant caravans, travelers, and refugees. The only way in and out of Sanction is by boat and even that is perilous. The black ships are attempting to blockade the harbor, but so far our ships are keeping them at a distance and escorting merchant vessels into Sanction in convoy. The maneuver seems to work.

The problem is many of the merchants from other ports are pulling out. They see the trouble in Sanction's future and do not wish to be a part of it. Only the Khurs are staying. Their connections with the Dark Knights may help them get caravans through to Khur and cities beyond. I just do not see how that will be enough. We have to keep the harbor open or Sanction will starve.

One good thing, I suppose—the number of refugees coming into the city has fallen to virtually none. The Temple of the Heart closed its camp for safety's sake and moved the remaining refugees into the city.

23rd day Sirrimont
37 SC

Dear Marli,

One positive thing has come out of this siege, the city has pulled together and become one. Under Lord Bight's leadership, the city council, the guilds, the remaining merchants, the Guards, militia, and sailors, the shopkeepers, and all the diverse population have put aside their bickering and banded together with one purpose: to save our city. The healers have set up a hospital for the wounded in a warehouse donated by a textiles merchant. Teams of volunteers come each day to help the healers, cook for the soldiers, tear sheets into bandages, haul water, and do whatever needs to be done. Shopkeepers and innkeepers have donated food and barrels of beer.

People have accepted the food rationing and water restrictions without complaint. Teams of firefighters patrol the streets in the stead of the City Guard who now hold their posts along the outer defenses. The city council has worked day and night to cope with endless details, orders from Lord Bight, and the needs of thousands of civilians.

Lord Bight, himself, has barely slept.

Several city officials suggested he move out of his new palace on the hill and return to the old one inside the city wall. The governor refused. His palace is vulnerable outside the walls, but it sits on a height above the city and commands a wide view of the area. The Guards use it as an observation post and a fortified bastion on the north side of the city. If it is abandoned and the Dark Knights bridge the moat, they could use it for themselves and take advantage of the height to bombard us from above. We plan to stay in the palace for as long as we are able to hold it.

13th day Reorxmont
37 SC

Marli,

The siege has been going for over a month now.

The economy is suffering, but the citizens are still in good heart. The blockade runners, the fishermen, and a few stout farmers keep our people fed and allow communication with the outside world.

Apparently we are not the only ones with difficulties. A Solamnic supply ship brought the news that Palin Majere is missing. That is dark news for all of us in Sanction. We had hoped he could find the reason the magic he discovered was failing so Lord Bight and our healers could possibly recover their power. I only hope he is not dead.

The news from Solace also informed us the Academy of Sorcery has been destroyed by the green dragon, Beryl. I could not help but think of Linsha Majere, Palin's daughter. Where is she now? Is she helping to search for Palin? Was she there when the Academy was destroyed? I have a feeling, insignificant as it is, that she will be back; that somehow, somewhere she will turn up to help Lord Bight. There was just something in her eyes . . .

22nd of Reorxmont
Harvest Come

Sweetest Marli,

There is no harvest this year and very little to celebrate. The Dark Knights have burned out almost every farm in the eastern half of the Vale and either taken or destroyed the crops and animals. Many farmers have fled to the city, but a few stayed to defend their farms and were killed. Their Guild Master, Chan Dar, has done what he can for the families, but almost all of this year's grapes, olives, apples, farm produce, wool, and cheese is gone. Another blow to the city's staggering financial woes. Without the food to feed the people or trade for goods, we shall be in serious trouble by spring, and who's to say we shall be free of war to plant another season?

2nd day Hiddumont
37 SC

Marli,

I must make this brief. The strange machines the Dark Knights brought were finally assembled and revealed to us. There are two monstrous, black trebuchets, siege weapons with enough power to hurl large boulders over the fortifications into the guard camps or, in one place where the moat creeps close to the city, over the high walls. By day these machines fire large rocks into our midst. The boulders have already damaged the wall and demolished houses, flattened tents, and crushed people. But at night the missiles are changed to bundles of burning hay bales, and I think at times those are the worst. The flaming bales burst and scatter fire across the roofs and walls of the neighborhood. The firefighters spend all night fighting blazes and checking for smoldering fires. Half a dozen houses and shops and a large section of the Guards' training field has burned. The area in range has been evacuated. The only thing that has dampened the effects of the fire bombs has been the intermittent autumn rains that blow in from the west.

I don't know how much more of this the common people can take. The siege is in its third month. Food is growing scarce and the casualties are mounting. People have begged us to destroy the trebuchets and tonight Lord Bight means to try. We will ride with him and if our luck is with us, we will burn the machines to the ground.

14th day Hiddumont
37 SC

Dear Marli,

It is difficult to write of these past twelve days. The arrow that pinned my arm to my ribs has, in an ironic fashion, done me a favor by forcing time upon me to heal before I had to face these words.

Amania is dead.

Gods, I can barely speak of it.

My friend, my companion. She has gone to join you and her own family wherever you may be.

15th day Hiddumont
37 SC

Marli,

I could not continue to write last night. Perhaps

now in the light of day I can face the truth and find the strength to put it into words.

The night of the 2nd . . . If the gods were here I would think they had a personal grudge against me, and I would have to wonder if I had done something heinously wrong. But they're not. We have nothing to blame, nothing to shake a fist at and ask "Why?" We are just here, thralls in a forsaken world gone mad, without guidance, destiny, fate, luck, justice. There is nothing left to stand on but honor and duty, and I am too cold to care.

The raid against the Dark Knights' machines began well enough. Lord Bight and Captain Janklin led two troops of Guards, one troop to each trebuchet. We went down under the city and the lava moat by secret ways Lord Bight knows through the realm of the legendary shadowpeople to the ruins of the Temple of Duerghast on the windy slopes of Mount Ashkir. From there we had to march east and north to reach the two machines. Our attack came out of the dark and took the Dark Knights by surprise. Lord Bight's men were able to set fire to one machine before they were driven back. Our squad was not so successful. The machine we were to destroy sat further away on a high hill near the guard camp. We captured the trebuchet and tried to set our fires, but a Knight of the Skull was close by and came to the aid of our attackers. He managed to work a spell that put out our fire and drove us back. Captain Janklin was killed in the first blast. The Dark Knights came after us like the furies of Chaos.

Only four of our squad made it back to the temple

with me, and the only reason I was with them was because they picked me up out of a pile of bodies and carried me back to safety. I spent the next five days in the hospital with the wounded and it was there, Morgan brought me the rest of the news.

I knew when I saw his face the news was grim, but Marli, I had no idea it would tear the heart out of me. When the second trebuchet was salvaged from the fire, the Dark Knights turned it on the city. Angered by our attacks, they fired fire bombs into the houses and shops of the south quarter. The fire-fighters hurried to put out the fires before they spread and as soon as they were among the burning buildings, the enemy switched to boulders and rocks that shattered on impact and sent chunks and slivers of rocks flying through the unarmed firefighters like scythes. Amania died the third night when a piece of rock crushed her skull. She was buried in a mass grave with others who have fought for this city, a grave that still lies open and waiting for more. The Dark Knights are already hard at work building another trebuchet.

29th day of Hiddumont
37 SC

Dearest Marli,

I will continue this journal for a while longer because I still find solace in thinking of you. I cannot yet keep Amania in my mind without the danger of losing what's left of my self-control. My arm and side are healing the natural way without magic. It is a slow, frustrating process because I cannot yet move my right arm without pain. The healers tried to help only to watch their magic fail. I have seen this happen time and again for them in the hospital. I don't know how they bear the frustration and helplessness with such resignation.

11th day H'rarmont
37 SC

Dear Marli,

The weather is turning colder now and so is the heart of the city. We have withstood siege and fire and death and fear for over four months and there is no end in sight. The Lord Governor has tried everything he can think of, nearly everything the city council advised, and even a few things the citizens suggested. Very little has helped. Since the trebuchets cannot move closer to the city walls, the area of damage is somewhat limited. Lord Bight, therefore, ordered every building in the entire zone of fire to be torn down and evacuated, thus creating a firebreak between the walls and the neighboring sections of the city. The protests were vociferous, but once the task was finished the number of fires and casualties to the firefighters has dropped considerably. So, too, has the demand on our limited freshwater supply.

Several elders asked Lord Bight if he could use his magic to make Thunderhorn erupt and destroy the camps of our foes. He said nothing would please him better than to see the Dark Knights swept away in the gale-force, grit-laden winds of a pyroclastic flow, buried under ten feet of ash, or incinerated in a massive flow of lava. Two years ago he might have been able to do it. Now he cannot. His magic is being sucked away he says and it is barely enough to keep the volcanoes stable and Sanction safe.

I hope if the time ever comes that the Knights of Neraka enter this city as victors, he will release the power of the Lords of Doom. I would rather see Sanction buried forever with her dead than rotting in the hands of Targonne's minions.

20th day H'rarmont
37 SC

Marli,

The Governor's Council met today. It was not a pleasure to watch. The unity of four months ago is cracking under the strain of the siege. Elders who once swore to stand by Lord Bight are urging him to seek help from outside the city. The Solamnics, they say, would send aid. Have the Knights not offered in the past?

"For a price," Lord Bight replied.

He agreed to consider their plea but made no promises. He does not and probably never will trust

the Solamnic Knights. Or the Legion of Steel, for
that matter. We know that clandestine group is in
the city and helping in the militia and the hospital,
but they have made no formal offer of assistance and
Lord Bight has rigorously ignored their presence.

We learned today that two guild masters and their
families slipped out of Sanction on a fast sailing vessel, leaving their guilds leaderless. Their members
were furious and immediately blacklisted both.

To what point? The guild masters are well out of
it and as safe as anyone can be in this dangerous
world. If Death has a sense of humor, maybe he'll
sink their ship. I hope to meet Death soon. I have a
few words to say to him.

5th day Phoenix
37 SC

I have moved into the palace and left our house
behind. It was too dark, too sad. Your garden is
dismal in the winter without Amania's care and I
can see her house through the bare foliage. It, too,
is dim and lifeless. I cannot bear to be near either
of them. So I have turned the house over to a family left homeless by the fires in the evacuated district and I live in the barracks, work twenty
hours a day, and bide my time.

The Knights of Solamnia have made another over-
ture to Lord Bight. The Council begs him to let them
come. The City Guard, who once resisted the idea of
outside aid, now adds their pleas to the council's. Its

numbers are exhausted, under strength, and low in morale. Perhaps they're right. The Knights of Neraka show no sign of leaving or weakening, and we are obviously losing the war of attrition.

20th day of Phoenix
37 SC

Marli,

A year to the day since their last visit and the Knights of Solamnia are back. Their war ships broke through the thin blockade and arrived in our harbor like heroes bearing supplies, medicines, food, and letters for our beleaguered population. What better way to win favor with the populace?

There will be no Hunt, no feast, and very little celebration for Yule this year. No one can even get out of the city to cut a Yule log for the fires. The Knights who arrived are respectful and complimentary in their conversation. They have toured the walls and the outlying guard camp and studied the distant lines of Dark Knights. They looked at the port facilities and at the surviving ships in Sanction's tiny fleet that help keep the harbor open. Lord Bight does not say very much. For once he is withdrawn and distant. I know he feels that to admit the Knights of Solamnia into the city as allies is a defeat of sorts, but I don't know what else we can do. Our economy is ruined, the treasury is nearly empty, the food supplies are dangerously low, and our soldiers are worn beyond exhaustion. We can't keep fighting alone anymore.

28th day Phoenix
37 SC

Marli,

It is done. Lord Bight signed a treaty with the Knights of Solamnia giving them open access to our harbor, our city, and our siege. I hope they make good use of it. The news was spread across the city and the people rejoiced. The Knights will come and bring an end to the war, they say. I hope they're right. I also hope that if the city is saved, Lord Bight still has a position of authority in his own government. In all reality, I cannot see the forceful, independent, authoritative Lord Bight working well with a committee of Solamnic Knights. We shall have to see.

16th day Aelmont
38 SC

Dear Marli,

The first ship of reinforcements arrived today as well as several freighters stuffed with grain, livestock, and foodstuffs. Solamnic ships have driven the black blockade ships further apart and opened a safer passage for freighters. A few merchants have returned to sell goods to our desperate citizens. Our people are ecstatic, and everyone expects the Knights to gather their forces and put an end to the siege once and for all. The commander of the Knights, Sir Ambrim Cuthney, is reserved and guardedly optimistic. He does not intend to attack soon, but he promises Lord Bight that he and his captains will study the situation and make their plans.

Lord Bight does not like him. Of course, I do not think Lord Bight would like anyone in that position. Meanwhile, the lord governor is still in command of the Governor's Guards, the City Guard, and the city militia. I hope that continues. I only stay here because of my duty to Lord Bight. If he is forced to dismiss us, I intend to remain by his side in any capacity he'll accept.

The newly arrived knights also brought the news that Tika Majere is dead. The Solamnic Knights already in the city declared a day of mourning and donned black arm bands. They are truly sad for the passing of a great woman. She was a Hero of the Lance, a mother of Knights and of the last great wizard, the grandmother of a Rose Knight. She will be missed. I wonder if Palin has been found and if he knows of his mother's passing. No one seems to know.

21st day of Mishamont
Spring Dawning

Marli,

Spring is dawning slowly this year. The cold rains

continue and the clouds have formed a permanent roof over the Lords of Doom. The city streets are awash with mud and muck and debris. People are trying to plant gardens in every available open space in the hope of growing some food, but the weather is making planting difficult. Stray dogs and rats are growing scarce.

The Dark Knights are stepping up their attacks on the Solamnic ships that bring us supplies, yet the Solamnic Knights have made no move to stop the sinkings. They march back and forth through the city and seem to do very little. No progress has been made in the siege—except perhaps for the Dark Knights. If they are waiting for us to crack, for our morale to plunge to the depths, and our affection for the Knights of Solamnia to turn to disgust, they won't have to wait much longer. The same people who cheered the Knights in the streets and called them heroes are now impatient, angry, and starting to murmur the word "cowards."

Sir Cuthney acknowledges the time he is taking and tells the city council he needs reinforcements. I guess he wants to have the advantage of overwhelming numbers before he attempts anything. But at this point, he should make some gesture. A sortie, a raid to burn the horrendous trebuchets, a breakout in the North Pass—something to show the people of Sanction some good faith! His men are fighting in the earthworks with our Guard and he has had some casualties, but beyond that the Knights of Solamnia are doing little to help. I think the Legion is doing more in its quiet, secretive way. They turned over another spy yesterday.

We shall see. Lord Bight fumes like the crater of Ashkir, but he is biding his time, too, and spends much of his energy keeping the volcanoes in line and maintaining the lava moat. Yesterday Thunderhorn shook the city with an earthquake, then erupted with a spectacular show of lava fountains and a new flow that broke out of the channel and spread toward the Zhakar valley. Lord Bight just sat back and watched it happen. Unfortunately, the flow was a small one and stopped before it did any serious damage to the Dark Knights' camps. The earthquake did more damage, flattening tents, toppling catapults, terrifying horses, and sending soldiers running. The quake has given us a respite for a day or two while the Dark Knights regroup.

Now if the rain would just ease up.

18th day of Bran
38 SC

Dear Marli,

Sir Cuthney and his knights have finally devised a plan to break the siege. It's certainly an interesting one. I am not permitted to speak of its details even in the privacy of this journal for fear the plan would reach the ears of Neraka spies and ruin the element of surprise that is so crucial to its success. Lord Bight approves of it and offers his full support. I just pray it works.

Mary Herbert

It is early in the morning. By the grace of some almighty power this palace still stands. A storm blew through here last night the likes of which I have never seen before. It crept up on our western horizon close to sunset, looking for all the world like a range of mountains newly sprung from the sea. The clouds were black and gray, edged with the fire of the descending sun and topped with towering thunderheads. They piled up against the distant sky, moving with the speed of the great dragons.

In the city, I was with Lord Bight and a troop of Guards preparing to leave the old palace after a meeting with the Solamnic Knights. We had just mounted our horses and were making our polite farewells when Lord Bight raised his head and stared at the west. He was silent for so long we all turned to see what he was looking at. The western sky was a solid mass of clouds, roiling and churning and tinted with that sickening green that presages a fierce turmoil. Sheet lightning flickered across its black ranges. It reminded me of a pyroclastic flow I saw once on Mount Thunderhorn and the sight turned my blood cold. The clouds moved as swiftly as that ash cloud, and in moments it had swallowed the sun. Sanction was plunged into an early twilight.

"Better come in here," Sir Cuthney called to us, but Lord Bight spurred his horse around. "Take a squad," he yelled at me. "Tell the City Guards at the west gate to sound the alarm and send a signal to the

Harbormaster. The rest of you come with me," and he set off at a gallop along the road toward the Guards' camp at eastern gate.

I and my men turned our horses west and made for the City Guards' Headquarters. The wind picked up as we rode and swirled around us with a bitter chill. It whipped up the dust, stripped leaves from the trees, and sent laundry soaring from the lines. People scattered frantically to find shelter or to calm their terrified animals and get them indoors. Still the wind strengthened until it howled around the buildings and keened a terrible song through the streets. Buffeted by the wind, we struggled on and reached the west gate just as the black clouds reared overhead. A crowd of City Guards milled around the open gate, fearfully gazing at the sky.

"Sound the city alarm," I bellowed to the nearest guard. "Keep sounding it as long as you can stand on the walls. And send a signal to the Harbormaster, there may be a storm surge with this one." I yanked my frightened horse around. "And everyone get under cover! This is a bad one."

We took just enough time to see the guard with his horn race for the stairs to the top of the wall before we spurred our mounts back the way we had come. By now the daylight was almost consumed by the black, racing clouds. Thunder rumbled an ominous warning. We rode like fiends, unmindful of people still in the streets or the wind that roared at our backs. We galloped across the city, racing the clouds, and arrived gasping and wind-beaten at the eastern gate of the city wall. There the City Guards were already on the wall. Commander Gethrik and Lord Bight hurriedly passed on orders to runners and the signal blowers. The warning horns sounded their blaring calls across the camps and the eastern fortifications.

Satisfied that the signal was being heard and sent along, Lord Bight finally agreed to return to his palace. We had no sooner turned our horses for the road up the hill than a tremendous bolt of lightning seared out of the black heart of the storm and exploded against the peak of Mount Grishnor. A massive explosion of thunder rocked the city.

None of us said a word. We simply leaned over our sweating horses and raced for the palace. A moment later another devastating spear of lightning struck, this time closer, and the thunder boomed like the voice of the volcano. The hail struck us a moment later in a curtain of flailing ice. More lightning cracked overhead until the sky was a sheet of black laced with the dancing cords of fire. The clouds consumed the sky over Sanction and darkness fell with a vengeance. Our poor horses were so terrified they pranced and reared in blind fear and tried to bolt, but they were war horses trained to follow their riders' every command and with spur and voice and whip, we managed to keep them moving behind Lord Bight up the road to the palace. Behind the hail came the rain in driving, horizontal sheets that drenched us in a heartbeat. It was so dark, we could not see the road but had to ride guided by the flashes of lightning.

When we cleared the woods and rode out into the open grounds around the palace, the wind nearly swept us out of the saddle. It was like a sentient creature determined to knock us to our knees. Thunder rolled around us, pounding us with sound. I didn't think it could be possible, but the rain fell even harder in a liquid wall that filled our ears and eyes and beat our exposed skin raw.

I don't how we made it to the courtyard behind the palace without losing a man or horse, but we did and I have never been so glad to see a stable. Strangely, by the time we dried off our exhausted mounts, saw to their needs, and bedded them down the worst of the storm had passed. We went to the palace and climbed one of the towers to watch the massive storm move east across the Khalkist range. We listened to its thunder rumble through the peaks and watched the lightning streak from mountaintop to mountaintop. We watched for a long time. Lord Bight stayed in the tower all night and watched the storm to its end.

It was an odd storm, Marli. There was something almost unworldly about its ferocity and speed and the intensity of the lightning, yet no one knows what spawned it or what, if anything, it might mean. The storm is gone now and the sun is rising in a clean blue sky.

This morning we must go out and assess the damage and make repairs while we can. I haven't heard from the sentries in the earthworks yet, but I imagine the Dark Knights in their tent camps suffered more than we did. I hope they take a long time to clean up. Perhaps this will work to our advantage. Our planned attack will be soon and with luck, the Knights of Neraka will not have time to recover.

Mary Herbert

22nd day of Corij
38 SC

Dear Marli,

The damage to Sanction was moderate and most we will ignore for now. The best news was the fleet in the harbor was not seriously damaged thanks to the swift action of the crews and the warnings from the Harbormaster. A storm surge did sweep through the harbor and sank a few of the smaller boats. The water swept up over the wharves and into the streets, but the roads are sloped downward for that very reason and most of the water simply swept back into the bay. We lost perhaps a dozen people due to lightning strikes, collapsed buildings, and a flash flood in the one of the old lava beds that swept away two kender. Over all we were extremely lucky. The plans for the attack on the Knights of Neraka go forward. In a few days time, if all goes well, we will be rid of them.

24th day of Corij
38 SC

Dear Marli,

I don't know how to tell you this because I am not entirely certain myself what happened this day. We sprang our trap as we had planned, and something went drastically wrong.

Our plan of attack began early in the cool, dark hours before dawn. In the harbor the ships of the Solamnic fleet made ready to sail on the morning tide. On their decks stood dozens of straw human-like figures wearing the armor of the Solamnic Knights and looking for all the world like an army preparing to depart. The Harbormaster employed every fisherman and dockhand on the wharves to march back and forth like soldiers and scurry around looking extremely busy. The docks were to give the distant Dark Knights the impression the Solamnic Knights were leaving Sanction.

To make the impression stronger, the Neraka spy captured by the Legion was allowed to hear certain unsubstantiated rumors that Lord Bight might be willing to surrender the city and in a moment of "gross negligence" was allowed to escape. He was followed back to his hide-out in the outer city where he immediately sent a messenger bird to the Dark Knights. The men who followed him promptly made sure he would send no more messages.

While the Harbormaster staged the Solamnic departure, the real army of Knights and what City Guards, militia, and Governor's Guards we could spare were making ready to spring the trap. Under cover of darkness we made our way into the earth-works outside the city walls and disguised our numbers in carefully hidden pits and bunkers. There we waited through the long, hot morning for the Dark Knights to see the departing the ships, hear the rumors, and—with luck—take our bait.

It was nearly noon when we heard a muted roar

issue from the direction of Beckard's Cut at the mouth of the Zhakar Valley. Trumpets blared from the enemy camps and a cheering rose above the hills. Outpost guards quickly passed the word, the enemy was on the march out of their valley. From the sound of it, the march seemed more like a charge or a free-for-all. In our hiding places we could hear the distant army like a rampaging horde coming closer with each passing second. Several of our sentries stared in disbelief then gleefully sent the word along. The army of the Dark Knights had taken our bait—hook, line, and sinker. Instead of an orderly approach as we expected, the ranks had broken loose and came charging toward us in a hungry, exalting mob without leadership or discipline. When they reached the lava moat, many fell into the molten river, but others (prepared for such a day) threw across sturdy, temporary bridges that allowed several to cross at a time. We watched and waited while the men filed across the lava moat like ants on a stick and we held our silence as they stormed over the earthworks and charged for the guard camp and the city walls.

The sky began to darken, and I noticed grim clouds were rolling in from the east over the mountaintops. Suddenly a single horn sounded from the high watch tower, clean and sweet, and a blessed release. Giving a great shout, Lord Bight climbed from his concealment to the top of the earth wall. He raised his hand and summoning all his energy, formed a powerful explosive blast and hurled it into the thickest crowd of oncoming soldiers. The explosion rocked the earth. The sunlight abruptly vanished behind the dun-colored clouds.

Our shout of war answered Lord Bight's and echoed through the mountains. Here at last was an enemy we could fight face to face, hand to hand. Here was the enemy who burned our city, starved our people, and killed our loved ones. A tremendous fury rose up in all of us and propelled us over the walls and into battle. Abruptly the gloating shouts of victory stopped when the Dark Knights and their forces realized they were facing a vengeful army, not empty walls.

On the city wall and in the guards' camp, archers appeared in ranks from their concealment and fired a swarm of arrows into the masses of foot soldiers. From the right came another clarion call that summoned the mounted Knights who had crossed the moat in the night and gathered on the Dark Knights' flank. The Solamnics cantered forward, their silver armor glinting in the dull light, their weapons flashing. Deadly silver light seared from the hands of their wizards and burned all it touched.

The crowded enemy wavered. Their officers exhorted them to stand and fight, but the surprise we had gained proved too much for their courage. Our foes broke and ran.

What an exhilarating, glorious feeling that was, to see these hated besiegers run like rabbits before our swords. The blood lust infected us all. Every Solamnic Knight and Sanction Guard on that field gave chase as the mob of fleeing soldiers headed for Beckard's Cut. I saw where they were going and rejoiced for I knew if we could trap them in the valley, we could decimate them.

Lord Bight knew it, too, and he plunged into the

running melee to keep the rabble running with his magic and his fearsome sword. His bodyguards stayed close to his side.

I will not apologize even to you, my love, for my actions this afternoon. You have heard the word berserker and know what it means, but you cannot understand how the grief of losing you and Amania, the pent-up anger, the frustration, and the hatred melded into one furious hot star within me that consumed my fear and thought. I lost sight of everything but the enemy before me and the desire to kill. Lord Bight told me later he had to struggle to keep up with me.

We drove the forces of the Knights of Neraka into the cut and rushed in to complete our victory. It was then something happened that changed everything.

The fleeing rabble slowed and even though they pushed and fought like animals to get away from us, something was blocking their way. The clouds shifted overhead and a single beam of golden light broke through to shine upon a high promontory at the head of the valley. There on its crest something bright caught my eye and I paused in my mad killing to look up. A warrior sat on a blood-red horse and held high a stained ruddy standard. The sun caught this person in a bright beam that gilded his armor with fire. At the foot of the promontory and on a ridge close by, Dark Knights and their men were gathering. To my surprise, I saw a line of archers firing on their own men. They seemed to be trying to stop the mad rout.

My fury cooled somewhat at that moment and I

stopped to stare at the strange apparition on the cliff. I realized I was bleeding from two deep cuts and a myriad of small ones, and my face was covered with blood and sweat. I ached in every muscle.

The crowds of soldiers in front of us slowed and milled in confusion. They seemed terrified by both the Knight on the hill and by our charge. We tried to push them on, but our own momentum slowed and ground to a halt.

Lord Bight, I, several other Governor's Guards and a handful of City Guards regrouped near the right side of the cut just behind the mounted Solamnic Knights. We wanted to try to flank those archers and maybe take down that strange Knight, but before we could make a move the Dark Knight on the blood-red horse gave a great shout and rode his horse straight down that steep hillside directly for our forces. I don't think anyone could believe it.

All at once there was a deep echoing cry of, "For Mina!" And all of the archers, knights, and soldiers who had gathered at her rallying cry turned and threw themselves back into the battle.

I won't say they routed us because we fought for every inch of ground and every body that fell, but when the battle ended sometime near sunset, we were forced to retreat back to the city. Our glorious victory turned to ashes in our hands. Shocked and mortified, the Solamnic Knights tended their wounded and burned their dead. Our people wept. Lord Bight managed to destroy the bridges over the lava moat, and the City Guards killed every enemy still on our side of the lava. But that is all. All those months of planning, all the deaths have led us right back to a stalemate. The Knights of Neraka do not have Sanction and we do not have our victory.

I don't know what the Dark Knights will do next. They suffered many casualties in the battle; I doubt they have enough left to overwhelm the city any time soon. And yet, what of this strange Knight we saw lead the rally and turn it into a victory? Some said it was a youth, some thought it was a young woman, a beautiful girl with a glorious face and a morning star that dripped with blood. No one really knows. The battle swept over us and turned our plans to turmoil.

The healers have tended me now and I cannot keep awake any longer. Good night, my love. I guess I must wait for another day to see you.

27th day Corij
38 SC

Dear Marli,

The siege continues as I feared. The Dark Knights did not retreat, but neither can they launch another attack. We do not know what has happened to their Mina or to the forces that followed her. One of our outland spies reported seeing a force leave the Zhakar Valley, but we cannot prove yet who left.

The city was devastated by the failure of our attack. Many people blame the Solamnics, but I cannot. We all gave our best and tried to do our duty. It is no one's fault that the tide of battle turned against us in such a way. Lord Bight rides through the city every day to talk to the people and tell them about the battle. He still does not totally trust the Solamnics, but he will not lay blame at their feet either. Our dead have been burned and repairs have been made. The siege settles back to its deadly drudgery. The catapults on the ridge have started firing again. If only the gods could tell us where this will lead.

Dumarian's note: This is the end of Sergeant Hartbrooke's journal. Unfortunately, the sergeant died a week after this last date, defending Lord Bight against an assassination attempt. The Lord Governor told me when he gave me the journal that Sergeant Hartbrooke had been buried with honor in the Guards' catacomb under the palace. At last he got his wish to be with his beloved Marli.

Bertrem's Note

Diaries, as the reader of this account may well have gathered by now, are the meat and drink of the historian. In no document does the ordinary citizen so tellingly reveal his or her hopes and sorrows, joys and fears.

My researchers have made ample use of these materials in their reports on Krynn in this age of war. Whether from the journal of an elven poet in Qualinost or of a frightened little girl in Solace or of a brave old soldier in Sanction, these entries are a window into the soul of Ansalon.

To conclude, then, it seems only fitting to reproduce a journal of another young soul, this time of an elf of the Silvanesti. Sister Nancy Berberick of our order obtained and edited this journal before handing it over to me, and, I think the reader will admit, she has done *an admirable job. Here again we see the ordinary emotions of a young girl on the brink of womanhood (a transition, I hasten to add, about which I personally know little or nothing but have received reliable reports from those in a position to understand) played out against the terrible story of the disasters that have overcome the Silvanesti people.*

The sickness of which Evelyne Stargrace speaks is the wasting sickness brought about by the shield that the dragon Cyan Bloodbane (falsely disguised as an elf) dropped over Silvanesti.

FROM THE JOURNAL OF
THE UNTOWARD GIRL

BEING THE JOURNAL AND DIARY AND RECORD OF THE
HEART AND THOUGHTS OF EVELYNE STARGRACE, WHO
IS THE DAUGHTER OF MERIAL ROWAN
AND LANGTHORN STARGRACE
AND HAS NOW LIVED FOR FIVE YEARS AND SIXTY.

[COME INTO THE HANDS OF SISTER BERBERICK, A
LIBRARIAN, BY STRANGE ROADS AND DANGEROUS, FOR
A WHILE TRAVELING TO PALANTHAS IN A KNIGHT'S
SADDLE BAG, IN THE BEDROLL OF AN ELVEN HUNTER,
AND FINALLY IN THE WALLET OF A FLETCHER'S
APPRENTICE, WHICH APPRENTICE PRESENTED
IT TO THE LIBRARIAN AS A TRUE ACCOUNT
OF TROUBLOUS DAYS]

I am so angry, Mother! I am so angry, and I—oh.

Near Alinost
On Dead Eye, for the Third Time
In Summer Home

(And do I have to write this annoying Notation every time I pick up my pen and stain these pages? Oh! I am so angry with Mother! I hate this—)

Stupid journal. I hate these pages. Creamy pages, she calls them, the soft, sweet creamy pages of a new book. They are like dark endless pits! They want to be filled up with words, and I don't want to fill them. I don't want to give them one taste of a word. This is some kind of punishment. No matter what anyone says, I know it. Mother has commanded: Evelyne, you will find a quiet place in your father's library and for an hour each day you will write in your journal. It will do you good.

No matter how I plead and beg and implore, she will not rescind her command. She knows I am not a creature of words, as she is. Well, not exactly a creature of words as she is. I am, in these summer days when we exist in this summer place without all the servants we are used to, I am my father's scribe. He thinks this is good training for me, for he and my mother imagine this is what I will become when I am grown—a scribe to some lord or lady of a higher house than our own. And, it is true, I love to read, and I love all the truths and tales to be found in Father's library, in the libraries of others.

I have been to the wondrous library in Silvanost, where we really live. *Li'lagalharegiannethrathol,* which simply means, The Library of the Silvanesti Upon Which House Cleric Is Attendant. It is like going to a temple.

It's funny about that name. Cleric—you always

think that has to do with temples and priests and priestesses and the kind of people who dedicate their lives to gods. It does, but it also means people who record things, tend the records of things, people who are scribes. And a long time ago the people who told stories—bards and poets and playwrights and actors, even the raggedy buskers in the streets who sing for their supper—they were all part of House Cleric. I suppose technically they still are, but those folk aren't easily contained and no matter what anyone else thinks about them, they think of themselves in their own strange way. The clerics at The Library, though, they know who they are and they make sure all the rest of us know, too. They believe their work is as holy as any work done in temples, some believe it is holier than that. I know of one or two of those librarians—maybe more, but one or two who admit it right out loud—one or two who say that if there were no Shield around the kingdom, no magical barrier to keep out all the uncouth and savage races of Krynn—if they could travel freely, they would risk all the dangers of the road to travel to Palanthas and apply to be even the humblest of clerks in the magnificent library there. It is the library renowned in all of Krynn, and they would bend the knee—proud elves of Silvanesti!—they would bend the knee to Bertrem who keeps that place and has kept it through wars and famines and plagues, and they would beg to work there, in any humble capacity.

(Of course, being Silvanesti, they are certain their worth would soon be recognized and they would be elevated by the end of the week in which they were taken on . . . And after all, why not? Elevation surely wouldn't come so swiftly as that, but no one can deny that we Silvanesti are the most refined, the most educated, the most sophisticated folk of all the kingdoms of the world. But, one hardly need explain, no one from here will ever go there. We do not wander the roads of Krynn. It is said the only Silvanesti you will see out there in the wild world are dark elves. The banished daughter of Lorac Caladon, her rogue husband—who might be dead, if some accounts are true—and her son whom she insists is our king. They are mad, and others fallen from the light are criminals. We, the sane and the safe, are committed to living behind our Shield, that wondrous magical boundary that serves us well. We are not harmed here, we are not beset by the madness of life without. Here, we are at peace, and this is our time of healing, for times have not dealt well with us . . . our Nightmare has been a long one.)

So, *Li'lagalharegiannethrathol.* That's the true name of the place, but anyone who lives in Silvanost just calls it The Library, making sure to pronounce the word so everyone knows they have an important capital 'T' and a grand capital 'L.'

I went there with Father once, for he had a gift to give them, a rare book written in the Age of Might, soon after the end of the Third Dragon War. It was a time when women gave birth to heroes and the spirits of the least of us soared upon noble wings; it was as though all the nation were peopled with kings. The book came to him from his grandfather's estate, a magnificent poem of 33,333 lines and a meter of such complexity only scholars truly appreciate it. Father thought it was far too valuable and important to exist outside the library. The clerics at the library agreed with their whole hearts. They were happy to have the book, but not so happy to have a half-grown girl in their holy chambers. They didn't let me read anything there, they didn't even let me touch anything. I had to stand in the center of the room with my hands behind my back. Well, I had to stand still, but the way they look at you there, all you can do to keep from fidgeting is to stand in the middle of the room with your hands behind your back. It keeps them quiet, the clerics and the hands.

But it doesn't matter how you stand in that place, you can feel all the tales and truths there, you can smell them and taste them and you can hear them whispering in the pages rustled by those who are allowed to touch the books. You can feel the spirits of the tellers and the stories all at once.

So, yes, I am a creature of words because I like to read words and hear them and learn from them. But I don't like to write words. Mother knows that, she has always known that.

When she insists I must write in this wretched journal, she is simply being cruel.

Words are like a stone tossed into water, she says, and one ripple follows another until something is made, a pattern of circles. Yes, that's very nice, but there is no water in this empty pit of a book. I have no stones to throw in.

Oh, well, she says, then draw upon the pages.

Take your pens and borrow your father's inks and illuminate your feelings. Contain them, Mother says, define your emotions, refine your heart. Don't simply wallow, Evelyne.

Here is a feeling, Mother: I am so angry!

I am an untoward girl, a troublous girl, a fractious, irritating girl whose ideas stretch beyond the bounds of her meager years and that . . . .

I am an honest girl, even my teachers, who have named me the Untoward Girl, admit that. In honesty, then, I have to admit that I am afraid of this book, these empty pages that will display the truth of the Untoward Girl.

From Windrace Which is Our Summer House Near Alinost
On Dream Dance, for the Third Time
In the Month of Summer Home

I saw and heard a shocking thing in the street when I was walking with Cyra who is my mother's niece and only a year or two older than I am.

She thinks she is nearly woman-grown because last year she had her Ceremony of Starlight, and she received the Star Jewel all Silvanesti women receive after that long night of watching under the stars. She wears it all the time, and—this is almost a scandal, or I think so—she wears it on the outside of her gown. I think she even chooses the colors of her gown to set off the jewel. Really, you're only supposed to wear your Star Jewel on important occa-

sions, or if you wear it all the time, you aren't supposed to wear it outside your gown but tucked modestly in your bosom beneath your gown. Not Cyra!
She'd been eager for the Ceremony since the first
time she heard about it. She talked about it for years,
saying how you're supposed to spy your fate in the
shadows and the starlight, you're supposed to know
what your life's path will be, who will be your
beloved.

(That means, your father will tell you who you
will marry, the deal probably being already made
and the last little details finalized while you sit peering into the night and wondering if something magical will happen, if your truest love will walk out of
the shadows and take your hand and lead you away
. . . or whatever little scene you like best from your
favorite story. Cyra tells me I'm cynical when I talk
like this. But I read, I am the invisible scribe who
draws the words of my father's thoughts and knows
how he speaks to his peers. I know how much of
things are magic and how much of things are business.)

On the night of her Ceremony of Starlight, Cyra's
father either made no deal, or her fate is somewhat
muddy. She remains unpromised—though her
father is wealthy and she really is very pretty with
her long silvery hair that falls all the way down past
her knees, and her eyes shaped like almonds. As for
her ears, well, I heard a young man say once that he
thought Cyra's were the prettiest ears he had ever
seen, and he didn't wear out that old phrase about
them being like shells. He talked about the petals of

a tender gardenia. You'd think he wanted to smell them, the way he went on about it. Cyra was unimpressed.

But never mind. She is very pretty, and she is nearly woman-grown, and even though I am a year or two away from my own Ceremony of Starlight, she doesn't treat me like a little girl. I like Cyra, even though she is being very foolish these days. Even a little bit scandalous. Maybe a lot scandalous.

She imagines she will be allowed to marry Bregin Fletch who shadows around in the garden when he knows she is there sitting with her embroidery or walking among the herbs. He stands in the shade. You can hear him breathing. You can hear her breathing change when she knows he's near.

She asks me to walk with her every day in the gardens and orchards at her parents' house. Sometimes in the morning, sometimes in the afternoon, once— she really is a dangerous girl!—once in the evening when the only light was the light shining out from the windows of the house and a wink of stars through the trees. She takes me with her for cover, I go to get out of this house where I live. This year, I hate it here. I hate it here.

Bregin Fletch he stands in the garden shade, he hums a tune under his breath. You'd think it was the breeze in the leaves unless you saw Cyra's cheek flush as she lowers her eyes. She thinks I don't know. Everyone thinks I know nothing about everything. I have my suspicions about some things, and I do know she wants to marry that Bregin Fletch. I know that.

This idea of hers, of course, is nonsense. She knows it, and she lets herself have it anyway.

Here is the shocking thing I saw and heard while I was walking with Cyra on the Street of Bakers in Alinost, I heard a busker singing in the little park across the way from Sustenance, one of the finer bake-shops in the town. This is what he sang:

Upon her hand, her hand, her hand,
Upon her hand I placed my ring.
My ring, my ring, my ring
Upon her hand I placed my ring.

Upon my lips, my lips, my lips,
Upon my lips she set her pledge.
Her pledge, her pledge, her pledge
Upon my lips she set her pledge.

And even as the busker sang, I saw Bregin himself walked out of the door of a shop as we passed, smelling like fresh-baked bread and something sweet. The busker tipped him a wink. Bregin didn't see that, for shameless Cyra flashed him a sudden glance, bright like sunlight on the river.

If Cyra's father knew she had made eyes at Bregin in the very moment that stupid song moped about lips . . . "Set a pledge upon my lips—"

Couldn't the song just have said she kissed him?

Nonsense, but I won't tell on Cyra. She would be sent away to her aunt who lives somewhere down by the Towers of E'li. Far away and with the length of the kingdom between them.

Why they wouldn't arrange for Bregin to be sent away, I can't imagine. Why is it Cyra would go? Why should she have to pack up her things and leave this lovely place of orchards where our families have their summer houses?

"I am sorry, my daughter, you sent an inappropriate glance to an inappropriate man, and now you must leave. No more twilight play in the peach orchards for you. No more dancing with the fireflies in the first dark beneath those sweet branches.

"Go! He is an inappropriate man."

I certainly think they'd just reassign the servant and sentence Cyra to a few hours a day in a quiet place to write in a journal.

Life isn't fair. Besides, he's not an inappropriate man. Oh, well, he is. Cyra is the daughter of my father's brother, a man whose wife's uncle is the head of a minor clan in House Defender—she is near to royalty, when you hear her tell it—and Bregin is a fletcher's son. His father makes the shafts of arrows and the steely tips, and Bregin sits all day among the best feathers, sorting to find the right one for the right arrow, then fletches the work of his father, cock feathers and hen feathers. He fills the quarrels—

I suppose you could say Bregin Fletch he is a quarrelsome man.

Whatever you could say, I am saying nothing.

This evening I went to attend Mother. The servant had brought her supper early and come to take it away again untouched.

I put flowers in the crystal vase beside her bed, stems of wisteria with the amethyst blossoms pouring down. The fragrance filled the room, and she smiled. I brought her a fresh pitcher of water myself, I filled the jade vessel with ice and then with water. I floated a little sprig of honeysuckle on top of the water. Mother always does that when she is filling the pitchers at the dinner table. A flower, she says, for the grace. I made sure the little jade cup was near to hand, I plumped her pillows, and I sat on the edge of her bed. Yes, I was careful not to crush the lace edge of the coverlet. It took me a year of days to make that lace, and I can see that the work at the end of the year is better than the work at the start of it, but Mother won't hide the ugly parts. She says it makes a pleasing whole.

Mother.

I asked her if she wanted me to read to her for a while. She said no, she would rather I held her hand.

She asked me if I wrote every day in my journal. It has only been two days since I was commanded to do that, and so I was able to answer honestly that I did write every day. She didn't ask me what I wrote, that wouldn't have been right. A person's journal is like a person's heart. No one comes in unless you let them in.

The skin of my mother's hand feels like parchment, dry and frail and with a kind of make-believe softness of creams and scented ointments trying to mask brittleness. The skin of her lips is dry, and when she tries to smile you can see that the skin cracks, little sharp separations, and it hurts her.

When she asked me to part the window curtains so she could see out to the river and the lights of Leylinost on the other side, I did that. She always says the lights look like golden stars come down to hang in the trees, we used to count them when I was a little girl, and we would guess which of the little lights shone from the windows of elves we knew. I hadn't sat back down for only a moment before Mother asked me to close the curtains, then close the window. Her fingers plucked at the satin edge of her blanket, and she said she didn't like the smell of the air.

It smelt like tangy summer air when the sky is thinking about rain. It smelt good to me, but Mother said she didn't like it. It made her feel nervous.

Windrace, Father's Library
On Winged Trade, for the Third Time
In Summer Home

I am so tired of writing this Notation at the start of each day of penance! All right, all right—*From* Windrace and *Near* Alinost—and why would anyone imagine I would look back on this miserable journal in the first place, let alone imagine I would want to remember this time if I ever did?

Penance. This is penance, to be shut up here for even an hour each day, and all the summer outside my windows.

When I am released from this awful punishment, I will burn this book in a great bonfire and dance around the flames laughing.

Cyra came to the garden gate this morning. She
leaned in through the wicket and watched me ~~fill up~~
fill—I say "fill up" too much—my basket with herbs.
We live like rustics here, Mother says that is part of
the fun of removing from the city to live in a summer
house. We have only three servants, so Father and I
must pitch in to help make the day orderly. I am
Cook's assistant, and I don't mind that. I enjoy going
into the town to run errands, but I think I like it best
to walk in the herb garden in the morning, wrapped
in a broad apron from the kitchen, soaking the hems
of last year's skirts with dew. I had my hands full of
basil, the rich purple kind and some of the common
green. I don't know what it is to get drunk on wine,
but sometimes when all the air around me hangs
with the scent of basil . . . I can imagine.

"You'd better start pinching back those plants,"
Cyra said.

(Well, she said something like that, but I have
been avoiding quoting anyone directly in this journal because while I can always remember the sense
of what they say, I can't really remember with perfect ~~accurateness~~ accuracy what exactly they said.
And my teachers at school warn that the punctua-
tion used to denote direct speech shouldn't be used
unless with unerring accuracy. But that's too bad. I
don't like being the only voice on these pages. I want
other people to talk on them, too. So—I will let them
speak and do my best to remember their words as
closely as I can.)

Cyra said "pinch back the plants," and when I
looked up at her, I thought someone had pinched

her. Or, well, not that, but her face had a pinched look to it. White and tight. There weren't but the first little knuckles of flower buds on the basil, and I wasn't going be the Gardener's girl as well as the Cook's girl, so I ignored Cyra's advice and told her to come and chew on some mint, she looked like she had indigestion.

She came into the garden, and she told me she'd had a quarrel with her Bregin Fletch, the quarrelsome man.

Oh, well, good, I thought. That's the end of that, and just as well. It really was bordering on scandalous, this shameless glancing and smiling at a servant. You'd think Cyra was nothing but a common tavern girl the way she'd been carrying on. Good. It's over.

~~But, it wasn't, it wasn't good. Cyra—~~
Cyra she cried a lot, in the shadows of the Windrace garden, hidden in the arbor all hung with Mother's wisteria. She cried until her face got all puffy and blotchy, and I have read about women who can cry so that the tears just leak from their lovely eyes and slide like silver down their alabaster cheeks, but my cousin Cyra isn't one of them. Cyra buries her face in her hands and shakes with sobbing, and she sounds like grief is being torn out of her bosom, or like something is being torn from her. She cried like that until I had to tell her to be quiet or Cook would hear. Worse, Mother would hear.

Cyra—it is awful and—well . . .
~~It is exciting, too.~~ No, no, not that. ~~It is~~
Yes, it is deliciously exciting. But I do, I do feel

sorry for her. Who could watch her wrenching her heart out sobbing and not feel sorry for her?

Cyra.

I didn't say that to her, though, that I think this between a woman of her station and her quarrelsome inappropriate man is exciting. I can't even believe I'm thinking that. So I only said, "Yes, it's awful," when she moaned that what had happened was awful. And I told her she probably shouldn't wish to die when she said she wished she would die. I patted her hand, I let her sit in our shadows and weep, and I did take the gardening chores that morning because Cyra's sorrow wasn't a thing servants should see.

And now, hours later, I don't feel like things are so deliciously exciting. I feel kind of sick at my stomach and I'm chewing on a lot of mint tonight to settle things down. I still smell like basil, the buds I pinched, the stems I stripped and the leaves I tied. When I attended Mother this evening, she tried to smile. She told me the perfume of the herb eased her headache, and I told her I was glad, though—and I didn't say so to her, enough people pester her about her appetite—I wish it had made her want to eat her dinner. Me, though, I don't much like the smell of basil just now.

What a contradiction! The perfume of basil cheered Mother, but it doesn't cheer me. It only makes me think of my cousin sitting in the shadows, hidden from the sunlight and shaking with sobbing she must keep very, very quiet.

Nancy Varian Berberick

Why can't one have a simple feeling, all by itself? Anger, or sorrow or fear . . . why do all one's feelings have to come in a tangling bunch till it's hard to tell what's being felt when or why?

Near Alinost, at Windrace, in Father's Library
On World Tree, for the Third Time
In Summer Home

At school they teach us the terms of venery. We must memorize these terms if we are to consider ourselves to be civilized creatures and not like the wild elves, those wanton, untamed Kagonesti who run around half-naked in the forests of Krynn like the very animals they hunt. We civilized elves—and I suppose you could say this about the Qualinesti, too, whatever else gets said about them, and a lot does get said—we civilized elves speak of a gaggle of geese, a pride of griffins, a paddle of ducks, a rage of colts, a kindle of kittens, a route of wolves . . . Someone has compiled a whole list of these terms—these collective nouns—and whether they know it or not, they left something off the list.

A confusion of feelings.

This journal was supposed to help me confine my feelings, define them, control them, understand them. Do something with them.

I am only confused. And today I'm trying to put in my hour, but all I can manage is to stare out the window into the garden and the rain coming down. There are a dozen fragrant herbs in that garden—thyme and lemon grass and mint and curly parsley and two kinds of sage and . . . oh, a dozen at least. All I can smell is basil. All I can think about is how a thing for joy can be also be a thing for weeping.

I wish I didn't know what I know about Cyra, her stubborn heart and her quarrelsome man.

Near Alinost, at Windrace, in Father's Library
On Gateway, for the Fourth Time
In Summer Home

On Dead Eye, at Silvanost:

Dearest Nephew, Esteemed Langthorne Stargrace:

I write with news that is good and ill. Your uncle has died, and I am bowed down with sorrow. You know the depth of my bereavement. And yet, nephew, I also trust that you realize how long and painful this illness has been. You know how the life has been ebbing from him, like a tide going slowly, slowly out. Ah, at last, the tide has gone. He stands no more upon the shores of the country of the living.

Dearest nephew, I write to tell you that my husband, your uncle, has particularly requested that you, of all his kinsmen, be the one to attend him at his funeral, the one to array him in his funeral garb, to speak the oration at his wake, and to see him decently settled to rest.

Will you come back to Silvanost? Will you come, nephew?

I am always and ever, your devoted aunt,
Leantha Sunglance

On Gateway, at Alinost:

To my esteemed aunt, in this her time of sorrow:

Aunt, you need not ask! I will come, and this letter won't long precede me to Silvanost. Be certain, aunt, that I am making all haste to join you at your home, to make this reading of the rite a proper ceremony. Never doubt that I will be there to sit with you and my cousin in your sorrow . . . .

Langthorne Stargrace

I have copied into this journal the text of a letter from my aunt to my father, I did it very carefully. I tried to imitate her actual handwriting—it is so lovely, like the vines of the morning glory twining on the page, and her ink is that same deep indigo of the wild morning glory, starting out dark from the inkwell, as the secret heart of the flower itself is dark, then growing lighter by degrees till she must refresh the nib.

You see that in the morning glory, too . . . paling at the edges, as though the flower had run out of color, right there.

I wonder if my uncle had run out of life, right there on the morning he drew his last breath and died.

I copied into this journal as much of my father's letter to his aunt as I could recall. He dictated in haste, I wrote in haste, for I could hear the bridle of the messenger's horse jingling even over the whisper of my pen on the page of his letter. And there was no time to make drafts, and so I haven't made a good record here. I will say this, though—he isn't a great one for expressing the first flush of his feelings, my father. He is well-reared, a noble elf of House Cleric who understands that the distillation of emotion is preferable to the first surges of the emotion itself. Distillation, to him, is well-considered action. And so he dictated his letter, in careful phrases, his words used with great precision, the abstract of his emotions, and this he did only after he had ordered our few servants to prepare us for a journey, to run with messages to Cyra's family and to, one of those servants, be ready to ride to Silvanost with his letter. He is a very precise person, my father. By the time he dictated his letter to my aunt, you would have thought he was composing an order to a tradesman.

Ah, Father.

We are to travel to Silvanost, my father and I. We will go down upon the river, the great Thon-Thalas. Cyra and her family will come with us. They are Mother's kin, of course, but they are making this journey back to the city to honor my father's family, to pay respect to the widow and her ailing son. ~~They do this because~~

This is an event ~~fraught with meaning~~—oh, a better word. Fraught is so . . . . This is an important event, for while it is sad that father's uncle has died—and it is, all my father's stories are ~~filled up~~ full of the doings of his uncle who was cleric in the days of the War of the Lance and he went north to fight against the terrible Dragonlord, Phair Caron and he was part of that band of white-robed clerics who went to minister to the mages who worked the magic of illusion crafted by the young mage who has since found the worst of all fates to befall an elf; he has become a dark elf, fallen from the light. This dark elf is wide-known in Krynn, rumor says so and rumor is one thing that cannot be stopped by our Shield. I have heard it said that people here, when they must make reference, know the appellation "the Dark" has been appended to his name.

My father's uncle had his part in the working of the mage's magic, and he was always proud to say so. Ah, that was scandalous, the working of red magic by white-robed mages! I wonder if our whole family is a scandal ~~and Cyra only the least of it~~

But, while it is sad that my uncle the cleric-who-walked-with-warriors is dead and not of a noble death but a wasting sickness, while it is sad, it is also a signal of change. My father's uncle had two sons, and one or the other of them should have been chosen to perform the funeral duties. In the regular course of things. But one has died, some years before and of the same illness that took his father. The other—

—No one really thinks the second son will live much longer. Father, my own father, will assume the duties as the head of our clan when he lays his uncle to rest.

It isn't a very great clan, the clan of Stargrace. Among the people of House Cleric, there are higher folk than we. Still, his will be a heavy duty for my father. I don't think he would like to know of scandal brewing.

Well. He won't hear about it from me. Neither will he guess it from any look or sigh or moan from Cyra. I have had a long talk with her. I shook my finger under her nose. I said to her, "You are going to a funeral, Cyra. Put on your best funeral face. I don't want to hear sighs for yourself. I want to hear sighs for my father's uncle." She looked at me with widening eyes, a long glittering stare of the kind I knew well. We aren't all that far apart in years, and yet it makes her smile indulgently to see me behave this way. Finger shaking, frowning. You look like your father, she says.

That might be, but when she widens her gray eyes and looks at me like that, she looks like my mother.

Mother.

Ah.

She cannot make this journey. She can do little more these days than . . . .

Ah, Mother.

Silvanost
Dead Eye, for the Fourth Time
In Summer Home

The sun came over the hill behind my aunt's

house at precisely the fifth hour of the day. It
warmed the air and seduced mist from the dewy
grass. Beyond, past Great-aunt's garden and the con-
fines of her estate, the tall towers of the capital itself
called the rosy light to themselves, embracing it and
flushing to receive it.

I looked at Cyra when I saw the towers blush. She
stood very pale between her mother and father;
between the two branches of my own family, mater-
nal and paternal, stood Great-uncle's bier.

The dew clinging to the grass touched my ankles
coldly. This is Summer Home, the dew should not be
so cold, but it is, and I don't think my imagination
chilled it. All of us, lord and lady and servant alike,
went out to the garden behind Great-aunt Leantha's
house dressed in our simple robes, silvery like the
color of tears, and around our necks hung the long,
red-bordered stoles appropriate for funeral wear. We
all went in sandals because though the morning was
chill—Well who had boots appropriate to that? We
had little soft boots for evening wear, velvet and
suede and leather suitable for gloves or a lady's tender foot. Those would be ruined in the dew, and
boots of heavier make were either stored away for
winter or existed only as orders in the leatherman's
shop. And so we went in sandals, and our ankles
were cold. I stood shivering a little, and Cyra looked
like she wanted to shift around from foot to foot but
she didn't. She stood with her head high, right
between her mother and father. She smelled like lily
of the valley, that pale flower of spring, and she
looked like my mother with her wide gray stare.

Father spoke the funeral rite, he said:

"We stand in this garden as people who stand between two worlds. We stand, and we hear our own breaths, the in-coming and the out-going sigh. We hear the echo of a sea of greater vastness than any water surging at the shore of any kingdom in Krynn. We hear that tide, that coming in and going out that some believe is the breathing of gods, and we mourn."

He spoke of his great-uncle, the brave man who had done his part in a long-ago war. He looked right at his aunt when he recounted the tale of the great effort of the Silvanesti against a Dragon Highlord. I was born after that time, in Silvamori where my parents and most of the kingdom had fled when the great effort failed. Someone said I was born on the very day King Lorac Caladon—of doubtful repute—inflicted the Nightmare on the kingdom and loosed from its magical prison the terrible dragon, Cyan Bloodbane, the beast who lurks still in the dark reaches of the kingdom.

About the dragon, I don't know. Wouldn't you think that squads of Kirath scouts and Wildrunners scouring the land would find something as big as a dragon? After all these years, no one has and I believe with those who think the beast is gone, a long time ago fled in the days of the War of the Lance, or killed in the Dragon Purge. About the day of my birth—I don't like to think that is true. Well, perhaps it is true, perhaps I was born on that day. But how could anyone know? No one survived the coming of the Nightmare.

I am kind when I say the old king's reputation is doubtful. He nearly killed his kingdom with his magic.

I am straying all over these pages . . .

If, perhaps, I thought well before I wrote, I would have a more cohesive account of Great-uncle's funeral. But—well, I am not my father, no matter how strongly everyone wishes I did think before speaking, before doing, before—I think afterward, and I don't much make them happy, my parents. But I will finish the account to make myself content.

He lay like a marble effigy upon his bier, my father's uncle who was three hundred years and seventy nine on the day he died. He should have lived longer, he was not young, but he was not old. The sickness robbed him of years he could have had, should have had. Everyone said so. The sickness robbed him from us. ~~The Sickness. You hear it said like that, with the great capital 'T' and the snake of a capital 'S.' It's like a plague, but no one wants to say so.~~

Great-uncle's face was sunken, for the blood no longer freshened him or gave him any semblance of a thing that had once been alive. The dawn light kissed the towers of the city, but it could not make his cheek flush. He lay with his hands folded upon his breast. Great-aunt had done that, made that placement, though Father hadn't thought it proper. He had said so when he took his uncle's funeral robe from the coffer in his bedchamber. We were all there, Great-uncle's kin gathered to watch Father take from him his bed-gown and to watch Great-aunt Leantha tend the corpse of her husband, to wash the body of the man she had lived with, oh, slept beside, for two centuries. We watched her wring cold water from linen cloths and wash his limbs. I had to look away, those tender motions were too much like caresses and I—I had to look away. I looked again when it was time for her to anoint his temples with oil of roses. And I watched with proper—and truly felt—awe when Father laid the funeral robe upon the bed and smoothed out the folds. It was a fine robe, made of linen dyed indigo and it had the voice of water when it moved, a soft sound like a brook distantly heard. Great-uncle began making his funeral robe the day he admitted to himself he had the sickness, that the sickness had him.

They say his last remaining son decided to do the same for himself on that day. They were alike, father and son. Mother always said of them, "One begins the thought, the other finishes."

And that's why my father's cousin couldn't perform the Enrobing for his own father. He was sick. A bed, a man who listened to the sigh of linen between his fingers and whose most difficult chore was to lift the needle and force it through fabric, in and out, out and in and up and down and—maybe that work has the sound of breaths being taken and let go, like the breaths of the gods.

Is he counting his own breaths, the dying man? With the cloth upon his knee, the green-dyed linen spilling, with each dip of the needle into a hem or seam, will he know by the end how many breaths he took from the day he began to sew his own funeral robe?

We buried him in his garden, Eaman Stargrace who was my great-uncle. There was no great weeping, not even among the servants who are not so nobly reared as we. There was no wailing or crying out to gods. There was sorrow, though, deep sorrow. I know. I saw how it was at the Enrobing, and before, when my great-aunt caressed her beloved for the last time.

A messenger came to my great-aunt's house at night, not in a clattering of hoofs or silver ringing of bridle gear. No one opened the gates from the courtyard to the street, no servant stood with torches to admit the word-bearer or take a sweating horse. A messenger came cloaked in shadows, his feet geared softly in stealth. He climbed the wall that separates the court of Great-aunt's courtyard from the street, he slipped across the cobbles and climbed up the sturdy trellis upon which white roses and red roses grow. He left some of his blood there, a bit of flesh from his hands, and he dropped lightly into the bower garden.

The bower garden . . . they call it that because there are secret bowers in every corner, one hung with purple clematis, the flowers as big as my two hands. Another is hung with wisteria, another draped in ivy, the last dripping honeysuckle.

He dropped down into the bower garden and moved like shadows on the ground, darker than night. I saw him from my window, here where I sit writing. I watched him, and I knew where he was going.

He found her window as though he had always known it, as though he had a hundred times come here shod in stealth to find her. I saw them because Great-aunt's house wraps all around her gardens and the suite of chambers she gave to Cyra and her family lies in a part of the house across the bower garden from where I sit writing. She didn't hold a candle in her hand, but a bank of candles stood on the table behind her, and she was golden in their light.

I don't know what he said to her, her quarrelsome man. I don't know what she said to him. This I do know:

Cyra opened the windows, she swung them out wide. She sat upon the sill and swung her legs over. They gleamed white, her legs, and her bed-gown shimmered right up to her thighs. He reached up his arms, and she dropped down into them.

It is the first hour of the new day, a starred hour, and they are in the honeysuckle bower now, my cousin and her inappropriate man. Bregin Fletch, her quarrelsome man. Sometimes they are two shadows, sometimes they are one. They are repairing their quarrel, while in a far chamber of this house, my great-aunt sits dry-eyed upon the edge of the bed she had shared with a man for many more years than I can imagine.

I will never fall in love.

People risk everything for it, and in the end, they cannot keep it.

I will never fall in love.

Here is something I'm putting into this journal. I read it on a parchment tacked to the public board outside the Rose and Star Tavern:

Wanted for Immediate Hire

Two Serving Women
Four Barmen
One cook
and a Boy to Carry Trash

And I have drawn three bold black lines under the word "immediate" because that is how it was drawn on the notice. It was as though the man who wrote it shouted it. This isn't the only notice of its kind I have seen in Silvanost. There are many, on tavern boards, in the windows of baker shops and milliner's shops and even out by the river where the chandler shops sit with windows looking inland and windows looking out to the water.

I pointed out these notices to Cyra but she, deep inside herself and her wrong-headed romance, said she imagines this is because everyone has gone to their summer homes.

Interesting idea, I thought when she said so. But

one can hardly imagine that the whole of House Servitor has suddenly become wealthy and removed to cooler places.

Where, then, are the people who work? I know where they are, though no one else likes to admit where they are. They lie behind closed doors in darkened rooms, for noise and light cause them great pain. Like my father's cousin, too ill to attend his own father's funeral, so ill he sits when he can and makes his funeral robe—like him, they sigh instead of breathe, they pick at their food and when those who feed them encourage them to do more than push their peas around on the plate, they make fretful sounds and plead to be allowed to sleep, please just let me—and they sigh, they sigh, weary, the life worn away from them, they sigh—Please, just let me sleep.

They are ill, and the sickness that has them is the same as that which turns Mother's breaths into sighs.

Sighs to sound like the coming in and going out of the sea, and there aren't so many people now to work in the shops and the taverns. There aren't so many lords and ladies strolling the streets of the city.

There aren't so many people here as used to be.

Silvanost
Winged Trade, for the Fourth Time
In Summer Home

I see these notices outside of taverns and shops

because I am again Cyra's walking companion. Together, we walk around the capital, the beautiful city of towers and palaces and gardens unlike any in the kingdom. We walk in the city of our birth but, oh, we don't call it walking when we are here, doing this. We are young ladies from good families, and so we say that we are Taking the Air. In rustic Alinost people gone to live in their summer houses may walk around the town. They don't have to dress in fine gowns, and they don't much care if they look like farm-girls with their hair caught back in kerchiefs, the hems of their robes dark with dew. In Silvanost we had slender chains of silver links descending from our belts to the hems of our gowns so we can give the chain a tug to gather and modestly raise our hems from the dew or an inconvenient puddle.

And in Silvanost, we would not bundle our hair in kerchiefs even if those kerchiefs were cloth of gold hemmed in silver thread. We wear our hair in fantasies of curls and jewels, piled up high if we are old enough; spilling down our backs if we are . . . my age.

(And it's true that Cyra should be letting her silver hair tumble down her back, just as I do. She isn't quite old enough, she isn't a married woman or a woman for whom a deal has been struck between father and lover. Still—the girl is a scandal waiting to happen. She does something with her hair each morning after the servant has finished with it. She takes the long locks at each side of her face and she braids them into silver plaits. Then she winds the

plaits round and round her head, like a circlet. Her
curls spill down from there, but she has made a small
defiance and put up her hair. A little. And that is
supposed to mean—what? Good day, I'm sort of a
virgin, more or less untouched by unsanctioned
hands . . . Why she doesn't just sail into her father
one day and declare that she is sleeping with the
fletcher's man—And I suppose I shouldn't even joke
about that. One day she might.)

The sort-of-virgin and I, we Took the Air in the
streets around the Garden of Astarin, those roads
and avenues leading out from the star-shaped garden
like ~~wheels from a spoke~~

Like rays from a star.

This used to be the finest of all gardens in our garden kingdom. It is not now. Now, nothing can stay
long alive in it. Only the Shield Tree stands, that
wondrous tree from which it is said the Shield itself
emanates. The rest, the rest is dying.

No one talks about that, though. And people
still—people still see the Garden of Astarin as a kind
of focal point. We don't stroll its paths, not too much
any more. But we walk to it, from it, around it. We
say, I will meet you at Astarin on the 10th hour; we
will decide whether we will go visit or perhaps go
down to the Silver Sail and dine while we watch the
barges on the river.

But we don't talk about the dying garden, or the
Shield Tree.

Naturally Cyra and I go to Take the Air in our
finest gear, flowing gowns of whispering linen that,

these days, reminds me of funeral wear. We ring, walking, for it is the fashion this year to wear many bracelets upon the arm—men and women—and Cyra and I wear arm-rings from wrist to elbow. We are fine young ladies of good houses who wear the signs of the wealth of our fathers on our bodies. Young men stop to watch us walking. Cyra has no time for them. She nods, she smiles, but these are chilly motions of formality. Cyra is all the time looking for someone she won't find in the part of the city where the Tower of the Stars looms high or the lovely buildings stand that are the seats of the various heads of Houses. For this reason, we don't haunt the precincts of the city where our parents would expect to find us. We show ourselves to the elves of the noble houses, young ladies at the pastime of promenading, and then we are gone from there, quick to the Market District in the south and west part of the city.

She is, and neither pretends otherwise, on the watch for her inappropriate man. But I wanted to see the Tree, the Source of the Shield. I hadn't seen it in so long, not since Father took Mother and me out to Alinost because, he believed, the air was better there and whatever ailed Mother would loosen its grip. Not many people like being in that poor garden. I don't much like it either. But the Tree fascinates me.

It is a lovely tree, that magical tree we know as the Source of the Shield. A great spreading oak—and what else than that, the tree whose heart is strength, whose roots are life, whose leafy branches are shelter, what else than oak?—the oak it grows in the center of the garden, and it is the work of the great skill and cunning of elven mages, a tree whose roots reach right down into the earth and whose energy surrounds us all, the kingdom and the people. As the magic of King Lorac Caladon—whom we are trained not to love, and it seems to me not much training is needed when a person hears only once the tale of the mad king who plunged our nation into the darkness of unrelenting Nightmare—as the magic of that misguided madman destroyed our dear Silvanesti, harmed us nearly to death, so does the magic of this wonderful Shield heal us and keep us safe.

There are dragons outside, beyond our borders. They do great damage to the peoples of Krynn, they have broken up the world in the Dragon Realms and Free Realms—

That is all well known, and I don't write about monsters in this book.

But whatever dwells outside our land, we are safe here, the Silvanesti who are the best beloved of the gods are safe within our Shield, and sometimes, sometimes I like to go and look at the tree, the mighty oak whose soul holds all of us tenderly in its keeping. Today, I wanted to do that, and I did, and looking at it, I saw little else. *Li'lagalharegiannethrathol*, The Library, stands not far away, just across the garden and near to the seat of House Cleric. I didn't see it. I saw only the Tree.

Cyra stood around impatiently while I stood before the wonder, feeling what I always feel—deep reverence and gratitude. Under her breath, she hummed a little tune, and slight though it was, it intruded, insinuating into my silent and reverent moment words I'd heard only once before:

Upon her hand, her hand, her hand,
Upon her hand I placed my ring.
My ring, my ring, my ring
Upon her hand I placed my ring.

Upon my lips, my lips, my lips,
Upon my lips she set her pledge.
Her pledge, her pledge, her pledge
Upon my lips she set her pledge.

And she added a verse, right there waiting for me, she added a verse just made, or one she'd contemplated and now knew how to fit. Soft, under her breath, she sang:

Upon my heart, my heart, my heart,
Upon my heart he laid his hand.
His hand, his hand, his hand
Upon my heart he pressed his hand.

Secretly, for only me to hear, Cyra was singing her lover's song back to him, and she gave it a verse of her own.

Well, that's the thing about a song like that, a busker's ditty, words swiftly knotted onto some old tune everyone has known since before they were born—once heard, the cursed thing stays forever in the mind. I turned from the tree, the wondrous spreading oak that was our Shield, and I told Cyra we might as well do what we'd come out from Great-aunt's house to do. We might as well go haunt the Market District and see if she could see her quarrelsome man.

It seemed a long walk to me, all the way from the Tree and out of the garden and past the Temple of Solinari and through the streets that run past the Wildrunner Barracks and the Training Grounds. I've made the walk in short time, in times past. It seemed like a long walk today.

But the sun is hot—right outside my window now the bower garden seems to be wilting in the heat. I feel something pressing against my temples, the air like hands pressing. High up in the sky the clouds hang very still. They are white clouds, the puffy kind that don't mean rain. But something in me, in my chest, my head, feels rain coming.

I wonder how Mother is, far away in Alinost. I have only been gone from her a handful of days, but I feel like I wish—I wish I was with her now. I wish I hadn't left her, not even for this funeral.

We saw him, Bregin Fletch hanging around the Wildrunners Barracks, we didn't have to go so far as the Market District. We saw him standing in the shade of the tall oaks outside the barracks, he was talking to a Wildrunner who sat carving a green-mask. The scent of newly cut wood, living wood, hung sweet on the air, and it mixed with the tang of elathas extract. That isn't one of my favorite scents, elathas, it makes me sneeze. But when you are around Wildrunners, particularly the Kirath scouts, you get used to it. They started making those green-masks right after we returned to the kingdom from Silvamori. They made the masks and infused them with magic to hide the wearer from the sight of the dragons who lived here then. Since that time—for there are no dragons here now, not with our Shield to keep us safe—since then the greenmask has become part of a Kirath's kit and each is expected to know how to make one. This fellow, a man who looked old enough to remember the time even before the War of the Lance, he worked hardly looking at his hands or the knife that shaved the wood he held. Quick glances, to be sure he was working well, that's all he spared. For the most, he looked at Bregin, and the two talked like they were well acquainted. They weren't, of course. Bregin had never been away from Alinost before this week, and when he was there, he didn't run with soldiers. Normally, the Wildrunner and the fletcher would not speak comfortably together, but they were each craftsmen. They spoke a language most didn't, that of making.

And, they were men, those two. One a soldier, one a servant, still they were men. The old Wildrunner had only to see the way Bregin's head lifted when he heard the sound of Cyra's footfall to know the conversation between craftsmen was over.

Silvanost
At the—

Oh! I don't know what hour it is! I don't know what day! I don't know—I don't know where Father is—I don't

Outside—what is that sound!

[Researcher's note: The date our diarist could not reckon is the same as the one upon which she and her cousin went walking in the city of Silvanost, the same as the one upon which she stood before the spreading oak and contemplated the Silvanesti Shield. The hour is difficult to fix, but when I calculate according to what I know of that dire day's events as they went forward in the world outside the Silvanesti kingdom, I make the hour a very small one. The child is obviously frightened. How odd that she would turn first to her despised journal before all else. But then, perhaps, not so odd. She is a daughter of House Cleric. What magic sparkles in the blood of the elves of House Woodshaper, that growing magic, that wondrous gift from a blending of the blood of these fair elves and nature spirits older than they, is often celebrated. We forget, we who record the histories of the troublous world of Krynn, that a certain kind of magic runs in the blood of those elves of House Cleric, a magic of seeking and knowing and telling. They are, after all, not just priests in temples. They are, after all, like those tellers of tales, buskers of ballads, diarists and record keepers of every nation, every race in Krynn They are, after all, and sometimes, the clear voices of their people. This girl was one such, in spite of herself.]

It rains, and it will not stop. The sky crashes in thunder and screams in lightning and it will not stop. The bower garden lies in ruin. Frames that held the lovely clematis lie in tangles, the wisteria is no more. The ivy is only a tangle of green and someone running from one wing of the house to the other has trampled the tender honeysuckle into the mud.

Last night, last night a bolt of lightning struck a tree right outside Cyra's window and the tree exploded! It burst into flames and slivers of wood flew as far as over the garden wall, past the courtyard and—

A woman running by in the street—perhaps a servant on an errand—a woman running by was killed by one of those slivers. It pierced her through the eye. She died before help could come. Great-aunt Leantha heard of this and had the body taken into her house and kept decently until kin could be found. It was hard, though, to get the servants to venture out to fetch the poor corpse in. They all feared the same fate.

Father says that is simply nonsense, the superstitious moaning of the ignorant, but I'm not certain I would have been happy to run out after a corpse for the sake of Great-aunt's idea of decency.

Ah, gods! The rain is like steel darts against the windows. The servants in Great-aunt's house go around wringing their hands and looking at each other out the corners of their eyes. They are too well trained to show more fear than that, but I know what they feel. Their terror each time another limb crashes onto the roof, each time a fresh wash of water pours in under the doors is like the storm itself.

I sit here, risking my poor inked pages to the rainwater spitting in through the cracks between the window and the sill. I sit here, watching and sometimes, across the dark garden where bowers lie like corpses, I see the little light of a candle in Cyra's window. She cannot get from her side of the house to this. There is a tree crashed down upon the roof and she is caught there. Her father and mother are with Great-aunt, they were when the tree fell. Cyra is there alone.

I lift my own candle and move it gently back and forth.

Cyra's candle mimics the motion.

She must feel so alone and frightened.

[Another Day]

I don't know how to note the days now. I haven't seen the sun in . . . a long time. Maybe two days, maybe not so long. I don't see the stars or the moon, it is all clouds and mist and gray. Father says he thinks this storm has lasted only a night and part of a day, and the rest is just rain, normal rain.

I don't think he is right. Nothing feels normal. I feel—it's hard to say. I feel as though something terrible has broken something precious.

No. That isn't it. Or, well, it is, but—those are hiding words. They don't say what I truly feel. I feel exposed. I feel vulnerable. I feel as though something sees me that shouldn't see me.

[The Day After, or Possibly Two Days After]

I write in this book when I am moved to, and I am not so much moved to. And, the truth is, Father is not here. He is gone to make his way north to Mother. We cannot stand not to know how she is. We cannot stand not to know, and we remember— Father and I remember—how she doesn't like storms. Even the small ones that come grumbling down the river at the end of a summer day trouble her. They always have.

What must this storm of days have been to her?

I wanted to go with him. He would not let me.

They freed Cyra from her room this morning, and she is to stay with me. It was a great effort to get her out, one of the roof-beams had collapsed, and walls are sagged so the doors between one wing of the house and the other wouldn't open and she dared not try to climb out the window. She'd have broken her leg falling without Bregin Fletch to reach up his arms to her.

She was in no danger of starving, there are larders in the small kitchen in that side of the house. She must have been lonesome, though. Maybe she wondered where her quarrelsome man was and if he is well.

He's well enough. I told Father he's in the city, and I told him I thought Bregin Fletch would be just the man to go up to Alinost with him.

Father thought that was a good idea. He found him in one of the taverns and took him away to Alinost. When I see Cyra, I'll let her know.

[Yet Another Day, and I don't think we are in Summer Home anymore. I think we are in Summer Flame.]

After the storm, one day passes much like another. In the gardens the tiny corpses of sparrows and mice, the sad and broken bodies of doves storm-killed in their little dovecote—these the servants gather to dispose. There are little fires in gardens all over the city, pyres for these poor victims of the terrible storm. I hate it here in Great-aunt Leantha's house. I hate it here in the city.

In the corner of the garden, by the peach orchards, the servants found something sickening. Great-uncle Eamon's grave has been—oh—

His grave has been washed open by the storm. So much water—rainwater, river water from the over-flowing banks—so much came pouring down the hill that it swept the dirt away. There was no turf, no grass or plantings to hold the soil. The coffin of Eamon Stargrace gleams in the little pale sunlight.

It's like naked bones. They can't cover it up with earth again because it's all mud. They've erected a pavilion over it, six strong poles and a cloth of indigo, the color of his funeral robe.

It's horrible. This morning I took Cyra out of the house, past the garden where we didn't even look and tried not to listen to the workmen figuring out the best way to secure the cloth in case a wind came up, and we went to see the Tree. I felt hopeful, walking, even though storm debris lay all around, shattered trees, washed out gardens, the foundations of ancient houses sagged because so much earth was washed away from the supporting stone.

You can see patches of blue in the sky now. I thought we would feel better walking. I wouldn't be worrying all the time about Mother, Cyra wouldn't be thinking about her Bregin Fletch.

That wasn't the case, and when we saw the Tree—

Oh, to see those noble roots naked to the light! Oh, I felt the pain of it right in my heart, I felt it like a hand squeezing, and it was like I couldn't breathe. And I had that feeling again, that feeling of being exposed, of being seen by things I don't want to see me. I have read it in books that the hair on a person's neck stands up with horror.

It's true. I looked at the Tree's roots, stripped of their earthy covering, stripped even of the tender pale skin so their fibrous insides lay exposed and the life drying out of them. I saw that, and the stench of small animal pyres hung in the thick air, choking me, and I felt it, the little nape-hairs rising to stir on my neck.

"Listen," Cyra said, plucking my sleeve. I looked at her, she pointed west across the Garden of Astarin, to the Tower of the Stars. "Listen, there are people gathering on the Tower grounds."

There were, and we went to see them, she drawn by the sound of voices, I because I couldn't bear to look at the Tree, the mighty oak whose great roots lay stripped, whose arms hung broken, the bark flayed from the trunk, the leaves torn from its noble crest.

Two hour later, only two hours—two hours later, the Shield Tree stood as it always had. Tall and strong, its roots reaching deeply into the earth, the bark grown upon its might trunk, and leaves—they are growing upon branches no longer broken.

We saw him walking in the one of the gardens of the Tower of the Stars. Just a glimpse, there were so many people crowded around the perimeter of the grounds. He had a clutch of people around him, elves in lovely robes of fine silk and satin and linen, their sandals adorned with silver and gold. We saw him, and noted him because he didn't seem so fine as those who surrounded him. You might think they attended him, knowing who he was. And they did seem to do that, servants with trays of fruit—where did they find that after the disaster of the storm? Perhaps from some secret cellar in the Tower or the Palace of Quinari. You see the damage those two places endured . . . but the fruit came from somewhere. And the servants had wine chilled in iced buckets—where did they get the ice?

You look into that scene, that clutch of servants and the tall young elf who was the center of their focus, and you had to wonder whether they'd stepped out of some world where the sky never stormed.

But then I got a look at him, just a quick glance. I won't say our eyes met, they didn't, but it felt like that, a little. I had an awareness of him, the way you do when glances actually meet, and pause, and consider.

"Silvanoshei," someone murmured, a woman standing near me. "That's—" Well, she couldn't say Alhana Starbreeze (I am wrong even to write her name here, for she is a dark elf) she couldn't say the name, she said, "that's her son." And she hung on the word 'her' so we all knew to whom the pronoun belonged. Her son. The grandson of the mad king, Lorac Caladon.

I shivered to see him, and in the same moment that flashing glance made me feel like the bottom was falling out of my belly.

No, no. That's not foolishness or a girl's giggle. That's—I felt like you do when you're standing on a dangerous edge and maybe the ground isn't so firm as you'd thought, or hoped. This one, this son of dark elves, he had a look about him of suddenness. He didn't look like one who did much thinking. I'm not saying the feeling I got of him was of a man who couldn't think well. That's not it. He just looked— he looks like a man who leads with his heart, not with his head.

I have read enough books to know that in kings, that wild bright quality is both glorious and dangerous.

And that's was he is. Silvanoshei, the son of the exiled queen and a banished prince, the grandson of an old and half-mad mage of a king—he is himself a king. He is here in the city, and I don't know how or why. They said he was living beyond the Shield, in the wild world outside the kingdom. And now he is here.

I thought of the storm, and that feeling I'd had of being seen by things I didn't want to see me.

"Cyra," I said. I grabbed her arm and I pulled her away. "Cyra. Something is wrong. The—" I said it, why not? "The king has come here from beyond the Shield. How? How did he pass through?"

She looked back over her shoulder, staring at the king and his little cortege of courtiers. She reminded me that no one passes through, no one comes in, no one goes out. Even as she said so, she shook her head, hearing her words and seeing the king.

There is a king in Silvanesti again.

I have a date again, a day, a place, and time!

Silvanost, at Star High
On Dream Dance, for the Second Time
In Summer Flame

Mother came home, and she brought me time again. She had kept a good record, up there in Alinost where there was little for her to do but watch the changing of the light and reckon the passing of days. There was great storm damage there, and all along the river. The fish-kill was terrible, all the poor fishes flung up out of the river and beached, some found as far inland as a mile. The great stench of their dying hung in the air for days. Father said it reminded him of what things smelled like here during the Nightmare.

Why? Why did it stink so bad there and not here. There are not so many folk in the little towns and in the forest itself to clean away the poor dried corpses. She and Father and Bregin Fletch came home, and I removed from Great-aunt Leantha's home to my own. Mother is paler than before, she is thinner. Her eyes are awful to see, like she is looking into some place where the light is too bright, too bright. A place no one else can see.

But . . . no. Not 'no one else.' My father's cousin, Great-aunt Leantha's poor son, he sees into that place, he sees things that make the eyes grow wide, the soul startle, like a candle's flame suddenly leaping high before the wick collapses and the light dims.

They are dying.

Silvanost, at Star High
On Dream Dance, for the Third Time
In Summer Flame

In the garden of my old home, of Star High, Cyra keeps her old habits, walking the muddy paths, lifting her hem from the draggled plants that will clutch it and tear. She doesn't walk with me now, though. She seems to have lost any idea that she must keep secrets. And Bregin Fletch, he walks with her. Look at them, lovers in the purple twilight. He reaches for her, she clings. She turns away, pulling herself from his arms, wrenching. He reaches for her. With a cry, she clings.

Cyra, she is like—ah, she is like what I said

Bertrem's Guide to the War of Souls

Mother is like, a startled light, a candle's flame leaping suddenly. I don't know why the light of her doesn't cast shadow. It's that bright. And him. Bregin Fletch, he is like a suicidal moth, reaching for her, burning.

This is who we are.

In my father's house, my mother lies dying. Across the city, his uncle is being interred again, his cousin sews upon his burial robe. Father will attend another Enrobing soon, and then one after that.

And no one says anything. In the city, in our two houses, no one says, "So many of us are ill!"

It isn't as though we don't know. We do. We sigh, and we mourn, and we pray. But we don't say anything, we don't wonder why.

I did, out loud to Father on the day he and Bregin Fletch brought Mother home. Bregin carried her in his arms, wrapped in woolen blankets, shivering though it is high summer. He was tender with her as Father led him into the house, through the foyer and along the marble corridors where servants came like shadows to watch. Bregin settled her on her own bed, he tucked the blankets around her, put pillows behind her. He piled them so she could sit, and when she sagged a little to the side, why, he piled more beside her. When she thanked him, Bregin Fletch lifted Mother's hand—the skin so thin now I can map the route of her blood's journey on the blue marks of her veins. He lifted her hand, and he touched his lips to it, just lightly as though he were afraid even that tender pressure would hurt her.

In Father's eyes tears glistened, and he turned

295

away. I followed after, and I said, "Father, look, she's dying. So many are dying. What—?"

He looked at me long, and all the tears were gone from his eyes. They did not shine. He said, "You were ever an Untoward Girl, Evelyne. Will you never learn peace?"

This is how he answered me, this is how he watched my mother die. As though . . . as though she were not dying. As if, if he pretended, she would not die.

[Now many days have passed, and I don't care about time.]

Now many days have passed. Now many days, and this is who we are: My mother barely eats, she only drinks a little. She has asked for the servants to bring her bolts of satin—it is her favorite fabric and she says it feels like water on the skin—she has asked, and they did, and she had a pattern for a gown cut from material the same color as the Thon-Thalas shimmering with the last sunlight. She can hardly lift the needle, and I must thread it for her. She works, though. She works, and when she is not dipping the needle into the rivery silk, she sleeps.

Cyra wanders our garden, but weeping. Her quarrelsome man is gone. I don't know where, but not back to Alinost. He will never go so far from her, and once in the city I went walking to market to fetch a basket of peaches to tempt Mother's appetite. I passed by the Wildrunner Barracks and I saw an old

soldier with a quarrel of arrows, sorting. I thought of
Bregin Fletch, and from somewhere—behind the
barracks, I think—I heard the old song.

Upon her hand, her hand, her hand,
Upon her hand I placed my ring.
My ring, my ring, my ring
Upon her hand I placed my ring.

Upon my lips, my lips, my lips,
Upon my lips she set her pledge.
Her pledge, her pledge, her pledge
Upon my lips she set her pledge.

Upon my heart, my heart, my heart,
Upon my heart she laid her hand.
Her hand, her hand, her hand
Upon my heart she pressed her hand.

He has changed her verse, that one she made to
sing back to him. He has changed it and made it his
own. And Bregin Fletch, he added another and as
the others, this new one he sang himself with no
busker to smooth his own rough voice.

Upon my soul, my soul, my soul,
Upon my soul she breathed her last.
Her last, her last, her last
Upon my soul she breathed her last.

In that way I knew it, I knew why it was Cyra
looks so like the light in my Mother's eyes. Cyra,

unpromised by her father, sworn to a man she must not love and could not help but love—Cyra has the Sickness.

In the city, the people go about with the name of the young king on their lips, and we see him sometimes, walking. He doesn't walk in the Garden of Astarin, but he does what we all do—he walks around it, and he looks at the Shield Tree. He tips his shining head back, he is a handsome young man and when the sun shines on his face I remember what I have read about reckless kings who heed the heart and not the head. They are dangerous, hopeful creatures.

This morning, he and I were there at the same time. He stood looking at the Tree, his head tipped back, the sun on him. I stood looking, and I was a little behind him. I made no sound, I don't think I even breathed, not then, full of the looking. But he must have heard something, or sensed me near. He turned, the king who is the son of dark elves. He looked at me, right at me.

Untoward girl! I looked at him. I said, "King, they say you came through the shield because the shield itself knew you and let you past."

He said nothing, I don't think he knows if that is true or it isn't.

I said, "King, if this shield is our protection— King, why is it we are dying?"

He turned and he looked at me, his eyes went right into me, far down deep, but he said nothing. Silvanoshei, the son of an exiled queen and an outlawed prince, he said nothing. I don't think he knows the answer.

At Silvanost
On Gateway for the last time
In Summer Flame

It is Midsummer, and each time I try to abandon time, time comes to find me. Midsummer, and midmorning. The morning is strange and cool, and Father makes me sit with him in his library, hour after hour. He composes letter that I write and send away with servants. He flings his letters far, to all the quarters of the city. A man of House Cleric, it is as though he must make many records of his thoughts upon this strange and frightening day. I have twice drained the inkwell at my little desk by the window, and still he composes.

The letters he ends beget letters, and these beget missives, which beget queries and replies and then more letters.

There have come dark Knights into the kingdom!

Upon the soil of the Shining Realm the iron-soled boots of the terrible Knights of Takhisis tread, and it is said by those who sniff the wind from the direction of the broken western border that the air reeks of Neraka.

I don't know what the air of Neraka smells like. Perhaps like the air in Star High, every room made unpleasant by the rank and bitter stink of fear.

Father writes:

Nancy Varian Berberick

I have heard the knights are massing on the western side of the Thon-Thalas. I have heard that they are led by a young human woman—a mere child!

A corespondent cries in shaking script:

It is true! A girl, a child—all in black armor and she goes with a minotaur beside her.

Another letter comes, and it is from Lady Gealia who is father's cousin. She is not one to scrawl or scribble or cry out. She murmurs:

The boy is as crazy as all his kin. [She means, the king, but she will not say so, for Lady Gealia is not one who loves the family of Caladon, that clan of kings whose most recent scion was Lorac the Bringer of Nightmare, he who loosed the dire dragon Cyan Bloodbane, said by some to be lurking in dark places of the kingdom still, magic-hidden, waiting to fall upon us, by others to have long ago died or fled. She won't call Silvanosei king, no matter who else does.] *I have heard it that he will lead the army against her, and the boy thinks he is a warrior because he wears pretty armor and can lift a sword without falling over from the weight of it. Do you see? He is like his grandfather. Mad. He breached the Shield, and—Look! See what has come in behind him . . .*

It goes on like this, hour after hour, parchments flying in and out of the house like brittle-winged birds crying back and forth for news, and armies meet upon the crest above the river, clashing in steel and blood, and they say the king has made a good plan, that he will defeat those four hundred knights.

Bregin Fletch and his father do nothing but fill quarrels with straight and deadly arrows. Cyra says so, and she saw him some hours ago, but I don't know how she managed that. He comes and goes, back and forth like Father's letters. He carries bundles of arrows to the riverside, and he brings back news for those with the wit to stop him and ask how the battles goes. Father has the wit, and he doesn't like the answer to his questions.

"The battle goes disgracefully," Bregin Fletch said. "Our soldiers have no discipline. If we win, we win in spite of ourselves."

My hand is cramping, the little muscles in my fingers scream.

I write letters for Father, and I write here, in this journal that will not let me go though I can hardly hold the pen now. My fingers are stained with ink, all the time blue as bruises.

Blue as Mother's lips, oh, cold lips, and her eyes so bright now, I cannot bear to look into them. When I am not with Father, I am with Mother. She asks only a little about the news that has set the city to hiding within doors or scurrying from tavern to back gate to garden wall, begging for news and always looking west.

In the morning I told Mother that the king had gone to engage the young human woman and her

four hundred knights and her minotaur. We heard
cries from the street beyond our walls, and I reas-
sured her that all was well, these were only the cries
of servants going forth and back with Father's letters. She didn't seem to understand why Father was
so engaged in his letter-writing, but she didn't press
to know an answer. She looked into other places,
Mother did, while armies massed by the Thon-Thalas and we wondered what fate had come to find us.

*[Researcher's note: Here the integrity of Evelyne
Stargrace's diary fails, though this must not be understood to mean that the integrity of the diarist herself
has failed. It has not. Though it cannot be said that Silvanost was a city under siege—for in the true sense of
the word, it was not; the battle for the city was over
before sunset, the disorganized Wildrunners won in
spite of themselves—Evelyne was herself besieged. Her
young life, in all its hopes and dreams and expecta-
tions, shook beneath the assault of an alien army at the
city's borders, and the long-familiar enemy of the Sickness within her mother's bedchamber.*

*The child made notes, in scrawls and scribbles in the
margins of drafts of her father's letters, in her own journal, of the capture of the human woman, Mina, of the
fall of the invading army. Her hand is thin, not the careful script of earlier days, and it is plain her fingers will
not hold her pen. Her quill tips are blunt, her ink watery,
and on the day she notes "It is said all about the city
that the king has taken an axe to the Shield Tree ..." her
letters can hardly be deciphered.*

I was a week of days reading the next line, with great

care trying to interpret not only the aching script, but the strange words: "... ah, look at the sky! There is only fire—!"

Tears obscured the next lines, the ink running like rain in splashes and sliding down the parchment, until the last line of the journal of Evelyne Stargrace became clear. I reproduce it below.]

Today, two days after the death of the dragon Cyan Bloodbane and the killing of the Shield Tree, Mother died.

Afterword by Bertrem

And there you have it. The true tragedy of our times may well be that when death comes upon us, we do not understand its true source. The pain of those elves who died because of the shield they thought had been erected to guard them, their agony cries out to us across the valley of death.

Yet I will not say that all hope is lost. Cyan Bloodbane, who created the shield that killed Evelyne Stargrace's mother, is dead. Beryl, the great green wyrm, is dead, though at a mighty cost to the elves of Qualinesti. The siege of Sanction drags on, with no end in sight, yet we may take some comfort in the fact that the armies of the Dark Knights have not yet penetrated its defenses.

Bertrem the Aesthetic

Ours is an age of change that much is certain. Whether it will end in disaster or in a new, glorious renewal of our land, no one knows. We stand upon a blade's edge, and who shall say which way we fall?

From Krynn in a time of peril, Bertrem the Aesthetic sends his greetings to all who, in happier times, may read this manuscript.

My hand is tired, and I have nothing more to say.

The War of Souls

THE NEW EPIC SAGA FROM
MARGARET WEIS & TRACY HICKMAN

**The *New York Times* bestseller
—now available in paperback!**

Dragons of a Fallen Sun

The War of Souls • Volume I

Out of the tumult of a destructive
magical storm appears a mysterious
young woman, proclaiming the
coming of the One True God.
Her words and deeds erupt into
a war that will transform
the fate of Krynn.

Dragons of a Lost Star

THE WAR OF SOULS • VOLUME II

The war rages on . . .
A triumphant army of evil Knights
sweeps across Krynn and marches
against Silvanesti. Against the dark
tide stands a strange group of heroes:
a tortured Knight, an agonized mage,
an aging woman, and a small,
lighthearted kender in whose hands
rests the fate of all the world.

April 2001

THE *CROSSROADS* SERIES

This thrilling new DRAGONLANCE® series visits famous places in Krynn in the pivotal period of time after the Fifth Age and before the War of Souls. New heroes and heroines, related by blood and deed to the original Companions, struggle to live honorably in a world without gods or magic, dominated by dark and mysterious evildoers.

THE CLANDESTINE CIRCLE
MARY H. HERBERT
Rose Knight Linsha Majere takes on a dangerous undercover mission for the Solamnics' Clandestine Circle in the city of Sanction, run by the powerful Hogan Bight.

THE THIEVES' GUILD
JEFF CROOK
A rogue elf, who may or may not be who he claims, steals a legendary artifact, makes an enemy of the Dark Knights, and rises and falls inside the Thieves' Guild in Palanthas.

DRAGON'S BLUFF
MARY H. HERBERT
Ulin Majere and his companion Lucy travel to Flotsam, get mixed up in a rebellion, and battle against a dragon terrorizing the local populace.

July 2001

THE MIDDLE OF NOWHERE
KEVIN KAGE
Kevin Kage's debut DRAGONLANCE novel tells a tale of irrepressible kender, a forgotten town, and an act of pure bravado.

December 2001

THE DHAMON SAGA
Jean Rabe

THE EXCITING BEGINNING TO THE *DHAMON SAGA*

— NOW AVAILABLE IN PAPERBACK!

Volume One: *Downfall*

HOW FAR CAN A HERO FALL?
FAR ENOUGH TO LOSE HIS SOUL?

Dhamon Grimwulf, once a Hero
of the Heart, has sunk into a
bitter life of crime and squalor.
Now, as the great dragon
overlords of the Fifth Age coldly
plot to strengthen their rule and
destroy their enemies, he must somehow
find the will to redeem himself.

Volume Two: *Betrayal*

All Dhamon Grimwulf wants is a cure for the painful dragon scale
embedded in his leg. To find a cure, he must venture into the
treacherous realm of a great black dragon. Along the way, Dhamon
discovers some horrible truths: betrayal is worse than death, and there
is something more terrifying on Krynn than even a dragon overlord.

June 2001

FROM BELOVED AUTHOR
ELAINE CUNNINGHAM ...

FOR THE FIRST TIME TOGETHER AS A SET!
SONGS AND SWORDS

Follow the adventures of bard Danilo Thann and his beautiful half-elf companion Arilyn Moonblade in these attractive new editions from Elaine Cunningham. These two daring Harpers face trials that bring them together and then tear them apart.

Elfsong
Elfshadow
Silver Shadows (JANUARY 2001)
Thornhold (FEBRUARY 2001)
The Dream Spheres

AND DON'T MISS ...

STARLIGHT AND SHADOWS

Daughter of the Drow
In the aftermath of war in Menzoberranzan, free-spirited drow princess Liriel Baenre sets off on a hazardous quest. Pursued by enemies from her homeland, she rests her best hopes of an ally one who may also be her deadliest rival.

Tangled Webs
Continuing on her quest, drow princess Liriel Baenre learns the price of power and must confront her dark drow nature.